VB+T

# Law of Return

## Also by the author

*Death of a Nationalist*

# Law of Return

Rebecca Pawel

Published by
Soho Press, Inc.
853 Broadway
New York, NY 10003

Library of Congress Cataloging-in-Publication Data

Pawel, Rebecca, 1977–
Law of return / Rebecca Pawel.
p. cm.
ISBN 1-56947-343-9 (alk. paper)
1. Police—Spain—Salamanca—Fiction. 2. Salamanca (Spain)—Fiction.
3. Biarritz (France)—Fiction. 4. Missing persons—Fiction. I. Title.
PS3616.A957L39 2004
813'.6—dc21     2003050378

10  9  8  7  6  5  4  3  2  1

For Chalcey Wilding,
who wanted more about Elena,
with all my gratitude

# Acknowledgments

To all my colleagues, past and present, at the High School for Enterprise, Business and Technology, my grateful thanks for preserving my sanity while I was writing this novel. A special thanks to Aria McLachlan for providing me with the necessary German. And to Xavier Vila and my classmates in Català, *els meus agraïments*. This book wouldn't have been written without the comic inspiration of *Digui Digui*.

# Author's Note

All characters and events in this story are completely ficti-
tious, with one notable exception: Miguel de Unamuno,
the rector of the University of Salamanca from 1901 to 1914,
and again from 1931 until 1936. Unamuno was born in Bilbao
in 1864, and became one of the greatest members of the so
called "generation of 1898." Novelist, poet, and philosopher,
Unamuno was also for many years a professor of Greek at the
University of Salamanca.

Unamuno, who had suffered exile under the previous dicta-
torship of Primo de Rivera because of consistently barbed writings, was a firm believer in freedom of speech, especially his
own. However, his deep Catholicism and his disdain for mass
movements, including democratic ones, made him initially welcome the right-wing coup in Salamanca in 1936. On October
12, at a public ceremony at the university commemorating the
*Día de la Raza*, the Falangist General Millán de Astray made a
speech glorifying Spain's conquests, past and present. General
Millán's followers applauded him with their slogan, "*Viva la
muerte.*" ("Long live death.") Unamuno, standing beside Millán
on the platform, turned to the general, and delivered one of the
great plays on words in twentieth-century history: "*Vencerá pero
no convencerá.*" ("You will win, but you will not convince.") An
enraged Millán had to be physically restrained from striking the
rector. Unamuno was promptly removed from his post at the

university. He died in December of the same year, perhaps of grief, like the faithful Orfeo of his novel *Niebla*.

According to Gabriel Jackson's book, *The Spanish Republic and the Civil War, 1931–1939*, Unamuno spent the last months of his life "sitting in his favorite café in the middle of the town . . . shouting his defiance of the barbarians, but his friends no longer dared sit with him." I have taken the novelist's prerogative to rewrite history, and invented a few stalwart friends who refuse to abandon Don Miguel.

# Law of Return

The landscape was already parched, even though it was only June. The fields were the color of cornhusk dolls, not a healthy golden yellow, but a pale, anemic reminder of green. If the train had been moving, it would have looked like a flash of pure light. As it was, the glitter of sun on siding was enough to blind an unwary observer. It recalled a giant, freshly scrubbed oven, with firelight glancing off its sides.

Inside, the train felt like that oven. The sun had been beating down on the stalled railroad cars for over three hours, and the cracks in the windows did little to let in a non-existent breeze. The passengers in second and third class were probably miserable, but at least in first class there was room to stretch out. Very few wealthy people took the Madrid-Salamanca line in the middle of the day in the summertime in this year of 1940. The first-class car was empty, except for two men, and they, too, should have been in third class. The Guardia Civil did not waste money buying first-class tickets for its junior officers. But the more senior of the pair had automatically headed for the first-class car, his subordinate had unthinkingly followed him, and the conductor, taking in the rifles and three-cornered hats that proclaimed them members of the elite police force, did not think it was wise to press the issue.

The pair had stowed their rifles on the empty luggage rack

above, and their three-cornered hats were now resting on the seats beside them. Each had taken off his jacket, and rolled up his sleeves in deference to the heat. The older man was sitting with his legs stretched out in front of him, apparently absorbed in a book. The younger had slid downward in his seat onto his spine, and was glancing desultorily at a newspaper spread out beside him. He straightened suddenly, with an exclamation of disgust. "In this heat, I swear you stick to the seat!"

His companion glanced up, nodded, and returned to his book. The younger man pushed himself to his feet, and peered out a window. "It doesn't look as if they're doing *anything*!"

"Leave the shades down," the officer advised, without lifting his eyes. "It keeps it cooler."

The youth gave a snort of disgust, and returned to his seat. "We should have been there two hours ago!"

The reader checked his watch, and then nodded, although in fact the guardias civiles were supposed to have arrived two and a quarter hours ago by his calculations. After a little while, he turned a page.

The youth drummed his hands on his knees. "What's that you're reading, Lieutenant?" he asked finally.

"Linde." The lieutenant did not look up.

"Is that by Carmen Iscaza, sir?" the boy asked, incredulous. He was unable to hide a disrespectful grin at the idea of Lieutenant Tejada reading romance novels.

The lieutenant snorted. "Not *Linda*. Linde. Otto Dietrich zur Linde."

"Oh." The youth was abashed. He glanced at his wilted newspaper, filled with similarly unpronounceable names. "Is that a German name?"

"Yes." Tejada sighed and surrendered to his companion's desire for conversation. "He's a philosopher, somewhat in the line of Nietszche, although they disagree on certain crucial points."

"Oh." The younger man hesitated. "Why?"

"Why do they disagree?"

"No, I meant . . . why are you reading his book?"

Tejada's mouth twisted. "Because, Corporal, we are on our way to Salamanca, which is—in case you didn't know—a town famed for its university, and I have no wish to appear an ignoramus when we arrive."

Corporal Jiménez flushed, and rubbed sweat from his face. The lieutenant normally didn't snap at him like that. But what he said made a certain amount of sense. The two guardias had officially started a tour of duty in Salamanca two and a quarter hours ago, and it made sense to learn the lay of the land. But there was no way that Jiménez was going to start frying what remained of his brain with German philosophers. "Is this Linde famous, sir?" he asked diffidently, trying to gauge the necessity of learning about the new name.

"Not yet." Tejada folded down one page, and closed the book. "But I suspect he will be. He's the first German I've read who can write a simple declarative sentence. Although maybe it's just a good translation."

"A Spaniard might have a natural affinity for it," the young man suggested. "I mean, if he's one of us."

The lieutenant glanced at the title page, and smiled. "This was published in Buenos Aires."

"Oh." Jiménez flushed again. "Well, what's the book about?"

"The place of intellectuals in the Movement." Tejada watched his subordinate's brow wrinkle in puzzlement, trapping little rivulets of sweat.

"Intellectuals?" Jiménez pronounced the word as if it were the name of a particularly dangerous type of insect. "I thought . . . I mean aren't they mostly subversives, sir?"

"Linde classes himself as an intellectual." It was difficult to tell if the lieutenant's voice was sarcastic.

"Oh." Jiménez wrinkled his nose. "Is he . . . you know, all right, sir?"

Tejada opened the book and read the flyleaf silently for a moment. "How old were you in 1927, Jiménez?" he asked finally.

"Six, sir."

"Well, Linde has been part of the Movement since 1927. He's had a distinguished military career, cut short last year by a tragic accident. He's currently a ranking officer at a prison camp in Poland. So yes, he's all right."

"Shame he was wounded," Jiménez said sympathetically, wisely sticking to topics he understood.

There was a sound like a giant sigh, and then the train jolted forward again. "Thank God!" Tejada said. "We're moving." He opened the book again, and left Jiménez to his own devices.

The corporal leafed through the newspapers again. They were all filled with news from Paris: photographs of German troops on parade in the Champ du Mars; excerpts from Hitler's speeches; a statement from the German embassy in Madrid; a statement from the Italian embassy; a statement from the British embassy. It was still hot. He returned to his thoughts about Otto Dietrich zur Linde. "I'd think it must be very frustrating to go from being a soldier to just dealing with prisoners," he said aloud. "I mean, sort of a comedown."

Seeing that his junior would have to be entertained for the rest of the ride, Tejada abandoned any hope of finishing the chapter. "May I remind you, Corporal, that one of the duties of the Guardia Civil is the transport of prisoners," he commented dryly.

"Well, yes, of course, but I mean . . ." Jiménez had the grace to look sheepish. "I mean, if you're used to combat, and all, it must be rather dull."

Tejada, who had considerably more combat experience than the corporal, reflected that dull was not necessarily a bad thing. Aloud, he said, "Germany's only been at war since September. So he couldn't have been that used to it."

"Still," said the younger guardia civil. "A prison camp seems like sort of a dead end."

"Those camps are dead ends." The speaker could not have been more different from Corporal Jiménez. Jiménez was barely twenty, and looked young for his age. This man was in his early sixties, and his stooped shoulders and halo of white hair made him seem older. Where the guardia civil had the bouncy energy of good health, this man leaned heavily on a table as he spoke, as if even supporting his own weight were an effort.

But the greatest difference between the two speakers was their tones of voice. Jiménez spoke casually, dismissing a minor misfortune. Guillermo Fernández Ochóa, speaking the same words a few days later in Salamanca, was frighteningly intense. "A dead end," he repeated heavily, tapping one finger on the table for emphasis, in a gesture that any of his students would have recognized. "*The foggy realm of Hades.*"

"All *right*, Guillermo," his wife interrupted, hoping that her impatience would mask her unease. Professor Fernández only quoted Homer when deeply upset. "I get the point. So what?"

Guillermo abandoned his rhetorical stance. "This is from Joseph Meyer." He tossed an open letter onto the table.

His wife went pale. "He's been imprisoned?"

"Read it for yourself."

The professor's wife silently leaned forward, and pulled the letter toward her. A forest of indecipherable gothic letters met her gaze. "It's in German," she pointed out gently.

"He really isn't as comfortable in French," Guillermo replied absently.

María Pilar Ríos de Fernández bit back her irritation. Her husband had been abstracted and nervous since the arrival of the morning mail. He had waited until they were alone in the house, and then had pulled her into the dark, unused parlor to discuss "something important." María had not objected to his cryptic manner. She had not objected when he began to lecture, without even pulling up the blinds in the dim and musty room. But now it was necessary to object. "What does he *say?*" she asked.

Guillermo picked up the letter, and read silently for a moment, translating in disjointed phrases. "My Dear Dr. Fernández, you must for the time without a letter forgive me . . . As for your trouble . . . I am sorry to hear of it, but . . . glad it is finished. Your last letter . . . did not reach me quickly because it was sent to Leipzig . . . but . . ." Guillermo Fernández broke off. "I don't exactly understand this part. I think it's something like a friend is getting my mail, and sending it on to me. And he says to please write to him care of a Monsieur Rosenberg at an address in Toulouse."

"In Toulouse?" the professor's wife interjected sharply.

"Yes. It goes on a bit, about what he's been doing lately, and he finally says, 'Perhaps, if you are still interested in the *Odyssey,* we might meet to work together on it. Finding myself in the position of Theoklymenos, I must ask if you hold an interest in Telemachus.' Something like that."

There was a short silence. The entire Fernández family was soaked in the epic poems that were Professor Fernández's passion and life's work. María frowned for a moment, trying to remember. "Theoklymenos? The diviner?"

The professor nodded briefly, awarding partial credit to an alert student. "Telemachus picks him up in Sparta, remember, and he explains that he's killed someone in Argos. '*Death stalks me through foreign lands. Give me refuge in your ship I beg. / Don't let them kill me for I know I am pursued.*'"

Señora de Fernández considered. Two quotes in as many minutes suggested that her husband was seriously worried. She did not know what words he would find comforting, so she spoke her thoughts, making her voice as gentle as possible. "We can't, Guillermo. You're still under surveillance by the Guardia Civil. You could go to prison again. And then what would become of Elena and me?"

The room, lit only by the golden sunlight that leaked around the edges of the blinds, seemed to rearrange itself around the letter on the table. The innocuous-looking piece of paper bled fear. "I won't reply if you think it's impossible," Guillermo said slowly. "But . . . we've been friends for twenty-five years."

"Colleagues," his wife corrected firmly.

"Colleagues, then. And his work on the Homeric Hymns . . ."

"Is it worth your life?" The woman's voice was shaking.

"Is it worth his?"

"Don't be melodramatic."

"He's the greatest living editor of Aeschylus," the professor said pleadingly.

María de Fernández sighed. Guillermo was so fragile. This was the first time she had seen him with anything like his old passion. But to risk everything for a foreign refugee . . . "What about his family?" she asked, without much hope.

Guillermo shook his head. "He says here his nephews are still in Germany. And that he hasn't had any news of them since '38."

María bit her lip. "I thought they were close."

"So did I," the professor replied, a little grimly. "He always said they were like sons to him. And you remember how he was with Elena and Hipólito."

"How who was?" A new voice broke in on the conversation.

Husband and wife both started, and turned to regard the young woman outlined in the doorway with a mixture of anxiety and affection. Her arms were full of packages, and she blinked slightly, trying to see in the dim light after having been out in the sunshine. María was the first to speak to her. "Do you remember Professor Meyer, Elenita?"

"Of course!" Elena Fernández had been worried by her parents' tone of voice as she passed the parlor, and had paused on the threshold. Now she came forward, smiling, and set her packages down on the table. "He gave me brown-eyed Penelope."

Smiles flashed across her parents' faces as well. Some twenty years earlier, Herr Professor Meyer had attended a conference in Salamanca, and had stayed with the Fernández family. The fair-haired guest had been much amused by Elena's loudly voiced disgust with blue-eyed dolls, and the dark child's insistence that "Dolls should have brown eyes, like regular people." Several months after his visit, a package had arrived from Germany, addressed in copperplate script to Fräulein Helenka Fernández. It contained a magnificent doll, with chestnut hair and chocolate-hued eyes, and a brief note in French, carefully written so that a child who had only studied the language for a few years would be able to read it without help.

Elena had never seen Professor Meyer again, but she retained a warm memory of the man with the comic accent and the quick smile, who had soberly taken notes as she taught him Spanish, and had patiently answered her older brother's endless questions about German aircraft. *That was when German planes were models in toy store windows,* she thought, as the smile died out of her eyes, *toys that no one could be frightened of.* She gazed at her parents. They were not smiling either. They looked as they always looked now: tired, and frightened, and old. "What's happened to him?" Elena asked, bracing herself for bad news.

Her parents exchanged wary glances. "Did we mention that he moved to France?" her father said cautiously. "A few years ago, now. When you were in Madrid."

Elena was lively only when she was happy. The more unhappy the situation, the quieter she became. She was still as a statue now. "Paris?" She hardly moved her lips.

Her father nodded. "Initially, yes. But he's in Toulouse now."

Elena gave a little sigh of relief. "He's safe, then."

"For now," her father agreed. Her parents exchanged another

glance, and Elena had the impression that they were consider-ing whether to tell her something. "He's just written to me." Professor Fernández added slowly, "He asks us to play Telemachus to his Theoklymenos."

Elena heard her mother's indrawn breath, and put a hand on her shoulder. The older woman reached up to grasp at the prof-fered comfort. Elena shared her father's love of the *Odyssey*, and identified the characters without difficulty. There was a long silence. "Why did he leave Germany?" the young woman asked.

"He's a Jew, Elenita," her mother explained.

"He lost his post at the university," her father said bitterly at the same moment.

Elena took the third seat at the table, and the scraping of the chair as it moved covered the silence that followed the profes-sor's statement. His wife and daughter avoided his eyes. The University of Salamanca had been Guillermo Fernández's life and love. His daughter had been living in Madrid at the time of his forced resignation, four years earlier. She had not been pres-ent when the Falangists who had ruled Salamanca since the beginning of the Civil War had ransacked the professor's library. Nor had she been present for his arrest as a subversive, or his release six months later. She had returned to her parents' home at the end of the war and found a frightened and embittered old man, who sometimes looked like her father, except for his white hair and stooped shoulders. Most of the time he was sim-ply frightened. It was only mention of the university that made him vitriolic nowadays. "Could he visit us again, maybe?" Elena asked carefully. "I mean . . . would it be legal?"

Her father frowned. "I don't know. If he has a German pass-port, maybe. If he's become a naturalized French citizen, I don't know."

"What if it isn't legal?" Elena's mother spoke quietly, looking down at her hands.

The only sound in the room was the ticking of the clock.

Elena rubbed her finger along the grain of the wooden table-top. Her father drummed his fingers. Her mother sat absolutely still. "We've known each other twenty-five years," Guillermo said, after nearly fifty ticks. His wife and daughter nodded in unison. "So I guess, if you don't have any objections . . . ?" Mother and daughter looked at each other, and then shook their heads in response to his question. "I'll go upstairs and write to him," Guillermo finished slowly.

# Chapter 2

"You're late, Lieutenant." Captain Rodríguez spoke crisply. Everything about Captain Rodríguez was crisp, from his neatly trimmed mustache to his polished boots. His uniform was unwrinkled, despite the heat. "You were supposed to be here at thirteen hundred hours."

"Yes, Captain. The train was delayed." Tejada met his commander's eyes steadily. His voice was neither apologetic nor annoyed, although Rodríguez clearly expected an apology, and Jiménez, hovering in the background, looked indignant.

"I expect punctuality from all my officers."

"Understood, sir." Tejada did not point out that there was no way he could have avoided the delay. The captain had sent a car to the station to meet them, and the car had waited, patiently, until the train finally arrived. Tejada, who had some experience scheduling patrols, knew that a sudden three-hour delay in one man's schedule could throw off half a dozen other tasks. Rodríguez had some cause for annoyance.

"And a military appearance," the captain continued. "Your uniforms look as if you've slept in them!"

Jiménez's face, already red with heat, turned purple. Tejada remained impassive, although he considered pointing out that he and the corporal had passed a June siesta in a stalled railway car. The captain was too angry. Either he had not wanted their transfer in the first place, or he was merely putting up a front to impress new subordinates. If the former, defying him could only irritate him further, and if the latter, he would soon relax. "Yes, Captain," Tejada said.

Rodríguez glared, as if annoyed at his new lieutenant's obedience. "Go get cleaned up," he ordered. "Corporal, you'll report for night duty at twenty hours. Lieutenant, I'll see you in my office in twenty minutes. Guardia!" He raised his voice to a bellow. The door opened, and a young man about Jiménez's age stepped into the room and saluted. "Show them to their quarters."

Tejada and Jiménez followed the nameless guardia. No one spoke, although several times Jiménez attempted to catch Tejada's eye to give his opinion of their new commander. "These are your quarters, Lieutenant," their guide said, opening a door off a long hallway. "The corporal will be two doors down and across the way. And the bathroom's down the hall and to your left. Will you need anything else?"

"No, thank you, Guardia." Tejada's eyes were already roaming over the room. Someone had placed his luggage inside. "I'm sorry. Your name is?"

"Molina, Lieutenant." He flushed and looked pleased.

"Thank you, Molina. If you'll excuse me, I have an appointment with Captain Rodríguez in fifteen minutes." In response to the guardia's stiff salute, Tejada nodded and then disappeared into the room.

Guardia Molina led the remaining officer down the corridor. "You'll be sharing quarters with Corporal Méndez and the sergeants, sir," he explained to Jiménez.

Jiménez, who was not yet accustomed to being called "sir," blinked slightly, and decided that he liked Guardia Molina. "Thank you, Molina," he said, doing his best to sound the way the lieutenant had. He failed miserably, but Molina, a tolerant man, decided that the corporal from Madrid might be a decent officer.

Jiménez unpacked slowly, giving himself time to think various uncomplimentary thoughts about Captain Rodríguez. In the meantime, Tejada, who had done all that he could to make himself presentable within a short period of time, was also further sizing up the captain. His thoughts were based on more information than Jiménez's, but they ran along the same lines.

The captain opened their interview with a statement. "Your file states that you spent much of the war near the front, Lieutenant." He tapped a heavy manila folder lying on his desk.

"Yes, Captain." Tejada glanced rapidly at the desk, and then raised his eyes again, and waited for permission to stand at ease. Permission was not forthcoming.

"And that you were in Madrid at the end of the war."

"Yes." Rodríguez glared, and Tejada hastily added, "Captain. That's correct."

"Your *file*," the captain placed a heavy emphasis on the word, "says that you've showed considerable competence in several instances. It seems you're quite zealous. According to your *file*," the captain's tone conveyed the impression that Tejada's file was almost certainly a malicious fabrication, "your commanding officers speak very highly of you. During your tenure in Madrid you apparently showed considerable . . . initiative. Which accounts for your quick promotion."

"Sir?" Tejada hoped that he sounded respectful. It was difficult to know whether to make a modest denial, or to offer further apologies and explanations.

"This isn't Madrid, Lieutenant." The captain slapped the folder for emphasis.

"No, Captain."

"The people of Salamanca are good, decent, law-abiding citizens."

"Yes, Captain," Tejada said, repressing the urge to add, *Then what are we doing here?*

"So, while your *initiative* may be very commendable in wartime, here you will confine yourself to following orders. Do I make myself clear?"

"Yes, Captain." Tejada reflected that Jiménez was perhaps not alone in his distaste for the more mundane aspects of policing. He had a shrewd suspicion that Captain Rodríguez's war record, though doubtless exemplary, was undramatic. "At your orders."

Rodríguez glared again, but was unable to find fault with the lieutenant's reply. He began to detail Tejada's duties in the terse bark of a drill sergeant. The lieutenant received his orders as if they were in fact vital missions, instead of routine paperwork, and saluted smartly when he was dismissed. Then he returned to his room, and unpacked, wondering if the transfer to Salamanca was the stroke of good fortune that it had seemed two months ago.

Tejada had more cause to wonder over the next few days. Captain Rodríguez seemed to go out of his way to give his lieutenant the most boring assignments possible. Tejada's promotion meant that he was no longer required to go out on foot patrol, and he found himself regretting the change. At the end of a patrol he felt that he had accomplished something. Four hours of tramping through a city was tiring, but at least it was good exercise, and gave him the opportunity to think. In fact, Tejada was persuaded that he thought better while he was walking. The same four hours spent behind a desk left him irritable, stiff, and irrationally hungry. *It's only for two years,* he told himself. *And maybe less.*

In the meantime, he began to go for long walks during his time off, to reacquaint himself with Salamanca. It was not the golden city he remembered from his days as a student. It had not been as heavily bombarded as Madrid, of course, but the Red shelling had been effective enough to destroy homes and businesses. Everywhere Tejada went he saw people repairing damaged buildings. Never rebuilding or renovating. Simply making them strong enough to withstand another winter. He found the shoddy repairs nearly as depressing as the long lines for meat and milk. Furthermore, though Tejada would never have admitted it to himself, Salamanca seemed smaller than he remembered it. Had the city been in good condition, its graceful buildings with their uniformly yellow sandstone facades would have been pretty. But they lacked the variety and interest of Madrid's ruins.

Still, the walks were the best part of Tejada's day. His promotion to lieutenant had only come with his transfer, but his work in Salamanca was not challenging. The Guardia Civil in Madrid was short staffed, and Tejada had spent a considerable amount of his time there at a post with no captain. The captain's duties had fallen to the lieutenant, and the lieutenant's duties had been divided among the post's sergeants. Tejada was thus accustomed to performing most of the tasks that Captain Rodríguez had given him. He scheduled patrol routes, and kept track of the lists of citizens requiring new ration books. He reviewed files on prisoners and made sure that they were up-to-date. And he assembled and catalogued the files of those citizens whom the Guardia Civil wished to keep under surveillance.

If asked, Tejada would have said that this was the most interesting part of his job. At least it occasionally involved dealing with people as well as paper. On his fourth day in Salamanca, Sergeant Hernández handed him a stack of folders with a typed list clipped to the top file. "Thursday and Friday are visiting hours," the sergeant explained with a slight smile.

Tejada smiled back. "Visiting hours?" he asked. He liked Hernández. The sergeant was near his own age, and seemed like a serious and competent officer. It was, Tejada thought, a shame that the sergeant was stuck with a commanding officer like Rodríguez.

"The ones we have on parole," Hernández explained. "They're supposed to report weekly. They have appointments. You just see them, and check off here that they've come in." He bent over the lieutenant's shoulder and indicated a box next to each name. "Also, you record if they ask for permission to travel, a new ration card, anything like that. If they *don't* report in, you note it *here*," he pointed to another box on the list, "and then you schedule someone to visit them and find out why. Then you . . ."

"Add that to their file," the lieutenant finished wearily. "Got it. How many do we have?"

"About seventy, seventy-five, give or take." Hernández shrugged. "We can get through them in an afternoon, at a pinch, but it's easier to follow-up on the paperwork if you schedule them over two days. Your choice though, sir. Should we change the appointments?"

"No, there's no need." Tejada was already counting Thursday's folders. "Benítez, Vargas, Ortíz . . . aren't these in alphabetical order?"

"No, sir. Captain Rodríguez preferred them in the order they were scheduled," Hernández explained.

Tejada was grateful for the tactful warning that the folders had been the captain's province before his arrival. He had opened Juan Benítez's folder, and was already on the verge of a disgusted comment on its lack of organization. "Very reasonable of him," he said instead. "But I'd like them alphabetized, Sergeant."

"Very good, sir."

"I'll read through these now." The lieutenant attempted to remove the top half of the pile of folders, and found that he had removed more than he had intended. As he tried to replace a few of the files, he realized why: a group of them were held together with a thick rubber band. He slid the attached folders out of the pile, and then removed the rubber band. "Why are these together . . . Arroyo, Fernández, Rivera, and Velázquez?"

"Which? Oh, the petitioners." The sergeant's voice was dismissive.

"Petitioners?" Tejada asked, with some interest.

"Bunch of professors," Hernández explained. Seeing that the lieutenant still looked politely quizzical he added, "I don't know if you heard of the fuss about the university rector, back in '36, sir?"

"A little," Tejada nodded. "He told off General Millán in the middle of a public ceremony, didn't he?"

"Yes, sir. He completely flipped out." Hernández shook his head. "Started insulting the Movement, the general, everybody. With all the top brass there. *And* foreign press."

"Very embarrassing," Tejada commented.

"Ah, well." The sergeant's voice was tolerant. "It was probably just softening of the brain. He was an old man, after all. But as you say: embarrassing. He was fired, of course. The Reds made a big thing of it, though they hadn't been any too fond of him before that."

Tejada, who had a few memories of the acerbic autocrat who had ruled the university during part of his student years, smiled slightly. "He wasn't too fond of them, either. But the petitioners?"

"I was getting to that. You see, a bunch of professors thought the way he was terminated was a bit high-handed. You know these university types. So they circulated a petition, protesting the treatment of their friend and colleague, after his years of distinguished service, blah, blah, blah. You can imagine the type of thing. We kept tabs on all the signers for a while, but we think these four were the ringleaders. Most of them haven't been up to anything lately, but we still keep an eye on them."

The lieutenant tapped the top folder thoughtfully. "Arroyo Díaz. Manuel Arroyo Díaz . . . wasn't he in the law faculty?"

"Yes, sir!" Hernández blinked at the officer with new respect. "How did you know?"

Tejada grimaced briefly. "I took one of his classes," he explained, unwillingly. He did not normally mention his years at the university to his colleagues, and he hoped that Hernández would have the sense to keep quiet about them. "As I recall, his specialty was international law?"

"That sounds right to me, sir," Hernández agreed, still looking at the lieutenant as if he had suddenly grown two heads. "Do you know any of the others?"

Tejada glanced at the names again. "Not offhand. What did they teach?"

The sergeant frowned for a moment. "Arroyo's the only lawyer. The others were all in the medical school, I think . . . Or, no, no, wait . . . Fernández was philosophy and letters . . . classics, I think."

"Then I wouldn't know them," Tejada said, fairly sure that he was speaking the truth. Something about a classics professor named Fernández fluttered in the peripheral vision of his mind's eye, but he was unable to focus on it. He had probably simply seen the name listed in a catalogue at some point. Or else he was thinking of someone else. "Guillermo" didn't ring a bell, and Fernández was a common surname, after all. He looked at the pile of remaining folders. "What time is the first appointment?"

Hernández responded to the change in his superior's tone, "Juan Benítez, fourteen hundred hours, Lieutenant."

Tejada checked his watch. "Fine. Send him in when he comes. Dismissed."

The sergeant coughed. "Err . . . yes, sir. When he comes, sir? At two?"

Tejada looked up, surprised. "Yes, that gives me a few hours to go through these, so that I know who I'm seeing when they show up. If I get caught up in something I'll let you know so you can tell him to wait."

"Yes, sir," Hernández looked embarrassed. "Only . . . well, two o'clock's lunchtime."

The lieutenant raised his eyebrows. "I didn't schedule the appointment," he pointed out.

"Errr . . . no, sir. But, well . . . Captain Rodríguez always said it didn't hurt them to keep them waiting."

It was on the tip of Tejada's tongue to retort that judging

from the state of the files, the captain must have taken long and frequent lunch hours, but he contented himself with replying gently, "And he's quite right. However, I'm afraid that I'm not as efficient as the captain. I've found that I generally fall far enough behind schedule to keep people waiting without going to lunch."

Sergeant Hernández swallowed a smile and matched his commanding officer's gravity. "Understood, Lieutenant. But we're a quiet little post here. After all," he grinned suddenly, "*this isn't Madrid.*"

Tejada snorted. "Dismissed, Sergeant. I'll call you at fourteen hundred hours."

When the door had closed behind Hernández he applied himself to the files. The folders were in a sad state of disorganization. Handwritten memos had been randomly slipped in among lists of parole dates met, photographs of the subjects, and copies of court transcripts and official documents. The lieutenant painstakingly organized the first couple of folders and then gave up, and began to skim the others rapidly, making a mental note to spend more time cataloging them at a later date. His task was not made easier by the total lack of common elements among the files. Juan Benítez had been a known Socialist sympathizer before the war. His more recent loudly proclaimed Falangist sympathies had spared him a prison term or worse, but the Guardia Civil had received a tip six months ago that his conversion was not genuine. Benítez was currently unemployed. Before the war, he had worked for the post office. Julián Vargas was the brother-in-law of a man who had been executed as a union leader during the war. Daniel Ortíz had just been released from prison for smuggling. The smuggling was merely the latest in a series of petty offenses, all of them of a nonpolitical nature. The earliest record of his arrest was dated 1932, and his antagonistic relationship with the law had been maintained through several governments. The list went on: family members of men who were imprisoned or dead, owners of businesses who had dealt with the Reds during the war, authors of articles or pamphlets deemed subversive, members of outlawed political parties, thieves, and delinquents. The lieutenant found himself stunned by the range and quantity of minor offenses it was possible for the people of a town of "good, decent, law-abiding citizens" to commit.

By two o'clock, Tejada was tired and disgusted. But he was also anxious to begin matching human beings to the files, so he was pleased when Juan Benítez was ushered in. Their interview was brief. Benítez had attended all of his previous interviews promptly, and had no requests to make, other than that the surveillance be dropped. Tejada made a noncommittal reply, and dismissed him. If Benítez was mildly stunned that he had actually been seen at two o'clock, he was wise enough not to show it. Almost all of the interviews were equally short and uneventful. Occasionally, someone was late or requested a new ration card. Tejada checked off names, and made notes to himself with the comfortable feeling that he was actually accomplishing something.

Still, by 4:15 the lieutenant was tired and not sorry that the next parolee appeared to be late for his appointment. He checked the stack of folders. "Who's next, Hernández, Ana López?"

The sergeant glanced at the list. "No, sir. Actually, she's at four-thirty. Professor Arroyo's due now."

"The petitioner," Tejada remarked thoughtfully. "Perhaps he's taking advantage of the academic ten minutes' grace."

"Maybe," the sergeant agreed. "Although he's usually prompt. Lawyers are well trained by judges, I guess. Do you think he's likely to recognize you, sir?"

Tejada shook his head. "I doubt it. I was one of a hundred students in a lecture hall a dozen years ago."

"Just as well."

Tejada was inclined to agree with the sergeant. The lieutenant had successfully put his student years behind him, and he had no desire to be recognized. But he was somewhat curious to see his former teacher, and to figure out what form of mild insanity had brought a formerly respected academic to such a pass. So it was with some annoyance, as well as a quickened interest, that he noted that Professor Arroyo had still not appeared when Ana López arrived for her appointment. By six o'clock, when the last of the parolees left the post, Arroyo still had not reported.

"Get me Corporal Jiménez," the lieutenant ordered, as he put the last of the folders back into their dilapidated file cabinet.

"Yes, sir." Hernández saluted and disappeared.

A few minutes later, Jiménez appeared, looking rather cheerful. The young man was enjoying his promotion—possibly, in Tejada's opinion, because it did not involve dealing overmuch with Captain Rodríguez. "Yes, sir?" he asked.

"You're on duty this evening, Jiménez?" Tejada had the Arroyo file open in front of him, and was scribbling something on a pad.

"Yes, sir. Starting at twenty hours, sir."

"Good, then I have a job for you. We have someone who skipped his parole appointment." Tejada tore a sheet of paper off his pad and held it out. "Here's the name and address. Take three men, and visit him tonight. Find out where he is and why he wasn't here this afternoon."

"Yes, sir. And if we find him, sir?"

"If he's home in bed with a broken leg, give him a warning, and tell him to send us word. If he's not home," Tejada paused, and glanced at the file, "get his wife to tell you where he is. Arrest her, if you have to."

"Yes, sir." Jiménez flushed with pleasure. This was the first time Lieutenant Tejada had actually placed him in charge of a mission. Swelling slightly with importance, and doing his best to sound nonchalant, he added, "Should we take anyone for a walk, sir?"

Tejada winced mentally, and wondered if he had overestimated the corporal's maturity. It was, he knew, a source of constant grief to Jiménez that he had been too young to take up arms for his country during most of the Civil War. The boy still tended to think of executions as dramatic moonlit affairs, cloaked in the euphemism *We're going for a walk*. Tejada felt a moment's compunction about inflicting the zealous corporal on an elderly lady who belonged, he suddenly remembered, to one of Salamanca's more socially prominent families. "No, Corporal," he said firmly. "This is not wartime. That will not be necessary. Nor should you arrest Señora Otero de Arroyo unless you see absolutely no other alternative. In that eventuality, you will be polite to the lady, and you will inform her that she is only being brought here to speak with the lieutenant about her husband's whereabouts. Do I make myself clear?"

"Yes, sir," Jiménez agreed, looking deflated.

"Good." Tejada suppressed a sigh of relief, and dismissed the corporal.

The lieutenant was more cheerful that evening than he had been since his arrival in Salamanca. Keeping the parolees' files updated and organized was a job of some interest though one that Captain Rodríguez apparently considered too undramatic to bother with. And Arroyo's absence was an intriguing anomaly. Tejada was inclined to suspect that ill health or accident had prevented the lawyer's appearance. The former academic was in his seventies, and it was quite possible that he had simply been kept in bed by a cold. It would, of course, be a different matter if Arroyo's fellow petitioners failed to show up the following day. Velázquez, Rivera, Fernández, Tejada thought. Why do I have the feeling that Fernández is *supposed* to teach classics? I wonder if I knew him through Arroyo? They must all have been friends . . . I wonder why Arroyo didn't show.

The lieutenant finally turned to other tasks, and dismissed the matter from his mind. Nothing to be done about it until tomorrow anyway, he thought. Although this did turn out to be literally true, it was not perhaps as true as Tejada would have liked.

# Chapter 3

"Lieutenant! Lieutenant Tejada!" Tejada started awake in total darkness. Someone, he realized, was rapping urgently at his door, and calling his name.

"Who's there?" he called, rolling out of bed. Years of practice had given him the ability to make his voice sound considerably more alert than his brain actually was. The knocking subsided.

"Corporal Jiménez, sir."

Tejada stubbed his toe as he fumbled for the light switch and suppressed a curse. He found the switch finally, and the glow of a bare bulb lit the little room. "What is it?"

"I'm sorry to disturb you, sir. But I'm afraid if you don't come I'll have to wake the captain." Jiménez sounded plaintive.

Tejada had already started pulling on his clothes. At the mention of Captain Rodríguez he began moving a little faster. He fully sympathized with Jiménez's desire to avoid finding out if Rodríguez tended to wake up in a bad mood. "Why will you have to wake him?" he asked, opening the door, and then sinking onto the bed to pull on his boots.

Jiménez lingered in the doorway, rifle on his shoulder, looking relieved. "It's that Professor Arroyo, sir," he explained. "He's not at home, and his wife says she hasn't seen him and doesn't know where he is."

Tejada blinked. "That could have waited until morning, Jiménez."

"Yes, sir." Jiménez looked miserable. "I know, sir. Only, it's Señora Otero, sir. I don't know what to do with her."

With a sudden sinking feeling, Tejada remembered his last instructions to the corporal. "She's here?" he asked, pulling on his coat. And then, as the corporal nodded, "You arrested her?"

"Ummm . . . yes, sir. Well, more or less. In a manner of speaking."

Tejada grabbed his hat, and followed the corporal out of the room and down the hall. "Define 'in a manner of speaking,'" he said grimly.

"Well," Jiménez gulped. "I was going to arrest her. I mean . . . you *told* me to if I couldn't think of anything else to do, sir. B-but then . . ." The young man flushed. "Then she said that if I thought a . . . a bunch of very rude boys could go around waking up decent people at all hours of the night, she wanted to speak to my commanding officer about it right away. And I *wasn't* rude, sir!" Jiménez added with some indignation. "You *told* me to be polite, and I was!"

Tejada was seized by a sudden premonition. He glanced at his wrist, and saw that he had forgotten his watch. "What time is it?"

Jiménez, somewhat disappointed by the lieutenant's lack of reaction, looked at his own watch. "Ten of three, sir."

"And what time did you pay a call on Señora de Arroyo?"

"About an hour ago." The corporal looked crestfallen. "Why?"

"And you were polite to her?"

"*Yes*, sir."

Tejada winced. "It didn't occur to you," he said, in a carefully colorless tone, "that it might have been polite to visit her at a slightly earlier hour?"

"Ummm . . . no, sir. I thought, I mean, her husband's a wanted man. And I thought . . . between midnight and three . . . I mean, in training they say . . ."

Perhaps fortunately for Jiménez, the two of them had reached the main civilian waiting area of the post. The benches were empty, except for three guardias, who the lieutenant guessed to be Jiménez's companions, and a gray-haired lady of about seventy. She was dressed in black, and the fact that her hat was slightly askew was the only hint that she had not dressed with perfect composure. Tejada correctly surmised that she had ordered the guardias to withdraw and wait until she made herself presentable before leaving her home with them. She rose to confront him and the three guardias stumbled awkwardly to their feet around her. She reached only the collarbone of the shortest. "Are you responsible for this outrage, young man?" she demanded, as Tejada stepped forward and bowed. The other guardias cringed slightly.

"Good evening, Señora."

The lieutenant suddenly remembered, with the preternatural clarity of someone jerked from sleep, that one of his textbooks on civil law had been written by a Judge Otero Martínez. Probably a father or brother of Arroyo's wife. He spared a moment to hope that Judge Otero was either deceased or shared the political convictions of Manuel Arroyo. "What seems to be the trouble?"

"I would think," said Señora de Arroyo icily, "that the trouble is obvious. It is bad enough that my husband has to submit to the indignity of having his movements recorded like a common criminal. But until now the Guardia Civil have always maintained at least a pretense of common courtesy."

Jiménez made a choking noise, and the lieutenant swiftly forestalled any comment. "Until now," he said coolly, "your husband has cooperated fully with the Guardia Civil, as do all law-abiding citizens. His absence this afternoon occasioned our visit to your home. I am sorry if this was the outrage that you referred to earlier, but it was an unavoidable if unpleasant part of our duty."

"Your duty does not involve waking the entire street in the

small hours of the morning, and threatening defenseless women at gunpoint, Sergeant!" she snapped.

"*Lieutenant*," Tejada said softly, wondering how much Señora Otero was exaggerating about waking the entire street, and kicking himself for entrusting Jiménez with anything.

Señora Otero de Arroyo drew a deep breath. Tejada met her eyes steadily. "You are new to Salamanca, aren't you, Lieutenant?" she said quietly.

The words were a threat. Tejada remembered Jiménez's unwillingness to wake the captain, and wished that he knew whether the lady was bluffing. He went on the offensive before she could continue. "Where is your husband, Señora?"

The words hit home. She paused for a few moments before replying, and then said, "I don't know."

"When was the last time you saw him?"

She pursed her lips for a moment. "Is it necessary to do this *now*, Lieutenant?" Some of the bravado had gone out of her. "I'm an old woman, and I tire easily."

Tejada would have liked nothing better than to go back to bed, but he knew perfectly well that now, while she was tired, was the time to question the professor's wife. "Why don't you sit down, Señora?" He ushered her to one of the benches. She sank onto it, still avoiding his eyes. Jiménez and the other guardias hovered silently, occasionally coughing or shifting from foot to foot.

"Am I being detained, Lieutenant?" Her voice was cold.

"I don't think that's necessary, at the moment," Tejada replied cautiously. "But . . ."

"In that case, kindly show me to the nearest telephone." Arroyo's wife was apparently gaining a second wind. "I would like to call my brother, and inform him of my whereabouts."

Tejada thought rapidly. "Give the number to Guardia Molina," he suggested. "He can telephone your brother while we talk, and ask Judge Otero to send someone to pick you up."

Tejada caught the quick smile on Señora Otero's face as he called her brother "judge." The guess had been good then. She willingly gave the telephone number, and added with only a touch of acid, "And please apologize on *my* behalf for waking him."

"And on behalf of the Guardia Civil," Tejada added to Molina's retreating figure. He turned back to face his unwilling guest. "Would you like some coffee, Señora?"

"Thank you, Lieutenant." Her voice was almost gracious.

"Jiménez." Tejada jerked his head in the direction of the mess hall.

Jiménez looked unhappy. "But, sir," he began doubtfully. "she's a pris—"

"Coffee, Corporal. *Now*," Tejada interrupted firmly.

Jiménez disappeared, and Tejada risked an apology to the professor's wife. "I am sorry for the inconvenience, Señora. They're new."

"*That* is obvious. I certainly intend to lodge a complaint against them with Captain Rodríguez in the morning."

Tejada wished that he had thought to demand two coffees from Jiménez. At least, he thought glumly, she had thus far excluded him from the complaint. But if she knew Rodríguez by name, there was a good chance that she would make good on her threat. The memory of the captain's voice sounded menacingly in his ears. "*You will confine yourself to following orders.*" He did his best to smile conciliatingly. "This must be very difficult for you, Señora. Especially since I believe you said you don't know your husband's whereabouts. When did you say you had seen him last?"

She cast him a look of withering scorn, and he unhappily remembered that she was the wife, the sister, and probably the daughter of lawyers. She would be adept at avoiding questions. "I didn't say. However, since you ask, I will tell you that I have not seen him for over a week, and that I have no idea where he is at the moment."

"A week!" Tejada repeated, startled. "But why didn't you alert anyone earlier?"

"I am not in the habit of reporting my family's business to the authorities."

There was something wrong with the supercilious statement, and had Tejada been fully awake, he would have realized what it was. Since he was not really alert, he only said, "What family business would that be, Señora?"

She did not reply immediately, and he was distracted by the return of the corporal, bearing a cup of coffee, and Guardia Molina, who expressionlessly reported that His Honor, Judge Otero Martínez y Arias, was very sorry to hear of his sister's ordeal, and was sending someone to pick her up immediately. Because he was a compassionate man, Molina did not add that Judge Otero had been quite upset by the phone call, and had threatened to call the minister of defense, whom he had referred to as Fidel.

An automobile arrived within minutes for Señora Otero de Arroyo. Tejada saw her out, apologized as gracefully as possible for disturbing her, and then returned to Jiménez and his men. The lieutenant dismissed the guardias, and then herded Jiménez into his office. "Sit down, Corporal," he ordered, taking a seat behind the desk, and rubbing his eyes wearily.

"Errr . . . I'm very sorry, sir," Jiménez ventured. "But you did say that . . ."

Tejada wished again that he had managed to get ahold of a cup of coffee. His head hurt, and all he wanted to do was go back to bed. He glanced automatically at his bare wrist again, wondering how many hours he had before he officially went back on duty. Then he reached for a pad and pen. "I'd like your report on your visit to the Arroyo house now, Corporal."

"I told you—"

"Your official report," Tejada interrupted. "Including the names of your men, your exact time of arrival, who you met at the house, etcetera. As if you were writing it up."

"Well, all right." Jiménez was puzzled. He had planned to write all of it down immediately anyway. It was odd that Tejada wanted it in oral form instead. He made his report, as Tejada scribbled notes, and wondered a little resentfully why the lieutenant was unwilling to let him write his own report. Tejada interrupted him a few times to ask questions, and then scribbled some more.

"All right," the lieutenant said finally. "Thank you. Dismissed, Corporal."

"Yes, sir." Jiménez saluted. To his surprise, the lieutenant opened one drawer of the desk, and drew out a sheet of carbon paper. Then he stood, crossed the room to the table where the typewriter sat, and began taking off the machine's lid. Curiosity got the better of formality. "What are you doing, sir?"

"Typing this up." The lieutenant glanced at his wrist again, and made a face. "What time is it?"

"A little after four A.M. sir."

"Shit." The lieutenant inserted the sheet carefully into the typewriter, and dragged a chair over. "Well, at least I should get it done before dawn."

"I could do it, sir," Jiménez offered. "I mean, you're not really on duty."

"No, that's all right, thank you." It took all of Tejada's self-control to refrain from making an acid comment about the tone the corporal's report was likely to take. If, as seemed likely, the report was going to be scrutinized by Captain Rodríguez, and possibly by higher officials, Tejada felt more comfortable writing it himself. He dismissed Jiménez, and began to pound away at his composition, carefully balancing respect for the Otero Martínez family, with insistence on the justice of the Guardia's actions in the case.

He finished writing a little over an hour later, placed the precious document in a locked filing cabinet, and stumbled back to bed, feeling as if his eyes were the size of watermelons.

Naturally, since he wanted to make the most of the few remaining hours available for sleep, his mind became suddenly alert. *How could a man under surveillance disappear for a week?* He supposed it was logical that Señora de Arroyo might not be overly anxious to involve the Guardia in her personal affairs, but most women would have been worried if their husbands suddenly disappeared. Unless she knew where he was, of course. His mind sharpened. She had denied knowledge of his whereabouts and he had believed her. *Why?* She might well be Arroyo's accomplice. *In what?*, the lieutenant asked himself, and received no good answer. Tejada could not remember any charges against the former lawyer aside from his signing of the petition four years earlier. *What else might make him want to disappear? And did it have to do with the other "petitioners"?*

*In the morning,* Tejada told himself, *I'll read all of their files again, carefully. And I'll find out what the standing of the Otero Martínez family really is. And if Arroyo's family are leftists. In the morning. And right now, I'll go to sleep so that I'll be alert tomorrow . . . today . . . in just a few hours . . . shit, stop wasting time. GO TO SLEEP!* Naturally, he tossed and turned until a few seconds before reveille, when he was forced to arise totally exhausted.

# Chapter 4

Breakfast readings were a tradition in the Fernández family. Guillermo always claimed that he wrote best in the small hours of the morning, preferably when facing a tight deadline. His children had grown up with the phrase, "Go to bed now. Papa needs to write." Frequently, the morning after uttering these magic words, Professor Fernández would appear at the dining-room table unshaven and with bags under his eyes, clutching a sheaf of papers. "It's done!" he would proclaim. "Would you like to hear it?" Then he would read the speech or article to his wife, pausing anxiously at the end to ask for her comments. As Hipólito and Elena grew older, they too became part of his morning audience, praising and criticizing with increasing knowledge and interest.

Elena had missed the morning readings when she returned from Madrid. She had relegated them to the irretrievably lost world designated as "prewar." So she felt a rush of relief and pleasure when her father appeared the next morning with his chin covered in gray stubble, holding a folded sheet of paper, and said as he reached for the coffeepot, "The letter's done. Would you like to hear it?"

Elena caught her mother's quick smile as well, and a knot in her chest tightened. It was almost painful to remember what her father had been like. "Of course," she said, and waited for him to declaim.

Professor Fernández had worked hard on the letter. It was reasonable to assume that it would be read by both the Spanish and French authorities before it reached its destination—if it reached Meyer at all. He had carefully cloaked any reference to taking in the refugee in allusions to the *Odyssey*. Even his daughter had to work to follow these allusions, and his wife had to interrupt him with questions. "What do you mean 'visit Sparta for news of Odysseus?'" María asked halfway through the letter.

"That's where Telemachus meets Theoklymenos," Elena explained impatiently.

"Yes, dear." Her mother shot her an irritated glance. "But I meant what does it *mean?*"

Guillermo smiled briefly. "I was thinking that you deserve a holiday from all the heat. How would you feel about a few weeks in San Sebastián this summer?"

"I suppose." María was dubious. "If you're given permission to travel."

The professor nodded. "It would be simple to pick up Meyer there, if he can slip across the border."

"I love the seashore." Elena smiled, pleased above all that her father was once again planning things.

The professor shook his head. "I meant your mother and I. There's no need for you to get involved, Elenita."

Elena was annoyed. I'm already involved, she thought, and then reproached herself for being ungrateful for her father's intermittent efforts to protect her.

The professor continued reading, unaware of her mutinous thoughts. "Well," he asked, as he reached the end of the much worked-over letter, "what do you think?"

"It's wonderful, Guillermo," his wife said sincerely. "No one who wasn't as obsessed with Homer as you are could understand it."

"I wonder." Elena was hesitant, but the old urge to critique the professor's work was strong.

"Yes?" Her father looked at her anxiously, but it was with his old anxiety about his writing, and she was not upset by it.

"Is it *too* obscure?" the young woman said slowly. "You don't want something that shouts it's a code. Because a coded message is sure to attract attention. *Because* it's coded, you know."

The professor nodded. "I know. That's why I didn't write in Greek. It would have been simpler, really."

"Censors aren't known for their subtlety." María spoke comfortingly. "I think it's fine, Guillermo. They'll probably just make some comment about absent-minded professors, and pass it along."

The professor looked relieved. "Maybe. What do you think I should change, Elena?"

His daughter shrugged. "I don't know. Probably not one censor in a hundred has studied the classics. So I'm sure it's fine."

"Probably not one in a thousand." The professor spoke with a trace of bitterness. "I'll go and make a clean copy then."

Elena nodded, trying not to wince at this break in the routine. In the old days, her father had always rushed out of the house without the time to make fair copies. His speeches tended to be crosshatched and doodled-over affairs, with arrows leading from paragraph to paragraph. But at least her father was moving with some purpose, even if it was only to recopy a letter.

Elena had come to dread the end of breakfast since her return to Salamanca. During her childhood, breakfast had been a hurried affair; her father had been perpetually late for his lectures, and she and her brother had been rushing to school. In Madrid, before the incident that had cost her her job as a teacher and forced her to return home, she had stopped eating breakfast entirely, and had simply prepared for work first thing in the morning. But now breakfast had no natural end. It was usually Señora de Fernández who finally stood, after it was no longer possible to pretend to linger over coffee, and cleared the cups away with a final air. Then Elena would cast an apologetic look at her father, and follow her mother out of the room, to help her with the housework that both of them hated. Guillermo Fernández would stare at his hands, or else stand and mumble something about going to his study. He seldom left the house in the mornings anymore. He had few errands to run, and aimless walks tended to attract unwanted shadows with three-cornered hats and rifles. On good days the professor had private tutoring to look forward to in the afternoons, and he would spend hours carefully planning how to pound basic Latin into the head of a wealthy and unwilling adolescent. On days when there was no tutoring he did not leave the house at all.

Elena hated the drudgery of cleaning and mending. But she hated watching her father's idleness even more. She knew that her mother sympathized with him. But María de Fernández had never had to leave the house in the morning for work and Elena suspected that she did not understand how miserable it was to *not* have to leave for work. Even though Elena's stay in Madrid during wartime had been filled with hardship, and even terror, especially when her students' families were persecuted by the Guardia Civil, Elena missed teaching. She had an unarticulated feeling that she understood her father better than her mother did. The professor's daughter had never discussed her insight with her parents, perhaps because she felt obscurely guilty about it. But she also felt as if her secret understanding made her somehow responsible for her father, as if she were the adult in the relationship.

It was this lingering sense of responsibility that made her say every Friday afternoon, with false cheerfulness, "If you're going out, Papa, can I come along? I'd like a walk."

The professor always accepted her company on his walks to the Guardia Civil post. Elena felt at her most maternal towards him on these walks. It never occurred to her that she might be a burden as well as a blessing to him when he reported to the Guardia Civil; that Guillermo Fernández might wish to protect his daughter even as she wished to protect him; that he hated the fear that made him cling to her arm as they approached the post as much as she did. Neither father nor daughter wished to tug at their tangled skein of love and resentment, for fear that it might unravel entirely.

The professor was more cheerful than usual this Friday. He emerged from his study and poked his head into the living room where Elena and her mother were working considerably earlier than usual. "I'm going to stop by the post office before reporting to my parole officer," he announced, waving an envelope. "Would you like a walk, Elenita?"

"I'd love one." Elena's alacrity was less forced than usual. She turned to her mother. "Unless . . . ?"

"You go along," María reassured her quickly. "You need the fresh air."

Elena enjoyed the walk. Father and daughter reached the post office shortly before it closed for the siesta, and mailed two copies of the carefully written letter: one to the address Meyer had specified, and another to the address in Leipzig where Guillermo had sent his previous correspondence. Then they dawdled in the empty streets, taking the shady way whenever possible. At this time of year looking for shade was more a game than a necessity. The professor shared his daughter's good mood.

"Of course, it probably won't even reach Meyer," he said, as they turned out of sight of the post office. "Things are so unsettled now, and if the Germans have sealed the borders. . . ."

"I'm sure he'll get *one* of them," Elena soothed.

"And you think that's a good thing?" The professor turned and smiled at her. She was a hair taller than he was, and he had to raise his chin slightly to meet her eyes. "And here I was worrying about protecting you and your mother."

"Of course it's a good thing," Elena said firmly. "I liked him a lot. It's the right thing to do."

The professor sighed. "I'm lucky to have such a daughter."

Elena squeezed his arm, both pleased and embarrassed, and her father patted her hand. They walked arm in arm without speaking until they reached the Guardia Civil post, topped by its watchtowers and red-and-yellow flag. Elena, who had been leaning on her father's arm, straightened, as she felt him begin to lean on her. She wondered, as she always did, if his stoop actually became more pronounced in the presence of the Guardia, or if she merely thought that he suddenly seemed much shorter. "Will you ask the Captain for permission to travel today?" she asked, to distract him from his fear.

"If he's in a good mood," her father replied without meeting her eyes.

Elena sighed. She had wanted to ask him to ask the captain to give her permission to travel to San Sebastián as well. *So I can keep an eye on them,* she told herself, knowing that her real motive was the choking fear that she would be abandoned in Salamanca without news, or even a letter, if her parents were arrested in the north. But she did not have the heart to make demands on her father now, when he was leaning so heavily on her arm, with his eyes fixed on the ground to guide his faltering steps.

The professor stated his name and business to the guardia on duty in a low voice that was almost a mumble.

"And you are?" The guardia turned to Elena, rifle held across his chest.

Elena held her breath for an instant, praying, as she did every week, that her father would say something. For once, her prayers were answered. "My daughter," Guillermo muttered.

The guardia stood aside to let them pass, and they entered the familiar waiting room. Elena looked about her with hatred. The ugly, hard-backed benches, the dirty floors, and the harsh lights were as disgusting as they had been last week. The room, however, was noticeably emptier. Elena recognized most of the civilians in the room as her father's fellow parolees, although only a few of them were present. She and her father easily found a bench for themselves. She wondered where the other parolees who usually clogged the room were. Perhaps their appointments had been changed. Perhaps they were no longer under surveillance. Perhaps they had been arrested. Her father was still holding her hand, staring fixedly at the ground, unwilling to meet anyone's eyes. Elena gritted her teeth. Surely they had not been arrested. The Guardia Civil were not doing sweeps anymore. No one had been executed in Salamanca for months now. Perhaps it was simply that another waiting room had opened up.

The door to the inner corridor opened and then slammed, and a sergeant whom Elena recognized from previous visits emerged. "Fernández!" he called. "Fernández Ochóa."

"Here, sir." Guillermo shuffled to his feet, and Elena rose with him, nervous at how short the waiting period had been. Either the Guardia Civil were unusually efficient this week or . . . she decided that they must be unusually efficient.

The sergeant nodded, and made a note on a clipboard. Then he gestured toward the door he had just walked through. "Come on, then, the Lieutenant's waiting." He recognized Elena as she had recognized him, and nodded to her. "Good afternoon, Señorita. You can come too, if you want."

Elena nodded, and barely managed a courteous reply. Her father's fingers were like claws on her arm. The steady tramp of the sergeant behind them was giving her a headache. Why the lieutenant? Elena wondered, temporarily forgetting her worries about Joseph Meyer in light of more urgent questions. In the past, the post's captain had seen them. Surely if it was something important we'd see the captain again? And they wouldn't let me come if they meant to . . . She cut off the thought just as they reached a closed door, and the sergeant ordered them to halt.

The sergeant stepped past them, opened the door, and saluted. "Guillermo Fernández, sir," he announced.

"Thank you." The officer behind the desk had his head bent

over a file, so Elena's first impression of him was his voice. For a dazed moment she thought she was dreaming. Then he looked up, and she wished fervently that fainting or being struck by lightning were acts of conscious volition.

"*Carlos?*" Fortunately, Elena's incredulous whisper was drowned out by the crash of Tejada's chair as he shot to his feet, tipping it over backwards.

# Chapter 5

Captain Rodríguez had summoned Tejada fairly early that morning. Their interview had been as unpleasant as the lieutenant had expected. "I thought I had made it clear that Salamanca's people must be treated as the loyal citizens they are," Rodríguez began.

Tejada had considered pointing out that Arroyo Díaz was not precisely a loyal citizen, which was why the Guardia Civil was interested in him. He contented himself with saying, "Yes, sir."

"Señora Otero de Arroyo was extremely shaken by her ordeal, Lieutenant," the captain snapped. "She's an elderly lady, in frail health. You don't appear to understand the effect such a visit could have had on her."

If Captain Rodríguez had simply admitted that he feared complaints from the Otero family, Tejada would have felt sorry for him. As it was, the lieutenant listened to Rodríguez with increasing annoyance. A few of Rodríguez's points might conceivably have some validity, but Tejada was damned if he was going to accept correction from a blustering hypocrite. He listened to the captain's tirade as little as possible, contenting himself by responding with monosyllabic answers. "I'll expect a full report of this, Lieutenant," Rodríguez finished, finally.

"Yes, Captain. It's on file in my office. I can give you a carbon copy." The lieutenant was carefully expressionless.

"You mean you've written it up *already*?"

Tejada took secret satisfaction in the captain's stupefied expression. "Naturally, sir. As soon as I realized the delicacy of the case I wrote everything down." Tejada was quite sure that the captain would have liked to smack him for smugness or insubordination, and equally sure that he had manuevered his superior officer into an impossible position.

"Well . . . see that you get me that copy then," Rodríguez barked, forestalled of his prey.

"Yes, Captain." Tejada saluted, and left, feeling that he had come out of the interview as well as was possible.

Unfortunately, by the time he returned with the report, Captain Rodríguez had moved on to a new grievance. It was intolerable, the captain complained, for the Guardia to be so lax with regard to parolees. While Lieutenant Tejada and his men had been busily offending a prominent citizen, they had let a dangerous subversive slip through their fingers unnoticed. Lieutenant Tejada's time might be better spent dealing with criminals than harassing innocent citizens. Tejada, who was by this time feeling the effects of his interrupted sleep, swallowed his rage with some difficulty.

By the time Tejada was free to return to the parolees' files it was nearly noon, and he was thoroughly exhausted and annoyed. To his disgust, they were completely shuffled out of order. Sergeant Hernández, following orders, had alphabetized them, and the files that Tejada recalled from the previous day were scattered among utterly unfamiliar ones. The lieutenant spent nearly an hour shuffling through the files trying to remember which names were familiar, and then gave up, and pulled the petitioners' folders out from the stack. He began to read Arroyo's with more care, making some attempt to put it into a comprehensible order as he went along.

The information was not terribly enlightening. Much of it

seemed to consist of calendars of parole dates (all of them
scrupulously met until yesterday's), and handwritten notes saying things like, "*M.A. visited by H.F. 22:26 Monday Dec. 30 re:
Negrín symp???*" He finally found a typewritten form giving
Arroyo's address, date of birth, marital status, and current
employer. Tejada noted, with mild interest, that Arroyo's employer was listed as one Eduardo Crespo, doctor of jurisprudence,
and wondered in what capacity the former professor was now
employed. Doctor Crespo was a bold man to hire Arroyo in the
teeth of the Guardia Civil. A cutting from some legal journal
had been paperclipped to the form. It contained a brief biogra-
phy of Manuel Arroyo Díaz: "A native Salmantino, Arroyo
received his doctorate from the University of Salamanca in 1889.
He has studied abroad in France and Germany, and is author of
numerous articles, and books including, *The Retroactive Mandate;
a Possible Role for the League of Nations in Cuba and Hispaniola* and
*A Study of the Taxation of Foreign Nationals with Accounts in Spain.*
Arroyo currently holds a chair on the legal faculty at the
University of Salamanca, where he pursues his interest in the
intersection of law and economics." Tejada sighed, and wondered what the chances were that an elderly academic had somehow managed to slip across the border and risk a transatlantic
crossing to Cuba—or Hispaniola. It did not seem likely.

When he was satisfied that the Arroyo file was in order,
Tejada turned his attention to the folders dedicated to Rivera
and Velázquez. As he had expected, the two folders were not
organized enough to be cross-referenced, but contained considerable redundant information. Twenty years separated the
two doctors, but Rivera was clearly a protégé of Velázquez, and
their careers had run parallel for the last decade: research interests in neurology, a flirtation with Viennese psychoanalytic theory, a string of publications in French and German periodicals,
and then a sudden drop into professional obscurity in 1936.
Velázquez, at sixty-five, was listed as "retired." He was a widower

who lived with a married daughter. Rivera was married and the father of three. He was employed in an unspecified capacity by a firm listed as Quiñones and Sons. Tejada, noting Doctor Rivera's relative youth, decided that he had probably been led astray by his old mentor. It was unlikely, given the generation gap, that he had been a moving force among his elders.

Unfortunately, neither file contained the slightest reference to any connection the professors might have had to Manuel Arroyo Díaz. Tejada gritted his teeth, and glanced at his watch. It was nearly two o'clock and the first of the day's parolees would be coming in less than an hour. He began to skim Guillermo Fernández's file with one eye on the time. Somewhat to his surprise, Fernández had a prison record. He shuffled impatiently through the folder trying to find out why the classics professor had been imprisoned while his colleagues had been allowed to go free, but found nothing. Annoyed, he sent for Hernández and demanded an explanation.

"It does seem a bit arbitrary, sir," the sergeant agreed. "But as I understand it, Fernández was thought to be a ringleader. Because he was a personal friend of the rector's, you see. And we wanted to set an example for the others, and then of course there was the whole issue of family connections."

"The Oteros," the lieutenant said dryly. "Do Rivera and Velázquez have those kind of connections, by the way?"

Sergeant Hernández looked sympathetic. "I don't think so, sir, but that wasn't quite what I meant. Fernández had some very dubious family connections."

"Oh?" Tejada raised his eyebrows.

"His son's a Red," Hernández explained. "Hipólito, his name is. He slipped through our lines during the war and fought on the other side."

"Did he survive the war?" The lieutenant was already searching through folders looking for another labeled Fernández.

"Yes, sir, so far as we know. He's an inactive file though."

"Why? Executed?"

"No, sir. He made it across the border sometime last year, we think. He's in Mexico now."

"How do we know that?"

"Professor Fernández has been getting letters from him," the sergeant said simply. "I think there's a copy of the first one somewhere in the file, sir. From August of '39 or thereabouts."

Tejada wrinkled his nose. "Hipólito Fernández must be an expert runner," he commented with some distaste. "Through our lines, over the border, all the way to Mexico."

"Yes, sir."

Tejada considered for a moment. "Are we sure it's Mexico, and not Cuba or the Dominican Republic?"

Sergeant Hernández blinked. "As sure as we can be, sir. I don't think anyone thought it was important. Why?"

Tejada shook his head. "Probably no reason. It was just a thought." He bent his head over the Fernández file again. There was the usual list of parole dates, each one neatly checked off, except for the last. He inspected the sheet more closely. "Why didn't you tell me that Fernández missed his last parole date?" he demanded, his voice suddenly sharp.

"What?" The sergeant looked startled. "What do you mean?"

"Here," Tejada pointed. "June fourteenth. That was last Friday and it's not checked off."

"It should be, sir." Hernández sounded uncertain. "At least, I think it should be. I remember seeing Fernández."

"Are you sure?" Tejada asked.

"Fairly sure, yes, sir. He always comes with an old maid daughter of his. I remember seeing her last week."

"Are you sure it was last week?"

"Yes, sir." The sergeant was frowning, troubled. "It must have been. The captain was a bit short-tempered, and he was annoyed that I'd let Fernández's daughter in with him. He made some comment about it being the last time he'd have to deal with the . . . er . . . the girl as well as the old man, something like that."

"The girl?" Tejada raised his eyebrows.

Hernández looked half-abashed and half-amused. "Well, the bitch, if you'll pardon my language, sir."

Tejada smiled slightly. "Understood, Hernández. Do you think the captain's annoyance might have made him careless about noting the date?"

The sergeant immediately became wooden. "It's not my place to say, sir."

"I agree." The lieutenant was bland. "But I'm grateful for your powers of observation, Sergeant." He picked up a pen, and checked off the June fourteenth date. "So, if none of them have missed any of their parole dates before, what do you think has happened to Arroyo this week?"

"I have no idea, sir." Hernández's tone was genuine, and apologetic now. He glanced at his watch and added, "The first of the parolees should be coming in any minute, sir. Should I let them wait?"

Tejada was tempted to continue examining the Fernández file, and even more tempted to take a nap, but a determination to upset the routines of Captain Rodríguez made him say. "No, show them in as they arrive. That way we'll finish with them on time."

Tejada's interviews with the first half-dozen parolees were uneventful. They were all more or less on time, and none of them had any special demands. The lieutenant, preoccupied with the problem of Arroyo Díaz's disappearance, was pleased to recognize the name of one of the petitioners as next on the list. "Is Guillermo Fernández here?" he asked the sergeant, half expecting (and half hoping) that Hernández would say that the professor was late.

"Yes, sir," the sergeant replied readily. "He's in the waiting room, with his daughter. Should I show them in?"

"Please." Hernández left, and Tejada bent his head over the

Fernández file, scrupulously checking off the appropriate date to avoid further confusion. He wondered idly why the professor was always accompanied by his daughter. Perhaps she was unusually fond of him. Perhaps he was afraid of entering the post alone. Perhaps they merely liked annoying Captain Rodríguez.

The lieutenant was shuffling through the file, searching for useful information, and wondering what kind of a man would bestow on his only son the archaic name of Hipólito, when Sergeant Hernández returned. "Guillermo Fernández, sir," he announced.

"Thank you." Tejada closed the file, looked up, and met a pair of wide, dark eyes set in a white, stricken face that he remembered only too well. Classics! he thought. Oh, shit. So *that's* how I knew the name. And then, somewhat unfairly, *Old maid?* I'm going to kill Hernández for that bit of misleading information.

Elena looked as if she were going to faint. Tejada stood rapidly, gauging the possibility of catching her if she fell, and overturned his chair with an embarrassingly loud crash.

Guillermo Fernández jumped slightly as the chair fell. "Err . . . good afternoon, Lieutenant," he stammered. "Is the captain . . . ?"

Tejada stooped, and attempted to pick up his chair by one arm while still keeping his eyes on Elena. Since the chair was a heavy, wheeled affair, it was impossible to set it upright one-handed, and his efforts were rewarded by a series of loud thumps, followed by another crash as the chair hit the floor again. Red-faced, the lieutenant dropped his eyes, wrenched the recalcitrant piece of furniture upright, and held out his hand to the man standing across from his desk, trying to pretend that he had only intended to shake hands in the first place. "How do you do, Professor Fernández," he said shortly. "The captain has transferred the duty of interviewing parolees to me. I will be in charge of your files in the future."

"Oh." The professor took the proffered hand, looking a little nonplussed. No guardia civil had ever offered to shake hands with him before, and it was unusual for a guardia to explain his actions so freely as well. "How do you do?" He became aware that Elena was still clinging to his arm, and added, since the lieutenant was so unusually well mannered, "This is my daughter."

Tejada looked hastily at Elena, waiting for some cue. She held out one hand mutely. He took it, wondering wildly if he should say something of their former acquaintance. They shook hands in mutually miserable silence. *Do something,* Tejada wanted to shout at the old man. *Say something. Offer her a chair, damn you. Can't you see she's upset?*

The lieutenant had given a good deal of thought to what he wanted to say to Guillermo Fernández, and had carefully planned out an interrogation, touching on the professor's relationship to Arroyo, to the other petitioners, and to his absent son, but he found himself tongue-tied. It was difficult to cross-examine someone properly when you had the nagging feeling that he might cross-examine you about your intentions at any moment. *I wonder if he knows my name?* Tejada thought. *No, probably not, or he'd have guessed why Elena was upset. But what did she tell them about Madrid? She must have said something. Perhaps she only mentioned the little girl, her pupil, but not me.* He took a deep breath. "Your . . . your political beliefs, Professor. I would appreciate it if you would state them for me." Even as he spoke he remembered Elena's voice, shaking with barely controlled hysteria, incriminating herself: "*I'm a Socialist, Sergeant!*" He stared at Professor Fernández to avoid her eyes.

Guillermo shuddered slightly and stared at the ground. The question was a familiar one, and somehow the strange lieutenant, who politely used the formal "you" and shook hands before interrogating, was far more menacing than the blustery, openly insulting Captain Rodríguez. "I'm a professor of humanities, Lieutenant," he said quietly. "Politics aren't my business."

"They were your business in '36, though." Tejada looked

down at the desk, remembering Elena's voice, as relaxed as he had ever heard it: "*My father is a very devoted admirer of the classics.*"

"No." Guillermo was aware of the quaver in his voice and hated it. No violence, he thought, remembering the blue-shirted youths who had dragged him to prison. Please, God, no violence. Not in front of Elena. "No, I was a friend of Don Miguel's. I acted only as his friend."

"And your son? Is he also apolitical?" (I never knew she had a brother. Of course, she wouldn't have told me.)

"I haven't seen my son since '36." (And is that an excuse for me to cling to my daughter? Why did I let her come with me?)

"What about your fellow petitioners?" Tejada asked abruptly, his mind only half on the question. ("*I haven't seen my parents since the beginning of the war,*" she told me. God, and I wondered why she feared me.) "When was the last time you saw Arturo Velázquez?"

"I don't know. A while ago." Guillermo frowned. (Why does he want to know this?)

"Tomás Rivera?" Tejada felt the awkwardness of the question. (Stupid way to go about this! But since you've started, you might as well continue.)

"I can't remember. We were never close." The professor felt himself sliding into the familiar pattern of interrogation. He stared fixedly at the stack of manila folders on the desk, knowing that he probably would not have the courage to ask the strange lieutenant for permission to travel. (I've already mailed the letter to Meyer. It's too late. Why do they want to know now? I shouldn't have written. I shouldn't have let Elena know about this . . . I can ask next week. Next week I won't let her come with me.)

"Manuel Arroyo Díaz?" Tejada risked a glance at Elena. She was staring at him, very straight-backed and white-faced. (Vouch for him, Tejada silently willed her. Tell me if he's telling the truth.)

"I don't know. Five or six months ago, maybe."

"Are you aware that Professor Arroyo is suspected of subversive activity?"

"No, I wasn't."

Tejada managed to jerk out a few more unrelated questions, and then closed the interview with relief. He sent for Hernández automatically.

"Well?" the sergeant asked, interested in his superior's impressions of Professor Fernández. "Do you think he knows anything about Arroyo?"

Tejada shrugged. "Probably not. But have someone follow him home, and keep an eye on his movements for the next couple of days, until we know what's going on."

"Yes, sir." Hernández, Tejada noted approvingly, carefully wrote the order on a small pad. "Just Fernández, sir, or the wife and daughter also?"

"Just Fernández," the lieutenant said hastily, and then recollected that it would have been wiser to ask if Hernández had a reason for wanting surveillance of the rest of the family. He swallowed. "Unless you think El . . . the girl knows something."

The sergeant shook his head. "No, it's not worth wasting a man on. Just checking, sir."

"Fine." Tejada heaved a sigh of relief. "Is the next parolee here yet?"

Hernández glanced at the list. "Ernesto Cárdenas? Yes, sir. I'll send him in."

"Thanks." Tejada pulled Cárdenas's file from the stack, returning to familiar routine with infinite relief. He devoutly hoped that he would not meet any more parolees' relatives he knew in the course of the afternoon. One was quite enough.

# Chapter 6

E lena walked home through the slanting afternoon sunlight blind to the buildings around her, and very nearly deaf to her father's voice. "I suppose I should have asked about traveling," Guillermo was saying, a little anxiously. "But overall, I don't think that went too badly. Of course, the lieutenant asked a lot of questions, but that's probably just because he's new, don't you think?"

"Yes." Elena had no idea what she was agreeing to.

"I was nervous there for a bit." In fact, Guillermo was calm enough to realize that his daughter was upset, and he spoke now in an effort to draw her out. "But I think it will be all right. What did you think of the lieutenant? He struck me as a bright man, for a guardia."

Elena nodded slowly. "Yes, he is bright." Now, she knew, was the time to tell him, before her silence became guilty. Logically, it should not have been difficult. Her father would not think of blaming her if she said casually, "*Actually, I was too startled to mention it earlier, but we've met before, right after the war ended. He was investigating a murder in Madrid that involved one of my students. He asked me for some information.*" She tried to imagine the turn the conversation would take next. "*No, no, I wasn't a suspect. Nothing like that. He was very kind. He's not bad as the guardia go.*" That was all that was necessary to say. Surely her father would not press her for more details. He would be concerned, but not overly curious.

Elena knew that she was lying to herself. Her parents would certainly be worried enough to ask other questions about her encounter with the Guardia Civil in Madrid. In fact, she would be able to set their minds at rest regarding her brush with a murder investigation. She might have to admit that Tejada had been very kind to her—he had fed her when she was starving—but even that would not be so terrible. The awful part would be explaining her last encounter with him. She had rehearsed the words a thousand times: "*I had dinner with Sergeant Tejada and then I went home. A couple of soldiers tried to get fresh. They were drunk, and, well, you can imagine the sort of thing. It could have been unpleasant if Sergeant Tejada hadn't been there. He followed me because he was worried about me. Very gallant—and very helpful as it turned out.*" She could practically hear her own lighthearted laugh, and see the casual shrug that would (of course) allay her parents' fears. "*I would have told you earlier, but I didn't want to worry you. No harm done, after all.*"

"So you thought so, too?" her father asked, after a sidelong glance to make sure that she was not going to say anything further.

Elena took a deep breath. "Yes. Actually, I . . ." her voice was a croak, and for a moment she felt again the rage and terror of that darkened street in Madrid. "Actually, I thought it was a bit funny, the way he tipped over the chair."

The professor laughed. "It's a treat to see them trip up once in a while, isn't it?" He glanced around and lowered his voice. "I only wish it happened more often."

Notwithstanding his white hair and distinguished appearance, the professor spoke with the undisguised glee of a schoolboy. Elena bit her lip. The worst part of telling her father that she knew the lieutenant would be reliving her brief encounter with the Falangist soldiers. But it would not be easy to admit that she had sobbed out her fear and confusion in Tejada's arms either.

María was waiting for them when they returned home. She immediately demanded news of Guillermo's interview with the

Guardia Civil, and the brief meeting was dissected minutely. Elena sat without listening and let her parents' voices wash over her. I have to tell them, she thought. He'll see papa again next week. And if he says anything . . . For the first time, Elena wondered what the lieutenant had thought of the meeting. She was sure he had recognized her. Perhaps he had already known that she might be there. Her father's file must include the names of his family. It was even possible that the Guardia Civil had started a file on her in Madrid, although going to so much trouble over a mere schoolteacher with left-wing sympathies seemed unlikely. Maybe he won't say anything, if he didn't today. Elena was too nervous to judge whether this was a reasonable hope. It did not occur to her that Lieutenant Tejada might have been as embarrassed as she was, albeit for slightly different reasons.

". . . can't think of a better idea," her father was saying.

"What do you think, Elenita?" her mother asked.

Elena blinked. "Sorry, what?"

Her mother looked at her with concern. "I was saying that if we do manage to make this trip to San Sebastián, we'll have to figure out a way to house our Theoklymenos. Your father thought maybe Hipólito could help."

Elena considered for a moment. "I'm sure he *would*," she said at last. "But I don't see how he can, exactly."

Guillermo frowned. "It depends on Meyer's passport, of course. If he can book a passage, then I thought Hipólito could meet him at the other side. If someone could arrange his entry into Mexico. . . ."

"What about money for the passage?" Elena asked.

"That was what I said." María's triumph was muted by worry over her daughter's apparent inattention.

"I don't know how much he'll be able to afford," the professor admitted, troubled. "And even if he has money, it's illegal to send it out of the country."

"And then there's the question of other expenses," Elena added dryly.

Her mother smiled at her. "We can feed him, Elenita."

Elena felt a flash of annoyance at her parents' naïveté. "I meant false papers," she said baldly. "And bribes, if necessary. You don't know the state of his passport, and unless you'd like to walk into the sergeant's . . . the *lieutenant's* office and ask about visas, I suggest you double the amount necessary for a legal emigration."

Guillermo winced and Elena's spark of irritation was snuffed out by guilt. It was cruel to play on her father's fear of the Guardia. Her mother moved on to another problem. "It's all very well to speak of a passage to Mexico, but even if money weren't a problem, where could he sail from? Even if the Guardia approve a trip to San Sebastián, they'll be suspicious of a request to travel to a port immediately afterward."

"He doesn't require a chaperone, María." The professor spoke with a certain grim amusement.

"Does he speak Spanish?" his wife countered.

Guillermo, whose conversations with Joseph Meyer had been essentially in classical Greek punctuated by French or German when necessary, blinked sheepishly. "He knows French and Latin quite well," he offered.

"Very helpful if he wants to communicate with monks!" his wife retorted.

Elena shook her head, trying to clear her mind of the memory of Tejada's voice saying with amused incredulity, "*Surely you don't actually know Latin?*" Her parents saw the movement, and turned to her expecting a comment. "Can't he stay here?" she asked. "One border crossing is complicated enough."

"Without a ration card?" her father asked.

"Mama said we could feed him."

"For the short term," the professor amended, looking at the sharply drawn planes in Elena's face, wondering if a generous impulse to a colleague was about to take food from his only daughter's mouth. "And it would be impossible to keep him in hiding indefinitely."

"I don't see how you plan to get rid of him though." María's voice was taut with strain.

Guillermo, who had the increasing conviction that he should never have replied to the fugitive's letter, did his best to speak reassuringly. "Maybe we won't have to. It's too early to tell yet. We'll have to see what happens in France."

"You'd send him back?" María asked sarcastically, knowing the answer as she spoke.

"The Germans only reached Paris last week," Guillermo replied in what he hoped was a placating tone. "And in the north the French relied too much on the Maginot Line. It may be different in the south. The Provençals are Catalans, really. Good fighters."

To the professor's relief, his wife and daughter seemed willing to let this shaky comfort stand. The Fernández family continued to worry intermittently about this topic throughout the evening, but little progress was made. Guillermo, whose courage was always at its peak on Friday evenings, when his next interview with the Guardia Civil was furthest away, promised to ask for permission to take "a family vacation" in San Sebastián the following week. Elena wondered uneasily if he was relying on her presence at the Guardia post the following week, and then, with a little spurt of alarm, remembered that she would have to invent an excuse to avoid Lieutenant Tejada in the future. María watched her husband's return to equanimity with pleasure, but was slightly worried by her daughter's withdrawal.

Professor Fernández's tenuous optimism was destroyed the following afternoon. The family was assembled in the living room after a depressingly frugal lunch. María was writing to Hipólito. Elena was rereading, somewhat listlessly, a novel that had been a childhood favorite. Guillermo was reviewing his monthly bank statement, a task made more interesting by the Guardia Civil's propensity for temporarily freezing his account without warning. The professor punctuated his calculations with occasional whistles between his teeth when perturbed. This had been an uneventful month though, and the task was finished relatively quickly, and with fewer whistles than usual. "Do you mind if I turn on the radio?" he asked, closing his accounts with a satisfied air, and pushing himself to his feet.

"Hmmm? No, it's fine." María glanced up, and returned to her letter. "Do you want to add anything to my letter?"

"Of course. When you are finished." The professor crossed the room to the radio, and paused with his hand on the knob. "Any requests, Elena?"

His daughter shook her head. "No, oh, music, I suppose."

"News is always bad," María agreed with a smile.

Guillermo flicked the switch and static filled the air, followed in rapid succession by the high singsong tones of General Franco, a combination of horns and strings that sounded vaguely jazzlike, static again, and the clipped English of the BBC. "Let me know when to stop," the professor said, still spinning the dial slowly, as a woman's voice crooned the last strains of a love song, and a warm bass said, "*You're listening to Radio Española.*"

"Something less sentimental," María requested.

There was another burst of static, and then the precise tones of a newscaster: "Once again, the surrender of Maréchal Petain's government to the German forces has been confirmed. In a statement made earlier today, the Maréchal said, quote . . ."

There was a thud as Elena's book slid out of her lap unheeded. Guillermo Fernández stood, one hand poised over the radio, as if frozen by some latter-day Medusa. María's pen slid in her shaking hands, blotting half a line. Their preference for music forgotten, the Fernández family listened intently to the news. Only when the announcer began detailing the casualties resulting from a bridge collapsing over the Ebro did Elena say, "It's

mostly lies, probably." Her voice trembled only slightly. "Radio
Burgos broadcast lies about Madrid all through the war.
Remember, I told you."

"They managed to get the date of the surrender right though,"
Guillermo muttered.

María shook her head. "It doesn't seem possible that they've
conquered France. I mean . . . *France* . . . it's . . . it's not a *small*
country."

Her husband looked grim. "Give me that letter," he ordered.
"I think it's a good idea to write to Hipólito about all this."

María handed over the paper, but with a pleading look.
"You'll be discreet?"

"Of course." The professor smiled briefly, paternal pride
glowing through current worry. "The boy knows enough Greek
to read a simple message."

"But—"

"I'll use quotes, María. Hipólito knows his Homer. And even
a literate censor will have trouble following if I slip something
extra into a citation."

The professor spent the better part of an hour writing to his
son. By the time he finished the letter, it was too late to go to the
post office. He accepted the delay with unexpected calm, and
proposed to his wife a stroll around the plaza. She accepted,
and Elena, feeling that her presence was unnecessary, stayed
home, ostensibly to read but actually to brood. Guillermo's calm
was unimpaired that evening, even though his wife had noted
that they were being discreetly tailed by a guardia civil.

María was almost unnerved by the change in her husband
over the next few days. In spite of the alarming news from
France, and in spite of the fact that the Guardia had almost certainly stepped up their surveillance again, he seemed more
decided and more contented than he had been in years. *He's*
glad *that Meyer wrote to him*, María thought resignedly. *It's like that
business with Don Miguel all over again.* It was noble of Guillermo

to take risks to help colleagues. His generosity was one of the things she loved about him. But she sometimes suspected that it would be more restful to have a husband who was content without taking insane risks. It was, María supposed, merely the law of averages that Elena seemed to be falling to pieces just as Guillermo pulled himself together. A family vacation! María thought, as her husband began to talk of writing to hotels in San Sebastián. It will be a wonder if we all come out of this one alive!

Guillermo's good mood received an abrupt check when the mail arrived on Wednesday afternoon. The postman had brought only one envelope. It was crumpled, but the address, in Professor Fernández's own handwriting, was still legible: *12 Rue de Lafayette, Toulouse.* One end had been slit, and resealed with the stamp of the Spanish censors, but the seal on the envelope remained untampered with. Stamped across the back of the envelope were the words: UNDELIVERABLE: SERVICE SUSPENDED, and a black stamp of an eagle perched over a swastika, its wings spread, with the words: OBERKOMMANDO DER WEHRMACHT.

Guillermo brought the letter into the kitchen without speaking, and held it out to María. She looked at the envelope that her husband had mutely offered for her inspection, half hoping that Guillermo's newfound and possibly suicidal determination would falter under this blow. Then she raised her eyes to his face. "Perhaps the mail is only disrupted for a few days," she suggested gently. "After all, a lot has happened lately."

Guillermo sank into a chair, shaking his head. "Wasn't that what you said about Madrid?" he remarked.

It was his wife's turn to wince. The nightmare months of Guillermo's imprisonment, when she had tried over and over again to write to Elena, too frightened to telephone her, and never certain if the letters went through, were all too vivid. "Try again in a few days," she pleaded, forgetting that she had hoped that the problem of Joseph Meyer might be solved by continued postal delays. "You don't have anything to lose."

"I suppose not." The professor sighed, and leaned his forehead on his hand. "But I don't see the point."

"We'll find a way." María spoke soothingly, and tucked the offending letter into the cookbook she had been reading, as if it were a bookmark, so that it would be out of her husband's sight.

"I don't see how."

The gist of this conversation was repeated at intervals during dinner, until Elena thought that she would go mad. She had noted the impending approach of her father's Friday interview with the Guardia Civil with increasingly guilty dread. Now, adding to her guilt, was the feeling that she should have been helping her mother to cheer her father.

"The letter to Hipólito was sent without any difficulty," María reminded him. "And Friday you'll ask about San Sebastián. . . ."

"My God!" The professor shuddered. "I'm not looking forward to that either."

"Perhaps you could ask the lieutenant if he knows anything about when the mail will be back to normal," Elena suggested without thinking.

Her parents turned to stare at her, and she flushed as she recognized the absurdity of her idea. But she succeeded in striking a spark from her father. "You ask him," he said, wryly, "since you're so at ease in his company."

Elena was grateful for the note of humor, but decided somewhat unhappily that this was not the best time to explain that she wished to avoid another meeting with the lieutenant.

# Chapter 7

Tejada spent a good deal more time than he would have liked thinking about his encounter with Elena Fernández over the next few days. He told himself that he was merely worrying about her to take his mind off of his work, which was proving irritating. He might, however, have devoted even more mental time to the professor's daughter had he not been so busy. Circumstances certainly seemed to conspire to bring her to mind.

In the absence of actual clues to Arroyo's whereabouts, Tejada had fallen back on careful scrutiny of the records of Arroyo's fellow petitioners. He instinctively and unconsciously avoided scrutinizing Guillermo Fernández's too closely, until a chance comment made by Sergeant Hernández on Monday morning about the failure to check on Fernández's associates made him aware of the oversight.

"What do you want me to do?" he snapped. "Send to Madrid to see if there's a file on his daughter as well? I'm sure *that* will help with Arroyo!"

"No, sir," the sergeant replied quickly. Hernández had quickly come to like the lieutenant, and he had not expected the sharp note in Tejada's voice. Because he liked Tejada, however, he risked another question. "How did you know she was in Madrid, sir?"

Tejada deposited the Fernández file in the filing cabinet, and slammed the drawer shut with slightly more violence than necessary. "Because, Sergeant," he said with careful formality, "you may recall that I interviewed Fernández on Friday and, despite your apparent opinion, I did my best to avoid negligence."

"Understood, sir." The sergeant knew when not to ask more questions.

To satisfy his conscience, Tejada persuaded himself that there was no evidence that any of the petitioners had had any contact with Arroyo recently. It was far more likely that his wife or his employer knew something about his whereabouts. The idea of another interview with Señora Otero de Arroyo was not attractive. Tejada looked up the address of Arroyo's employer, and set out to meet the man who had hired Professor Arroyo after his enforced retirement from the university.

Tejada found the law offices of Doctor Eduardo Crespo without difficulty. They were on the Rua Mayor, in what had been a wealthy neighborhood, halfway between the Plaza Mayor and the university. Like all of Salamanca, the row houses along the Rua Mayor were made of yellow-gold sandstone. Unlike much of the city, they were in excellent repair, clean and golden, instead of sooty. A discreet and highly polished brass plaque proclaimed that Eduardo Crespo, Doctor of Jurisprudence, would be found on the main floor of number eight. The concierge who opened the door bowed the lieutenant up the stairs to a large set of rooms overlooking the street.

A fair-haired man in a gray suit sat behind a desk in the outer office, typing something. He was not an expert typist, and his index fingers hovered over the keys like pistons, pouncing occasionally. He was apparently absorbed in what he was doing. Tejada coughed to get his attention. The man looked up. His eyebrows rose as he took in the lieutenant's uniform, but all he said was, "Yes, Señor Guardia? Can I help you?"

"I'm looking for Eduardo Crespo." Tejada did not waste words.

"Do you have an appointment, Señor?"

"I am here in an official capacity." Tejada's voice was absolutely calm, but he was somewhat puzzled. People very rarely asked uniformed guardias civiles if they had appointments. Crespo's clerk (or secretary, or junior partner) was either exceptionally brave or exceptionally stupid.

The fair-haired man held Tejada's gaze a moment longer, and then stood up. "I'll see if he's available."

"Thank you." Tejada, watching the young man's progress towards an oak-paneled inner door, noticed a slight limp. War wound, thought the lieutenant, revising his estimation of the clerk.

The door closed briefly, and then opened again. The fair-haired man emerged, and a voice spilled after him, saying, "Show him in then, man!"

Tejada's first impression of Eduardo Crespo's office was of a blizzard of papers. Files were stacked on top of bookshelves and filing cabinets, on chairs, and scattered across the broad mahogany desk in the center of the room. Since the lieutenant was accustomed to less than pristine offices, the general air of chaos did not prevent his forming a second impression, which was of wealth. The leather-bound, gold-embossed legal tomes on the bookshelf behind the desk lost only a little of their dignity by being buried beneath large manila folders laid sideways on top of them. Tejada had a shrewd suspicion that the freestanding telephone sitting near one corner of the desk was worth the better part of his monthly salary, and the brass lamps flanking it were probably of equal value.

Crespo himself gave off the same aura of disorganized opulence. He was in his mid-forties, and even his excellently tailored suit could not quite conceal a small paunch. As he came around the desk his unbuttoned jacket flopped sloppily back to reveal a gold watch chain spanning his vest. "Good morning, good morning." Like most lawyers, his voice was a shade louder than necessary. "Forgive the mess. My partner is on vacation and we're short staffed." He held out his hand. "A pleasure to meet you. I'm sorry, I'm stupid about ranks. Captain? Lieutenant Colonel?"

"Lieutenant," Tejada said, wondering why he resented having his rank inflated. If it was honest ignorance there was no reason to be irked by it, and if it was a clumsy attempt at flattery, then Crespo was clearly trying to be friendly.

"No, really?" Crespo was still genial. As he shook hands Tejada noted that he wore a ring on his smallest finger that looked like it bore the insignia of a fraternity of some sort. "Well, no doubt you have a great career ahead of you. What can I do for you, young man?"

He waved the lieutenant to a seat in front of the desk, and then returned to his own. Tejada sat, and realized why he had resented the lawyer's assumption that he was a captain. He implied that he wouldn't ordinarily deal socially with anyone below a captain's rank, Tejada thought. His sense of humor rescued him. *I'm sure he would enjoy dealing with Rodríguez.* He smiled slightly as he replied, "I'm here regarding a criminal investigation, Doctor Crespo."

"Criminal?" The lawyer's voice was still loud and jovial, but Tejada noticed that he no longer leaned back in his chair. "I'm afraid I can't help you very much, Lieutenant. I have a strictly civil practice."

"The Guardia Civil retains its own legal counsel," Tejada remarked dryly. "I am actually looking for a missing person. That is, there is a gentleman whom the Guardia is looking for. I believe you may have information as to his whereabouts."

"Who would this be?" To Tejada's satisfaction, Crespo looked considerably less comfortable now.

"Manuel Arroyo Díaz." Tejada inspected Crespo narrowly as he spoke.

The lawyer sighed. "Professor Arroyo?" The inflection of his voice made the words a question, but he did not seem overly shocked.

"Are you surprised?"

Crespo shook his head. "Quite frankly, no. I've been afraid

that something was amiss with him since he didn't show up for work."

"He didn't show up for work when?" Tejada took out a notebook with a feeling of satisfaction. Crespo might be obnoxious personally, but he was proving more helpful than anyone else had been so far.

"I'd have to check the actual day." The lawyer was apologetic. "As I mentioned, we're short staffed, and things have been chaotic around here. But he wasn't in at all last week. I'd meant to telephone him and ask if something was wrong." He nodded at the phone on the desk. "But I'm afraid it slipped my mind. And now I gather that something *is* wrong."

"Were you aware that Professor Arroyo reports to the Guardia Civil on a weekly basis?" Tejada asked, struck again by the ease with which some people accepted mysterious disappearances.

"Yes, yes, of course I knew," Crespo admitted. "The professor's never made any secret of it, poor man. Not that he could."

"Yet you didn't report his absence to the Guardia?" Tejada asked. *It's bizarre,* he thought. *A man disappears for a week, and neither his wife nor his employer thinks of reporting it to the Guardia. I could understand it in Madrid, if they were Reds, but these are respectable people.*

The lawyer sighed and leaned forward, placing his elbows on the desk. "May I speak frankly, Lieutenant?" He was attempting to use a confidential tone.

"It would be appreciated."

Tejada's gentle irony appeared lost on Crespo. The lawyer's voice dripped with sincerity as he said, "I didn't report Professor Arroyo's absence to the Guardia Civil because . . . well, in all honesty, I suspected that he might not want me to. He was always a proud man and he still is, now, in spite of everything. I respect him too much to . . . to run to the Guardia to tell on him like a child tattling to a teacher."

Once again, Tejada's sense of humor saved him from

annoyance. That, he told himself, must be the truth, because no one who went through law school would be capable of inventing such a clumsy lie. Aloud, he said, "Of course I have to respect such loyalty, even if I do feel that it is a bit misplaced." He allowed the pause after these words to become slightly tense before continuing. "You speak as if you've known the professor for some years, Doctor Crespo. Could you tell me something about your connection with him?"

"Certainly." As Tejada had expected, relief made the lawyer voluble. "I was Arroyo's student, oh, twenty years ago. Nearer twenty-five now, actually. Hard to believe that. He was one of the few truly inspiring professors I had. A brilliant mind, but also such a passion for teaching. He could ignite a lecture hall. It's impossible to explain, if you haven't experienced it."

Tejada, whose experience with Arroyo's lectures had inspired only somnolence, nodded understandingly. "And you've kept in touch with him over the years?"

"Well, naturally more frequently when I first graduated." Crespo became cautious. "He took me under his wing, as it were, for the first couple of years. We saw less of each other as time went on, but I've run into him and his wife socially over the years. At Christmas parties, and things like that. A friendly acquaintance, you might say."

"And how did he come to work for you?" Tejada asked, puzzled. The sort of relationship described by the lawyer was perfectly plausible, but did not explain the dogged loyalty that would make a man stand by a convicted Marxist during the bitter days of the war.

Crespo sighed. "Well, I suppose you know what happened to him at the university." Tejada nodded, and the lawyer continued. "He could have retired completely, you know. He wasn't badly off, and his wife's family are also comfortable. But he wanted to work. One of the endearing things about him is his determination to keep himself busy. Naturally, an academic career was out of the question, and it was impossible for him to practice law on his own, and well, feelings here ran rather high during the war. No one wanted to take him on as a partner, and since, as I said, he'd been something of a mentor to me, well, you understand, Lieutenant, I didn't agree with his politics, but I couldn't just stand idly by and let him lose all self-respect. And it's worked out very well."

"Of course." Tejada felt the glimmerings of a grudging respect for the stocky lawyer. "What title does he hold in your firm?"

"Maintenance director," Crespo replied unhesitatingly. "I can't tell you what a pleasure it is to have a janitor who's literate, and can be trusted not to shuffle everything out of order." He waved a hand at the piles of paper. "And he gets on well with the charwomen too." Then, since Tejada seemed bereft of speech, Crespo continued, "I'm fond of Arroyo, Lieutenant. He's some-one you can't help liking, even when you know he's being pig-headed as he was over that university business. I hope you can see now why I didn't run to the Guardia Civil."

"Of course," Tejada said automatically, his mind still reeling. He glanced at his notes, thinking of the little biographical sketch in Arroyo's file, and then said slowly. "So, you're saying that Professor Arroyo has been working here as a *janitor* for the last three-and-a-half years?"

"That's correct." Crespo opened his desk, and withdrew a damascene-inlaid cigarette case. "He comes in three evenings a week, generally after everyone's gone home. He has a key, of course, and this way he doesn't meet any of our clients. Some of them might be uncomfortable with having him—a man of his political sympathies—working here." He lit a cigarette and inhaled deeply. Something in Tejada's expression must have struck him, because he held out the cigarette case with an air of embarrassed contrition. "I'm sorry, Lieutenant, you must think I'm terribly ungracious. Do you smoke?"

"No, thank you." Tejada resisted the urge to add that the

ration books of the Guardia Civil were extremely generous, and that he would not dream of using a civilian's tobacco coupons, though he would have staked his career that the cigarettes were contraband. Recalling his duties, he said, "You don't have any idea where Arroyo may have gone? Or why?"

The lawyer exhaled a few thoughtful streams of smoke. Then he said slowly, "No. No, I don't think . . . well, no."

"You don't think?" Tejada prompted.

Crespo sighed. "I have a guess. But it's purely unscientific. Not the sort of evidence that would hold up in court. Or even be admissible."

"No one is on trial," the lieutenant pointed out. Very gently he added, "Yet."

"I am fond of Arroyo," Crespo admitted again. "I—if I could claim attorney-client privilege I would."

"Given that the professor is your employee and not your client, however . . ." Tejada could not completely suppress the sarcasm in his voice.

"He's been abstracted recently," Crespo said slowly. "I stayed late a few weeks ago to finish up some work, and also just to have a chat, and he seemed very upset about . . . well, about the news from France. It was right after the Germans captured Verdun, I think, and he was quite concerned. He mentioned something about looking forward to seeing a colleague of ours, a Frenchman, who I'd lost touch with years ago. I assumed he meant that he was expecting a visit, but . . ."

"You think he may have been planning to flee to France?" Tejada said, reflecting that this did not seem like a wise, or even a sane, course of action.

"No, of course I didn't think that," Crespo protested. "I told you what I thought. And I told you that it wasn't the sort of thing that could be considered evidence. The only objective fact that I can tell you is that for the last month or so Arroyo has seemed unusually nervous."

"Like a man planning to disappear," Tejada said grimly. He rose, and took a perverse pleasure in seeing Eduardo Crespo hastily stub out his cigarette, and stand also, looking surprised and vaguely uncomfortable. He's used to dismissing people, not to being dismissed, the lieutenant thought. "Thank you for your time," he said. "You've been very helpful, Doctor Crespo."

"You're most welcome, Lieutenant." The lawyer's voice was once again jovial, and slightly avuncular. "The Guardia Civil are the bulwark of our nation."

"That being the case," the lieutenant smiled slightly, "we would appreciate it if you would contact us if you hear anything from Professor Arroyo. Or if you gain any further information or insight into his whereabouts. I, personally, appreciate your loyalty to an old mentor," he added, "but my superiors may not see it that way."

"Of course, Lieutenant. Understood." Judging from the lawyer's unimpaired good humor in the face of this threat, Tejada guessed that he knew Captain Rodríguez personally. "Good day to you. And good luck." Crespo smiled, and held out his hand.

Tejada glanced at the hand, sketched a salute, and left. It was past noon, and shops were closing. He felt that he needed something to eat before tackling another interview. And preferably a bath as well. Crespo had left an oily aftertaste. At least you know where you are with the Reds, Tejada thought with disgust, as he returned to the post. Fernández wouldn't have acted that way. Not if he's like Elena. When *she* didn't want to answer a question she just kept quiet. And she volunteered information too. Not that she has anything to do with this. Or her father, probably. Just a coincidence that he signed that petition four years ago. And even if it's not a coincidence, she was in Madrid in '36, so it has nothing to do with her.

A hasty lunch and a brief rest did not make the idea of calling on Manuel Arroyo's wife any more appealing. Arroyo's brother-in-law was hardly a pleasing prospect either. Tejada smothered his guilt by telling himself that he would interview the Oteros the following morning, and set off to meet with Arroyo's fellow petitioners. Instinctively, he decided to visit the medical doctors first. I don't know them as well, he thought, although in fact his brief impression of Guillermo Fernández on Friday had been almost completely obscured by shock. I'll stop by to see Fernández on the way back, if there's time. Or send Hernández to interview him.

Giving due respect to seniority, Tejada visited Doctor Velázquez first. He found Velázquez's home, or rather, the home of his daughter and son-in-law, by consulting a map of the city's outskirts. The door was opened by a woman in her mid-thirties who froze at the sight of him. "Señora Velázquez de Carrillo?" he asked.

"Yes?" The familiar sullen hostility was a relief after Crespo's effusive welcome.

"I'm Lieutenant Tejada. I'm looking for your father."

"He attended his last parole date." The woman stepped backward to let him into the house, in spite of her defiant words.

"I know," Tejada replied soothingly. "I wanted to ask him a few questions that are unrelated to his parole—at least, I believe they are unrelated."

Velázquez's daughter clearly disliked having the lieutenant in her home, but she offered no further protest. She led him through the entryway and up two flights of stairs, to a landing with one door ajar. "Through there," she said, her voice still hostile.

Tejada pushed open the door, and found himself in a low-ceilinged, sunlit room, with a bed, a desk, an armchair, and an improbable number of bookshelves, crammed with everything from medical texts to popular novels. The window was open, and the room was no more than pleasantly warm, although it probably became unbearably stuffy later in the summer. Seated in the armchair was a balding man whom Tejada recognized as Dr. Velázquez. Perched cross-legged on the bed, next to a checkerboard with a game in progress, was a boy of about eleven, wearing what Tejada recognized as the uniform of the Falangist youth, minus jacket and cap. Both looked up as the lieutenant entered. The boy became saucer-eyed. The man rose to his feet, somewhat stiffly, and moved to stand in front of the child.

The lieutenant nodded politely. "Good afternoon, Doctor."

"Good afternoon." Dr. Velázquez appeared to be at a loss.

The boy slid off the bed, and stood next to the doctor with an air of defiance. Tejada smiled at the indignantly quivering little body. "Your grandson?" he inquired.

"Yes." The doctor turned. "Run along, Agustín. You don't want to be late for your game this afternoon. And the lieutenant and I have business."

The boy looked as if he would have liked to argue, then he obediently headed for the door. It swung shut behind him. There was silence for a moment, and then Dr. Velázquez said, a little more loudly, "I said, run along, Agustín." He smiled apologetically at the lieutenant as the creaking of the stairs signaled his grandson's retreat.

Tejada laughed. "He's very devoted to you."

Velázquez shrugged. "Keeping Anita's children amused is one of the few things I'm good for nowadays." The bitterness beneath his words was unmistakable. "What brings you here, Lieutenant? Surely I haven't committed any new crimes since Friday afternoon?"

"No." Tejada gestured for the doctor to be seated, and then realized that there was only one chair available in the little room. He loomed over Velázquez for a moment, and then sat on the other side of the checkerboard, in the place on the bed vacated by Agustín Carrillo. "I'm here because one of your colleagues is missing."

"One of my colleagues?" Velázquez was faintly amused. "As

you are aware, Lieutenant, I am retired. I am not in close touch with any of my colleagues."

"I didn't mean a medical colleague," Tejada said. "I meant Manuel Arroyo Díaz."

Velázquez sat absolutely still for a moment. Then he said quietly, "I know nothing about such a disappearance."

"Perhaps you could tell me the last time you saw Professor Arroyo?"

"The last time I saw him, Lieutenant, was over six months ago." Velázquez sighed, and continued before Tejada could speak again. "It was a chance meeting in a tobacco shop. I hadn't seen him for some time before that, and we exchanged no more than greetings. I may have asked after his family. I believe he asked me about Anita. As you must remember, I gave you all of these details on Friday, when you asked me the same question."

Velázquez had in fact said exactly the same thing on Friday. Tejada pressed ahead instead with a new question. "Where do you think he might go, if he were to, for example, try to flee?"

"I have no idea." The doctor sounded tired.

"Would you be surprised to learn that he had been involved in politics recently?"

Velázquez's gaze flickered over the checkerboard between the two men. His mouth twisted. "Checkmate, I think, Lieutenant. If I say I am not surprised, you will ask me what Arroyo's involvement consists of, and if I say that I am surprised, you will ask me how I can be so sure. Well done. I concede the game."

"You haven't answered the question," Tejada pointed out.

"And no answer is equally damning as a yes or no."

Tejada raised his eyebrows. "If I didn't know better I would think that you were deliberately trying to provoke me."

"I would be extremely stupid to provoke a guardia civil." There was venom in the doctor's voice.

"Yes," Tejada agreed. "You would be. So why are you doing it?" He felt a strong urge to slap Velázquez and tell him to stop behaving like a silly child, but he found the doctor's open antagonism easier to bear than Eduardo Crespo's subtly patronizing friendliness.

The doctor turned his head away from Tejada for a moment, and the lieutenant followed his gaze to the face of a small clock on one of the bookcases. "Are you planning to arrest me, Lieutenant?" he asked, and suddenly his voice was no longer mocking, but tired, and old, and somewhat frightened.

"That depends on whether you answer my questions," Tejada replied evenly.

"If you are planning to take me into custody for further questioning, I'd rather that you did so immediately." The doctor's voice was almost pleading now. "My granddaughter is having lunch at a friend's house, and I'd rather leave before she returns, and before Agustín gets back from his soccer game."

Tejada considered for a moment. "Suppose that you simply answer the questions," he suggested finally. "That way your grandchildren need not be distressed by your absence."

The doctor sighed, defeated. "I don't know anything about Arroyo. But I doubt that you'll believe that."

"I haven't decided whether I believe that, yet," Tejada replied. "But I do have a few other questions. For a start, how exactly did you meet Professor Arroyo in the first place?

Doctor Velázquez thought a moment, and then shook his head. "I don't really know." He saw the lieutenant's skeptical look and added despairingly, "I'm not trying to avoid the question, but I cannot tell you exactly when I met him. Close to a dozen years ago is the best I can do. I assume it was at some university function. Or we might have simply struck up a conversation at a café. One gets used to seeing the same faces around the campus, and sooner or later one talks to them. After thirty years in the same place pretty much all the faces look vaguely like acquaintances."

Tejada nodded, briefly wondering what it would be like to

remain in the same place for thirty years. Thirty years with Rodríguez, he thought with a shudder. And then, speculatively, thirty years in Toledo . . . in Madrid . . . ? "And when did you and Arroyo become friendly?"

"We never really did." Velázquez looked almost apologetic. "As I said, we were acquaintances. We had lunch a few times. My wife and I went to one of his open lectures once. We lost touch after we both resigned from the university."

"And how did you both come to resign?" Tejada asked.

"To become partners in crime, you mean?" The sarcastic edge was back in the doctor's voice. "In retrospect, I can only say that we must have shared an extremely ill-timed—or well-timed—self-destructive impulse." Seeing that Tejada looked impatient, the doctor continued with some bitterness. "In 1936 Unamuno was older than I am now, you know. Are you aware that General Millán tried to strike him, in full view of the assembled audience? And that the day after being assaulted and publicly insulted he was summarily dismissed from the institution he had given his life to? And that—"

"Are you quoting?" Tejada interrupted coolly.

"No. But no doubt you have my exact words on file."

"No doubt," the lieutenant agreed. "But you are once again avoiding the question."

"A number of those present in the audience were shocked," Velázquez said stiffly. "And the day after Unamuno's dismissal a number of us met, coincidentally, and discussed it."

"Coincidentally?" Tejada raised his eyebrows.

"As I said before, the university world is a small one."

"Who was there?"

Velázquez snorted. "You tell me."

"If I do have to take you to the post for questioning, I'll make a point of waiting until your grandson returns," Tejada said quietly. "I'm sure you wouldn't want that."

The doctor froze. Then he said very quietly, "Myself.

Arroyo. A classics professor named Fernández. And one of my former students."

"By the name of?" Tejada prompted. There was a short silence and then he added, "I think Agustín would be upset if he were to return and find, say, his checkers game overturned, and possibly a few of the bookcases? He's a bright boy. He might deduce a struggle."

Velázquez's fists clenched briefly. "Tomás Rivera," he said quietly. "But I suspect that Rivera's indignation had more to do with my convictions than with his own."

Tejada, who suspected much the same thing, moved on to another question. "I assume that you knew Fernández in much the same way you knew Arroyo? A casual acquaintance?"

Doctor Velázquez, who had wearily decided that fighting the insistent questions was impossible, would have been gratified by the knowledge that his next words seriously shook the lieutenant. "Actually, no. I knew Fernández through his daughter. My daughter Anita was a teacher before she married, and Elena Fernández was one of her first students. They became friendly after Elena graduated. They're close in age, you see, and Elena's also a teacher."

"I see," Tejada said shortly, mentally placing the woman who had shown him upstairs next to Elena. "And you say that you lost touch with each other after the incident of this petition?"

"Fernández was in prison," Velázquez pointed out dryly. "The rest of us didn't want to be arrested for conspiracy, or worse."

Tejada changed the direction of his questioning abruptly. "Do you know of any professional connections Arroyo may have had in France?"

The doctor blinked at the change in subject, but he answered readily enough. "No, but that doesn't mean anything. As I say, we were never really close. I know that Arroyo visited Geneva several times. With regard to the League of Nations. I suppose he might have met French colleagues there."

Tejada suddenly saw a possible explanation for Eduardo Crespo's surprising statement. It was extremely unlikely that Arroyo would think of taking refuge in France now. But if he were using France as a way station on the way to Switzerland, he might well follow news of the war anxiously. "Thank you." Tejada stood. "If you hear anything from Arroyo, please contact the Guardia Civil."

Doctor Velázquez rose also. "If I hear anything from Arroyo," he remarked, smiling slightly, "I suspect that the Guardia will already know about it." Seeing Tejada's startled look, his smile widened slightly. "I've been under surveillance intermittently for the last four years, Lieutenant. I am aware when I have a shadow."

"You're very observant." Tejada smiled back. "Have a good evening."

"Until Friday," the doctor replied.

The lieutenant decided to postpone further interviews until the following day. Sergeant Hernández had been making dire predictions about the inadequacy of two new recruits for patrol, and there was a pile of paperwork on Tejada's desk that he had already neglected for too long. He headed back to the post, wondering idly what subject Ana de Carrillo had taught Elena.

.

# Chapter 8

In his interview with the former professor the preceding Friday, Tejada had established that Quiñones and Sons was a construction company, and that Doctor Rivera was employed there as a bookkeeper. He did not learn that Ramón Quiñones was Rivera's brother-in-law until the following day, when he set out for the business offices of the company.

"He doesn't do anything political," Quiñones explained nervously to the intimidating uniformed figure who appeared in his private office Tuesday morning. "Just balances the accounts, and makes sure the men get paid. With respect, sir, your predecessor never had any objection."

"No, I gather not," Tejada said.

Quiñones shifted his weight and wished that the lieutenant would be a little more forthcoming. "Of course, I have nothing to do with his politics," he offered worrriedly. "Maybe I shouldn't have hired him. The only reason I did was because of the kids. I mean, Cristina's just sixteen this winter, and he's got two younger ones, and they're my sister's children as well as his, after all." The contractor talked himself to a standstill.

"That was very generous of you."

Quiñones flushed painfully under the lieutenant's impassive stare. "He couldn't work anywhere else. I did the best I could for him," he muttered. "I mean, you've got to have a job to get ration coupons, so that was something. And honest to God,

Lieutenant, he never did any real *harm*. He's never been a Communist, or anything like that."

Tejada reflected that Quiñones seemed unsure whether to apologize for not doing enough for his brother-in-law or for helping him at all. Randomized guilt, the lieutenant decided, definitely made people much easier to interview. "Of course," he said, meaninglessly. "I'd like to speak to Doctor Rivera now, if you don't mind."

"Certainly, certainly." Señor Quiñones led the guardia civil into a cluttered and windowless office, crammed with three desks and an ancient filing cabinet. Although the cabinet looked as if a slight breeze would make it collapse in a heap of rust, and the desks were chipped and scarred, the room was scrupulously neat. The stack of papers beside a typewriter had been squared off with mathematical precision, and even the telephone on the wall had been carefully hung in the exact center above the filing cabinet. A female secretary was seated at the desk with the type-writer. Two men occupied the other desks, and Tejada recognized one of them as the fourth of the petitioners. Quiñones wove his way between the desks and murmured something in his brother-in-law's ear. It was a useless piece of discretion. His other employees were openly staring at the guardia civil.

Doctor Rivera wordlessly closed the ledger on his desk, capped his pen, and made his way to where the lieutenant stood waiting. "You wanted to see me, sir?" His voice was dull, and he kept his eyes on the ground.

"I wanted to ask you a few questions." Tejada glanced at Quiñones, who was hovering at his brother-in-law's elbow. "In private, if possible."

"I'll take you into my office," the contractor said hastily. As they moved toward the door the typist raised her voice. "Tomás! I-I meant to tell you. I'll take that recipe over to Cristina at lunch today."

"Thanks." Rivera's smile came and went so quickly that

Tejada missed it completely. But the lieutenant suddenly understood that Rivera's normal expression was terribly sad.

Tejada patiently asked Rivera the same questions he had
asked Velázquez. As he had expected, the answers were not sub-
stantially different. Rivera thought that he had been intro-
duced to Guillermo Fernández by Doctor Velázquez. Or they
might have met casually elsewhere. It had all been years ago.
He had only met Manuel Arroyo in 1936, when they had
cosigned the petition. No, the petition had not been his idea.
No, he had not seen Professor Arroyo in years and had no idea
where he might be. "We've never been close," Rivera
explained, in the weary monotone he used throughout the
interview. "He belongs to a different generation, a different
profession . . . a different class." For the first time there was a
faint edge in the doctor's voice.

"Oh?" Tejada asked, pursuing the edge with some interest.

Rivera shrugged, once more indifferent. "My father was a tai-
lor, Lieutenant. I was the first of my family to graduate from a
university. And Arroyo . . ."

"I've met his wife," Tejada offered helpfully.

Doctor Rivera looked up, and met the lieutenant's eyes for
the first time during the interview. "Well, then, you can see."

"Yes." Tejada considered mentioning that the aristocratic
lawyer had spent the last three years as a janitor, but decided
against it. "How long have you worked here?" he asked, his
mind still running on professions.

"Since the end of '36."

"You're fortunate," Tejada commented.

"Fortunate?" Doctor Rivera repeated. Bitterness temporarily
colored his gray voice. "I was planning to spend that winter in
Vienna. I had the money. I'd exchanged letters with the
Psychoanalytic Society there. I was looking at schools for the
kids. I started working for Ramón at just the time when I
thought I'd be packing my bags."

There was, Tejada felt, nothing more to say. *You were a damn fool to meddle in what didn't concern you*, seemed apt, but unnecessarily cruel. "Thank you for your time," he said instead. "If you *do* learn anything of Arroyo's whereabouts, please contact the Guardia Civil."

"Yes, sir." Rivera stood and followed the lieutenant to the door like an obedient child. As Tejada went out the doctor cleared his throat suddenly. "Lieutenant?"

Tejada turned. "Yes?"

"Am I under surveillance again because of Arroyo's disappearance?"

"Yes."

"I . . ." Dr. Rivera stared at the ground. "Would it be possible for it to be a bit more discreet? It's only . . . my daughter . . . well, she's at an age where—where if she goes out her friends are likely to notice and well . . ."

"I can't make any promises," Tejada said slowly, recalling with something akin to guilt that he had specifically excluded Elena from her father's surveillance. "But I'll see what I can do."

Tejada left Quiñones and Sons feeling vaguely depressed, for reasons he did not bother to analyze. He returned to the post, examined his desk with distaste, and then considered who else he could question regarding Arroyo. The professor's wife and brother-in-law were high on the list. And Guillermo Fernández. The lieutenant decided that delegation was the key to successful command. He sent for Sergeant Hernández. "Go and talk to Guillermo Fernández about the Arroyo business," he ordered. "Find out when the two of them met, how they became involved with the other petitioners, everything you can. And see if Fernández knows anything about Arroyo's connections to France or Switzerland."

"Yes, sir." Hernández nodded. "Right away, sir?"

"No." Tejada shook his head. "Call Arroyo's brother-in-law, and set up an appointment for me first."

"Judge Otero Martínez y Arias, sir?" the sergeant asked.

"Does he have other brothers-in-law?"

Hernández shook his head. "Well, no one can say you shirk the hard jobs," he commented.

"Thank you, Sergeant. Remind me to delegate more of them in the future."

Hernández laughed, and reached for the telephone on his desk. His conversation with Judge Otero, or rather with Otero's secretary, was lengthy and (judging from his expression) frustrating. After nearly ten minutes he hung up the phone. "His Honor can squeeze you in for half an hour at five-thirty tomorrow," he said dryly, "if you will meet him in his chambers."

"Well done," Tejada said, because he felt that the sergeant deserved some recognition for the phone call. "Give me the address, and then go talk to Fernández."

Sergeant Hernández saluted and then left, and Tejada turned his attention to other tasks. He managed to successfully distract himself from the Arroyo case until a few minutes before five-thirty the following afternoon, when he knocked on the polished oak door of Judge Otero Martínez y Arias.

A few minutes after six an obsequious secretary entered the waiting room, gave the lieutenant a nervous half-bow, and said that the judge was currently free and would the Señor Guardia be so kind as to state his name. Tejada, who had spent the better part of twenty minutes thinking of cutting things to say, contented himself with replying quietly, "Lieutenant Carlos Tejada Alonso y León. I had an appointment for five thirty." The secretary, who was used to being the butt of people's frustration, merely bowed and announced him.

Manuel Arroyo's brother-in-law was seated behind a mahogany desk that might have been the twin of Eduardo Crespo's. This desk, however, was completely clear. No ink stains showed on the blotter, and the only paper in sight was a small memo pad, placed carefully in one corner. The judge, Tejada thought sourly, did not look overly busy.

Judge Otero rose to greet his guest, and Tejada saw that although he grasped a silver-handled cane with one hand, he stood remarkably straight. The silver handle matched his hair, which was neatly slicked back. "I'm sorry to keep you waiting, Lieutenant." His voice, unlike Crespo's, was quiet.

"It's nothing, Your Honor," Tejada lied politely.

Dark eyes regarded him from under bushy silver eyebrows for a moment. "You will forgive an impertinent question, Lieutenant, but your surname . . . are you related to Enrique Tejada de la Vega? Of Granada?"

Tejada mentally ran through the catalogue of his relatives. "My great-uncle, Your Honor."

"Ahh. I had the pleasure of meeting your great-uncle during his tenure as a deputy in Madrid. Is he still living?"

"Unfortunately, no, Your Honor. He passed away some years ago."

"I am sorry," the judge said politely. "Do sit down. Now, I take it that you are here in regard to my unfortunate brother-in-law."

"Yes, Your Honor." Tejada waited. After a moment, it became clear that the judge was waiting also. Feeling slightly awkward, the lieutenant coughed, and said, "We are, of course, interested in his whereabouts."

"You may well believe that I am too, Lieutenant." The judge resumed his seat, sounding slightly rueful. "Manuel has been eccentric in the past, but this disappearance is far beyond what is permissible."

"Eccentric in what way, Your Honor?" Tejada asked, surprised. His fellow petitioners had drawn a portrait of Arroyo as an eminently conventional man.

"Most notably for the event which first drew the interest of the Guardia Civil," Judge Otero replied, with a certain wry humor. "But I might add that his decision to continue working after his retirement from the university was somewhat unusual."

"For Doctor Crespo?" Tejada confirmed.

"Clerking for Eduardo Crespo might have been understandable," Judge Otero said simply. "Cleaning his office is completely insane."

Since Tejada found himself totally in sympathy with the judge, he risked a question. "Why do you think he does it? Or did it, until last week?"

"Because he is eccentric." Judge Otero's tone was half amused and half annoyed. "He always mutters some nonsense about the dignity of labor but frankly, Lieutenant, I suspect that he would cling to any excuse to remain in a law office."

"The law is so important to him?" Tejada asked, curious.

"Paramount," said the judge flatly. "Manuel has spent most of his legal career in an academic setting, you know, and he has remained quite idealistic, in a way that those of us who have chosen other paths cannot afford to be."

"The League of Nations?" Tejada suggested.

"Exactly." Judge Otero nodded. "And his work on Cuba. You're too young to remember 1898, I suppose?"

"Yes, Your Honor," Tejada said, privately marveling at how frequently people who seem perfectly capable of simple arithmetic asked if he remembered an event that had occurred a dozen years before his birth.

"Well." The judge shook his head. "Manuel's writings about it are interesting, but completely impractical."

"I understand that your brother-in-law traveled frequently to Geneva, though?" Tejada said casually.

"Not since the early thirties," Judge Otero corrected gently. "Although if you're thinking he may have fled to Geneva, I suppose it's possible."

"Do you think he did?"

The judge pursed his lips. "I'd rather think not," he said slowly, "if only for my sister's sake. She's had a fair amount to bear because of Manuel already." He flashed a grim smile at Tejada. "Although she did mention that the lieutenant on night duty seemed to have the rudiments of common courtesy."

Tejada did his best to keep his face expressionless. He suspected that he failed, because the judge's smile grew wider. "I believe my sister is acquainted with your great-uncle's daughter Barbara," he added. "I must tell her. She'll want you to convey her respects."

"So you think it is unlikely that Professor Arroyo would flee the country?" the lieutenant said, a little stiffly.

Judge Otero became serious. "I don't know," he said. "I would have said it was unlikely. I would still say that it's unlikely, but I'm afraid that's merely my desire to believe that my brother-in-law is merely an embarrassment and a nuisance, and not a disgrace. And since Crespo mentioned that he's been upset lately . . ."

"When did Crespo mention this to you, Your Honor?" the lieutenant asked, hoping that the judge would offer a more precise date than Arroyo's employer had.

"Monday evening," the judge said, dashing his hopes.

"*This* Monday?" Tejada said, suddenly alert. "But I assumed that neither you nor Dr. Crespo had seen or spoken to Professor Arroyo since the week before last?"

"That's correct," Judge Otero agreed. "Crespo telephoned me on Monday to let me know that he had spoken to you and that you were likely to call. That's why I was able to fit you in at such short notice."

Tejada sincerely hoped that his face remained blank at the phrase "short notice." He managed a few more questions, and then ended the interview as gracefully as possible.

"I do hope you find Manuel promptly, Lieutenant," the judge said, as Tejada left. "He's not an unlikeable man, but he has become quite an embarrassment to the family."

Tejada escaped from the judge's chambers with a feeling he had not had since visiting his maternal grandparents as a small child. When he returned to the post he found that a letter was waiting for him. The censor's seal only partially covered the return address: *Sr. Juan Andrés Tejada Alonso y León, Finca Dos Cabras, Granada.* If asked, the lieutenant would have said that he was very fond of his elder brother. The two men did in fact have a remarkably calm relationship. Possibly the fact that the lieutenant had never in word or deed doubted Juan Andrés's position as heir and favorite contributed to the lack of friction. A letter of any sort was a welcome diversion though, and Tejada felt that his interview with Otero had earned him a break. He took the letter to his office, closed the door, and sank into his desk chair to read.

Dos Cabras
24 June 1940

Dear Carlos,

Congratulations on your promotion! Mama has almost forgiven your decision to join the Guardia Civil, and Papa has actually been heard boasting of "my son, the lieutenant." If you send him a photograph of you in your new uniform with which to impress the crowd at the club you will complete your status as the new favored son.

I'm thinking of turning the old north vineyard into grain next season. I hate to do it, but these are hard times, and we have to feed our people. We're settled back at the farm for the summer, although Rosa has stayed behind in Granada until the baby comes. Unfortunately, the rebels continue their campaign in the hills, and she feels safer in the city. Now that you are a lieutenant Mama will doubtless be agitating for you to come home and defeat them single-handed. (Note: Andrés informs me that if you will wait until he is big enough he will help you. He also says to tell you that he is getting a hunting rifle for his birthday this year, which is a surprise to me.)

What do you think of the news from France? *Entre nous,* I found the timing almost providential, because Rosa has been nagging at me to take her to Paris for our anniversary, and I now hope to persuade her that your colleagues at the border will make any travel north more trouble than it is worth. At any rate, a quick war is better than a drawn-out one, and these Germans seem to know what they're doing.

I hope you're enjoying Salamanca. I imagine you must be, if it's the town I remember from my university days. Better than Madrid, at any event, which sounds like a hellhole at present. Speaking of which, your little protégé and her mother are doing fine, though the little one claims that she misses the capital. Do you intend to send her back to school in the fall? And what are your long-term plans for her, if one may ask? If she turns out to be pretty, I suppose you might eventually find someone to marry her in spite of her mysterious background. Do I get let in on the mystery anytime soon, by the way? I can't say she takes after you especially, and I wouldn't have said that the mother was your type, but don't ask me to believe that fairy tale about a soldier father, and your promise to a dying man, because I know as well as you do that all war orphans are cared for by the state, and certainly don't need your assistance.

Mama and Papa send love, as do the children. Don't get into trouble, *hermanito.*

Your affectionate brother,
Juan Andrés

Tejada read most of the letter with tolerant amusement. He frowned slightly over the last paragraph, however. He had not precisely lied to his brother about the child Juan Andrés was pleased to term his "little protégé," but he had suppressed certain crucial facts, and it disturbed him that his brother was sharp enough to sense this. He would have been less disturbed by his brother's casual needling had the memory of the little girl not reminded him painfully that in searching for her he had found her teacher: a slender, dark-eyed, courageous, distressingly left-wing Elena Fernández.

He was debating whether and how to answer his brother when someone knocked. Tejada hastily folded the letter and thrust it into his coat pocket. Then he picked up a pen and opened his notebook. "Come in."

Corporal Jiménez entered, shepherding a young guardia who Tejada had never seen before. "I beg your pardon for intruding, sir." Corporal Jiménez seemed pleased with himself. "But Guardia Falguera has something he wants to tell you."

Guardia Falguera cast a paralyzed look at the corporal. Jiménez beamed back at him avuncularly. "Go ahead, Guardia."

"W-well, sir, you know the district down by the river? G-guardia P-Pérez and I were on p-patrol there and w-we were hailed, sir. B-by concerned citizens." Falguera blushed painfully.

"Yes?" Tejada said, as encouragingly as possible, wondering why Jiménez did not simply summarize the stuttering guardia's story and save them all time and grief.

"There's a warehouse down b-by the river, sir, that's b-being repaired. And it seems some of the construction w-workers found a b-b-body there this afternoon."

"Not dead of natural causes, I take it?" Tejada interjected.

"No, sir. His head was b-b-bashed in. So Guardia P-Pérez and I contacted the c-contractor, sir, and only his b-b-bookkeeper was in, b-but the b-b-b-book . . . but *he* said to call the lieutenant."

Something clicked in Tejada's brain, and he made a desperate attempt to fend off another stuttering recital. "This would be the bookkeeper for Quiñones and Sons," he said.

"Y-yes, sir!"

"By the name of Tomás Rivera?"

"Yes, sir."

The lieutenant's half-formed suspicion gained shape and substance. "Did you identify the body?" he asked.

"N-not positively, sir. He's b-been dead a long time." Guardia Falguera's face twisted briefly in memory of the stench. "B-but the c-cards in his wallet say Manuel Arroyo Díaz."

# Chapter 9

E lena pleaded a headache on Friday afternoon to avoid visiting the Guardia Civil post again. It was not entirely an
excuse. A sleepless night and a fair amount of sick dread had
combined to make her genuinely uncomfortable. She watched
with relief as her father set out, and began vigorously to clean
her room to satisfy her conscience. She did her best to avoid
reflecting on what the lieutenant might think about her
absence. She had finished, and was just deciding whether it
would be a good idea to iron all of her clothes, when there was
a tap on her door. Elena turned, brushing a strand of hair out
of her eyes. "Come in?"

María stood in the doorway. "Your father's not back yet."

Elena had lost track of time but she knew that checking
the clock would only increase her mother's agony. "Well, we
were unusually quick last time, you know. There's probably a
line again today."

"The evening news is on."

Elena checked the clock then. It was past six-thirty. More
than an hour past the time when she and her father usually got
home. "Maybe they got behind schedule last week," she suggested. "And so it's longer today." The words had a hollow echo,
even to her own ears. *I should have gone with him*, she told herself,
and turned away, afraid that her mother would read her guilt.

María bit her lip. "I *told* him yesterday, after the sergeant came around asking all those questions, that he shouldn't ask about traveling now."

Elena tried to shepherd her mother toward a chair. It was too difficult to watch the older woman shifting nervously from foot to foot. "Probably it's just the new lieutenant," she said soothingly. "Papa said the sergeant yesterday only asked old questions about the petition, and Professor Arroyo, and things like that. So maybe Tej—the lieutenant is just trying to be conscientious."

"Maybe. Probably." María sat down, and then immediately stood up again. "I'm going to pack up some things for him." She moved toward the door.

Elena detained her, out of fear and not kindness this time. "What do you mean?"

María patted her daughter's arm. "They let me take him things last time. And he'll want clean clothes, a toothbrush, that sort of thing." She saw Elena's frozen face, and spoke gently. "It's just a precaution, Elenita. He'll probably be back by the time I'm finished."

"Mama . . ." Elena's voice trailed off. She wanted to deny the idea that her father had been arrested again; to scoff at it, to belittle it. She was used to being the expert, and defending her parents from the new world that the war had brought. But María had lived through her husband's arrest once, and now she was the experienced one. "Mama," Elena repeated, feeling like a child, and hating herself for it.

"Do you want to help me pack?" María had heard her daughter's childish tone and responded to it.

Very slowly, Elena nodded. She followed her mother into her parents' bedroom, feeling the same fleeting guilt that she had on entering their room when she was little. María opened a chest of drawers and began pulling out clean shirts. "I don't think they'll let him have a razor," she said. "But he'll want his pipe, don't you think? Run downstairs and get it, will you, Elenita? The tobacco is in the tin in the sideboard drawer, that's right, good girl."

The small bundle was quickly packed. Elena watched it sit in the middle of her parents' bed, as carefully as if it were a cobra poised to strike. María picked it up, and her hesitance seemed to return. "Well," she said. "Well, it's done. I guess he isn't back yet. So maybe we should go see what's happening at the post. Just in case he needs it."

Elena felt her stomach clench in terror. "What if he's on his way home?" she suggested desperately. "We can't both go. We might miss him in the street. And then," she tried to laugh, "think how worried he'd be to find an empty house."

María nodded slowly. "Yes. Yes, you're right. It's better if one of us stays behind, just in case."

There was a long, awkward silence as both women weighed their prospective roles: waiting alone in an empty house for God knew how long, or going alone to the Guardia Civil post to find out what had happened. There would probably be a delay at the post, Elena thought. The Guardia were not generally forthcoming about the whereabouts of prisoners. It might well mean hours spent alone. And then, whoever's left behind may set out for the post, looking for the other two, she thought. And then there will be none, like in the nursery rhyme. At least going to look for her father would be doing something. "I'll go," she said quickly. "I'd like a walk. And you must be tired."

You can't send her to a post alone! María thought. They might well arrest whoever shows up. My God, a girl alone among them would be completely defenseless. "What about your headache?" she said aloud, trying to hide her own fear of going to the post.

Elena looked at her mother's face and read terror there. "I'd *rather* go than stay here and wait by myself," she insisted.

"If you're sure." Her mother spoke doubtfully, while an internal voice said, *It was your idea! How can you send her into danger?*

"Positive," Elena said.

She hurried out of the house before her mother could argue

further, ashamed of leaving her mother behind in the more difficult role. As she drew nearer to the post, she realized why she had
assumed that her own task was easier. It had not occurred to her
that there would be any problem in speaking to the lieutenant.
But as she reached the entrance to the post, and an armed
guardia stepped forward to meet her, she felt her courage desert-
ing her. "My name is Elena Fernández," she managed, in answer
to his challenge. "I'm here . . ." she hesitated, wondering how she
could best ask about her father without arousing suspicion.
"Because I'd like to see Lieutenant Tejada," she finished finally.

"Is he expecting you?" The guardia looked dubious.

"No." Elena was uncomfortably aware that her answer had
not been calculated to increase the guardia's confidence in her.
She tried to think of something else to say, but her tongue
seemed glued to the bottom of her mouth.

"Through that door." The guardia gestured towards the entrance
Elena usually used. It led, as she knew, to the waiting room.

The room was nearly empty when she entered. She saw no
sign of her father. Taking her courage in both hands, she
approached the desk at the far end of the room. The man
behind it looked up. "Yes?"

Elena managed to stammer her name and requested
Lieutenant Tejada again. The guardia's eyebrows rose at her
mention of Tejada, but he picked up the telephone on the desk
and relayed the message. A few minutes later another guardia
escorted her to the lieutenant's office.

Tejada was standing behind the desk when she entered. His
expression was completely unreadable as he said, "Thank you,
Estrada. Dismissed."

The door closed behind Guardia Estrada. The lieutenant came
around the desk, holding out his hand. "It's good to see you."

Elena stepped backward instinctively and then cursed herself
for tactlessness. Tejada dropped his hand and froze. She took a
deep breath. "I came about my father."

"Of course." He retreated to the desk, hoping that his voice sounded businesslike. "We have a few extra questions for him this week."

"Has he been arrested again?" Elena raised her chin, and forced herself to enunciate each word carefully, as if she were speaking to a small child.

"You'll be notified." Tejada risked looking at her face, and immediately regretted it. She was too proud to cry in front of him, but tears would have been superfluous. Her eyes were deep enough to drown in. "I understand that you were planning a trip to San Sebastián," he said abruptly, to forestall another question.

"Yes." Elena was too nervous to remember that her father had been adamant that she be excluded from the trip to the north. Papa must have asked, she thought, and he said we *were* planning, so that means Papa can't go. Please God let it just be that permission's denied.

"I'm afraid it's impossible for Professor Fernández to leave Salamanca at the moment." Tejada stared down at his desk, embarrassment making his voice brusque. "But if you and your mother wished to escape the worst of the heat . . ."

"And my father?" Elena spoke very quietly. "What's happening to him?"

She watched the lieutenant's face intently, trying in vain to snatch some clue to his thoughts. When he spoke, his voice was courteous, but cold. "We have some questions for your father, and a number of the other parolees. I think you would be more comfortable waiting for him at home."

"I am here now," Elena pointed out. "And my mother will be anxious for news."

"Elena . . ." The lieutenant sighed, uncertain how to finish the sentence, and his voice trailed off.

The professor's daughter took a deep breath. "I'd like to see him," she demanded, making sure to pronounce each word slowly and clearly, so that her voice would not tremble. "And my mother has packed a bag for him in case he needs it."

"I can take you down to see him now, if you like." The meaning of life might have been written on the surface of the lieutenant's desk, so intently was he studying it.

"Really?" The word slipped out before Elena could contain her relief.

"Come on."

Tejada ushered her through a maze of hallways and into an adjoining building. With a slight chill, Elena saw that they had passed from the administrative section of the post to the prison. The number of guards increased, and the lieutenant was forced to answer an increasing number of challenges. Finally, at the head of a flight of stairs, he paused and turned to her. "It's not really a place for a lady. Are you certain . . . ?"

"*Yes.*"

He shrugged and led her down the stairs. Elena was not sure what she had expected: a medieval dungeon, complete with skeletons perhaps. What she found was a bare hallway, lit only by the glow of widely spaced bulbs. There were quite ordinary-looking doors lining the hall on both sides. Pairs of bored guardias lounged outside a few of them, but straightened to attention hastily when they saw Tejada. Elena drew a long breath, prepared to let it out in a sigh of relief. Then someone screamed. It was not a scream of rage, or even fear, merely a wordless exhalation of pain. Elena froze where she stood, trembling slightly.

"Come on." Tejada took her arm, unconsciously giving it a reassuring squeeze.

It took all of Elena's self-control to keep from wrenching her arm from his grasp and fleeing. She followed him down the corridor, eyes fixed firmly on the bare floor, wishing that she could stop up her ears. The scream was repeated. Or perhaps it was a different person this time. *How can the others stand hearing that?* the professor's daughter wondered. *How can the guards* stand it? Tejada was hurrying her down the corridor, almost running. Finally, he stopped in front of one of the closed doors with a pair of guards in front of it. "We're here to see Guillermo Fernández." The lieutenant's voice cut across the muffled cries. Elena wondered with sudden fear if she would shrink away from her father when she finally saw him. No one who made noises like the ones echoing in the corridor could still be whole and unhurt.

"Very good, Lieutenant."

As one of the guardias unlocked the door for them, Tejada half-turned to Elena. "These are the interrogation rooms." He caught a glimpse of her face and added hastily, "Professor Fernández and his colleagues haven't been questioned. It's simply a convenient place to hold people who haven't been formally charged yet. Just a secure waiting room."

There was a mutinous spark in Elena's eyes, and she might have answered him, but the door swung open at that moment, and Tejada stepped into the room, raising his voice as he did so. "Professor Fernández. Your daughter is here."

Elena raised her gaze from the floor and took in the "secure waiting room." Like the hallway, it was windowless, and was lit only by a single light bulb. It was empty except for a table, a chair, and three men. Her father had hurried to the doorway, holding out his hands to her, his expression both grateful and pleading. Arturo Velázquez, who had apparently just risen from the chair, was a step behind him. The third man in the room was slumped in a corner with his knees drawn up to his chest. He raised his head at the sight of her, and after a moment she recognized Tomás Rivera. In spite of the shadows, she saw that Rivera's lip was bruised and swollen. To her infinite relief, that seemed to be the only injury among the men. The door closed behind them, muffling the unpleasant sounds of the other interrogation rooms, but not completely.

Her father touched her cheek. "Elena! Sweetheart! What are you doing here?"

"I . . . I came to bring you some things Mama packed." Elena held up her bundle, as if it were a mute explanation.

"Then, you're not . . ." Her father's voice trailed off as he looked past her.

Elena was puzzled until she heard the lieutenant say quietly, "Señorita Fernández is free to go when she wishes."

"Elena!" It was Doctor Velázquez, imploring, "Will you tell Ana and Augusto what's happened? They must be frantic by now."

She nodded automatically, and then said slowly, "But what has happened?"

There was an awkward pause, filled by a cacophony of screams. Three pairs of eyes fixed themselves on a point just beyond Elena's left ear. Then a voice near that ear said, "It seems that Manuel Arroyo Díaz was murdered sometime last week. We're beginning our investigation by questioning his associates."

Elena turned. "Who?" The word "murder" had shaken her, but she could not immediately place the name Tejada had given, and fear and puzzlement combined to make her voice almost accusing.

"He was a professor of law," Tejada explained, rapidly deciding that her question was the result of genuine confusion. Of course she wouldn't know him, he thought. She was in Madrid when this whole petition nonsense started and there was no reason for her to have known him before that. Relief colored his voice, and made his tone closer to what Elena remembered from their first acquaintance as he added, "His signature appeared on a certain document your father also signed."

"And you think that one of *us* killed him?" Elena demanded, outraged.

"We have no definite suspects at the moment," Tejada replied. He considered reassuring her that her father was not a serious suspect but decided against it. Actions spoke louder than words, and Fernández would be released soon enough.

"We're only asking questions. We won't make an arrest until we have more information."

Against all logic, Elena found the lieutenant's words comforting. Murder might be a capital crime, but at least it was a specific one. And she was sure that Tejada would stay within the boundaries of the law. Her father and his colleagues might be imprisoned for a long time but she could not believe that Tejada would allow them to mysteriously disappear. She turned back to the prisoners and took a few hesitant steps toward Doctor Rivera. "Would you like me to send word to your wife, also?" she asked, suppressing the urge to kneel beside the doctor as she would have knelt beside a frightened child.

He looked up at her through eyes swollen by bruises and perhaps by tears, but his voice had the calm of despair. "No, thank you, Señorita Fernández. I discovered Professor Arroyo's body yesterday. My wife knew that I probably wouldn't be coming back today."

"Well . . . if you're sure. . . ." Elena stooped awkwardly and her hand rested briefly on Rivera's shoulder.

He did not respond, but Doctor Velázquez, who had watched the interchange with some anxiety, came to stand beside her. "I'm sorry to put you to the trouble, Elena. Thank you."

"It's nothing."

Velázquez embraced his colleague's daughter, and murmured as he did so, "Don't pay any mind to Rivera. Tell his wife what's happened."

Elena smiled at him, and nodded. Then she turned reluctantly to her father. "I have to go. Mama will be waiting for news."

Guillermo managed to smile at her. "You tell her that I'm fine. Better, now that she's sent me my pipe."

Elena hugged him, realizing as she did so how thin he had become, and wondered how long it had been since she had thought of him as tall. "I'll come again," she promised. "If I can," she added, with a sideways glance at the lieutenant, who had been studiously observing the floor.

The door swung shut behind Elena and her escort, and they were in the hallway of screams once again. At the top of the staircase, when the last sounds had died away, Elena heaved a sigh of relief.

"Come back to the office for a moment," Tejada said, breaking in on her thoughts.

She followed him mutely, glad that she was not responsible for finding her way, or meeting the eyes of the uniformed men in the corridors. When they had returned to the office, Tejada went to his desk, opened a drawer, and drew out a form. He wrote silently for a minute or two, and then folded the sheet into an envelope and held it out to her. "This is a permission to travel, for yourself and your mother," he said quietly. "To San Sebastián. For three weeks. You deserve a vacation."

Elena took the outstretched piece of paper automatically. How could he think that we'd go on vacation and leave Papa in that place? she wondered, confused. Then she remembered that the "vacation" in San Sebastián had another motive, and she shuddered. How could any of the Fernández family take further risks, with her father already entangled in a murder investigation?

Tejada held the door of the office for her. "Good-bye," he said awkwardly. "I hope your mother is reassured by your news."

As a matter of fact, María de Fernández was so incredibly relieved by her daughter's return that she hardly asked for news. It was nearly nine o'clock when Elena reached her home, and the sun was setting. María, who had spent the last two hours staring at the clock in an agony of guilt and suspense, greeted her daughter almost with euphoria. Elena summarized her trip to the post over dinner, tactfully limiting her impressions of the interrogation room where her father was being held to a strictly visual description. María was relieved by her account but began to giggle a little hysterically when Elena mentioned that the two women had received permission to travel. "A trip to San Sebastián!" María hiccuped. "A nice little vacation while Guillermo is in prison for murder! Because we deserve a vacation!"

The stress of the day had started to tell on Elena as well. She began to laugh also. Mother and daughter chortled helplessly for some time, wiping tears from their eyes. Finally, Elena pulled herself together. "It's pointless anyway," she reminded her mother. "The letter to Meyer didn't go through, remember."

"True enough," María admitted. "Although there's always the copy that was sent to Germany."

"Yes, but nothing's likely to come of that," Elena pointed out reasonably but quite incorrectly.

The next morning, a little after 9 A.M., the Fernández's doorbell rang. María, hoping that Guillermo had been released, flew to answer it, and was unexpectedly confronted by a boy in a dark uniform. "Telegram, Señora," the boy said, holding out his message. "For Guillermo Fernández."

Controlling her disappointment, María signed for the telegram and took it into the kitchen. She had barely opened the message, and was brooding on its contents, when the bell rang again. This time it was Elena who answered the door.

"Papa!"

The young woman's joyous cry brought María from the kitchen at a run. Guillermo Fernández, unbathed and unshaven but otherwise unharmed, was enthusiastically hugged, kissed, and dragged into the kitchen for breakfast. The professor himself seemed dazed at his good fortune. "We've all been released," he explained, in response to the eager questions of his wife and daughter. "I don't know why. But none of us are allowed to leave Salamanca until further notice. That's not a big hardship though." He smiled warmly. "It's enough to be home."

There was a sudden, awkward silence. "What is it?" Guillermo asked, sensing the changed atmosphere.

"Mother and I have permission to travel to San Sebastián," Elena explained.

"We just this morning got a telegram." María spoke at the same moment.

"A telegram?" Guillermo echoed. "From whom?"

With a reluctant glance at her daughter, María held out the message. Guillermo took the telegram from his wife's hand and read: THANKS. STOP. WILL PURSUE RESEARCH IN BIARRITZ LIBRARY. STOP. WIRE ME AT POSTE CENTRALE CARE OF JEAN SAMUELS. STOP. THEOKLYMENOS.

# Chapter 10

"Y̶ou've what?" snapped Captain Rodríguez.

"I released them this morning, sir." The lieutenant was impassive. "We had no further cause to hold them."

"You don't call murder 'further cause'?" The captain spoke with what was intended as blistering sarcasm.

"We have no evidence that any of them are involved in Arroyo's death," Tejada pointed out. "We haven't even positively identifed the body found in the warehouse."

"Observe the facts, Lieutenant." Captain Rodríguez spoke with the false sweetness that some men feel obliged to use with children and idiots. "Manuel Arroyo Díaz disappears. The Guardia Civil spend a week apparently doing nothing to try to find him. A body appears with a wallet containing calling cards with Arroyo's name on them. The body is found in a location with ties to a known Red, who is also known to have ties to Arroyo. The Red and his associates are brought in for questioning. Then they are released. *Where is the flaw in logic here, Tejada?*"

Tejada had not been totally happy with his decision to release the three former professors, but his commanding officer's reaction made him feel that it had probably been wise. "With respect, sir, I believed that they had answered all of our questions satisfactorily," he said. "They'll remain under surveillance, of course, as we continue the investigation."

Rodríguez, confronted with an excessively reasonable answer, made a dismissive gesture. "You might at least have arrested Rivera!" he said disgustedly. "For goodness' sake, Tejada, he's a Red. He practically discovered the body, and it was found at a construction site belonging to the company he works for."

"We still don't know if the body found in the warehouse entered it alive or not," Tejada replied. He did not point out that only a very foolish man would choose to dispose of a body at a site that would so obviously link him to his crime.

"Well, he's damn well guilty of something," Rodríguez retorted. "We can't allow Reds to go around murdering prominent citizens because the evidence is only circumstantial, Tejada!"

It occurred to the lieutenant that in this instance the Red and the prominent citizen had been colleagues of a sort. Captain Rodríguez apparently believed in speaking no ill of the dead. "Very true, sir," he said quietly. "I'll devote all of my energy to the case. And I'd like Sergeant Hernández to assist me, if possible."

"I should assign the case to Sergeant Betances and be done with it," Rodríguez barked. Tejada stiffened slightly, wondering if he was about to be relieved. Then the captain added ungraciously, "But since Judge Otero seems to think you're competent, I suppose you'd better clear it up."

"I'm honored by the judge's confidence, sir," Tejada replied smoothly, concealing his surprise. Otero must have contacted Rodríguez sometime yesterday, he thought. But why? And why go out of his way to mention me?

"I just hope it isn't misplaced." The captain stood, ending the interview. "Don't mess this up, Tejada. Arroyo was a distinguished man, and his family is very upset by this whole thing. I want this solved fast."

"Yes, sir." Tejada saluted formally, and then left feeling pensive. Arroyo was a janitor for the last three years, he thought. And his family want this solved fast. So they can bury him and be done with it? "An embarrassment," Judge Otero had called him. How much of an embarrassment? Had the captain guessed at Tejada's thoughts he would almost certainly have removed him from the Arroyo case, and would probably have tried to commit him to an asylum. But Tejada had judged hastily—and wrong—before, and had lived to regret his mistakes. He settled himself in his office, and reached for the telephone. Sergeant Hernández had left Judge Otero's phone number clipped to the top of the Arroyo file. Tejada dialed and waited. There was no answer.

The lieutenant thought for a moment. The judge might well be at home for the day. He picked up the phone again, and called the operator. "Do you have a phone number for Jorge Otero Martínez?" he asked.

"Yes, sir. His listing is four two zero one." The smooth voice confirmed the number that Tejada already had, and then added, in a slightly less formal tone, "But Judge Otero is never in his office on Saturdays."

Tejada, who had deliberately avoided mentioning Otero's profession, winced at this further proof of the judge's standing in Salamanca. "Thank you," he said, resigned to a delay in speaking with Otero.

"You're a guardia, sir?" The voice on the phone was chatty.

"Yes."

"I suppose I could give you his home number, then, if you like."

"Please," Tejada said, surprised. He had heretofore considered helpful operators to be in the same category as griffins and unicorns.

"One zero zero two." The reply was gratifyingly prompt. "He was the second one to have a phone installed in his home in that sector, after the doctor."

"Really?" Tejada said, since the disembodied voice seemed to expect some reply.

"Yes, sir. In the winter of 1919. His daughter was taken ill with the flu, and he wanted to be able to call the doctor at any hour. Or so people said, anyway."

"Oh," Tejada said. And then, before his confidant could

expand more on the history of the telephone in Salamanca, "Perhaps you could put through the call now?"

"Yes, sir. Right away."

Tejada counted the rings, making a mental note not to discuss anything that he did not want retailed to the next person unwary enough to place a call that afternoon. On the fourth ring, a woman answered.

Tejada stated his name and business, and asked to speak to the judge. After a rather lengthy pause, he heard a click, and Judge Otero's voice said, "Good afternoon, Lieutenant. I assume you're calling regarding the same unfortunate business we last spoke about?"

"That's correct." Tejada guessed that the judge had experience with Salamanca's operators, and was alert to the dangers of indiscreet communication. He relaxed slightly. "Naturally, we're all anxious to have it cleared up, Your Honor. I wondered if I could interview you again briefly?"

"I'll be at home this afternoon," the judge replied. "My sister has been staying with us since the unhappy event, and she'll be here, too, should you wish to see her."

"That's very considerate of you," Tejada said. "Shall we say, four o'clock?"

"Agreed." Judge Otero was brisk.

Tejada thanked the judge, and broke the connection, wondering if "four o'clock" in fact meant 4:30. After some consideration, he decided to err on the side of promptness. The Otero family lived in a handsome townhouse opposite the Church of San Martín. Tejada allowed himself ten minutes for the walk, made a point of dawdling, and arrived just as the clocks were striking 4:15. A servant opened the door, and led him across a wide hallway, and up a flight of stairs to a large parlor, furnished with the same subtle opulence that characterized Judge Otero's office.

The room was exactly what Tejada had expected. He could have made shrewd guesses at the titles of the sheets of music lying on the closed piano, and the names of the painters of the family portraits on the walls. Even the diamond-patterned wallpaper felt familiar. His rapid and unconscious assessment of the room left him free to focus on the three figures within it. Judge Otero had stepped forward to meet him, lightly swinging his silver-handled cane, followed by two women. Tejada recognized one of them as Manuel Arroyo's wife. The other woman was unfamiliar to him, but he guessed that she was Otero's wife.

The judge confirmed this immediately. "Good afternoon, Lieutenant. Thank you for coming. May I present my wife? Josefina, this is Enrique Tejada's nephew. He's investigating Manuel's death."

Tejada automatically acknowledged the introduction and took the seat offered, while thinking rapidly. Señora de Arroyo was wearing mourning, as were her brother and sister-in-law. And the judge had spoken of "Manuel's death" as if it were a settled fact, although Sergeant Hernández had made it clear to him the previous day that the body found in the Quiñones warehouse had not been positively identified. He wondered exactly what Judge Otero had said to Rodríguez about closing the case. "Now, do you have any information for us, Lieutenant?" the judge asked.

"I'm afraid not," Tejada answered carefully. "But if it isn't too much of a bother I do have some questions."

"Of course." The judge was gracious.

Tejada turned to Señora de Arroyo. At three in the morning, as an unwilling guest of the Guardia Civil, she had been merely self-possessed. Now, at ease in her brother's home, she was formidable. "I am afraid, Señora, that it is likely that the man found on Thursday was your husband," he said carefully. "I'm sure this must be a terrible blow."

"I've been prepared for the worst since Manuel's disappearance." The presumed widow spoke calmly.

"Very wise," Tejada agreed. "But we would like a positive identification of the body as that of your husband."

She raised her eyebrows. "Are you implying that my husband may have staged his own death?"

"No, no." Tejada reassured her hastily. "You understand, it's only a formality. But—forgive the question, Señora—did your husband have any distinguishing characteristics? Apart from facial ones, I mean?"

"No. Not to my knowledge." Her voice was disgusted.

"Perhaps I could view the body, once your men have finished with it," Otero interjected. "I knew Manuel for many years, and I'm sure that I would recognize him."

"Thank you, Your Honor." Tejada decided not to press the point. It would not, he thought, be tasteful to explain that Arroyo's skull had been fractured, and much of his face had been rendered unrecognizable even before decomposition had further damaged his body. "I do apologize for asking such a distressing question, but I was hoping that we might be able to expedite Professor Arroyo's death certificate."

"Is there likely to be any further delay?" Somewhat to the lieutenant's surprise, it was Señora de Arroyo who had spoken, and rather sharply.

"Not a long one," Tejada replied. He decided to needle the widow a little. "In cases like this, it could be oh, six to eight weeks. But perhaps we could issue one in, say, a month, given the special nature of the case."

The lady was frowning heavily now. "I would like Manuel's affairs settled more quickly if possible, Lieutenant."

Tejada wondered what affairs needed to be so urgently settled, and took a shot in the dark. "Did your husband leave a will, Señora?"

"Yes." Once more, it was Judge Otero who answered. "It was a simple affair really, as there were no children to be considered. My sister is the sole beneficiary."

"You are aware of the contents of this will, Your Honor?" Tejada raised his eyebrows.

"I'm his executor."

"I see." Tejada's eyes passed over the Persian carpets, and rose to the claw-footed side tables with their lace antimacassars and porcelain shepherds, until they once more encountered Señora de Arroyo's face. "Forgive me, Señora, but would a delay in putting your husband's will through probate leave you in any financial difficulty? Naturally, if that were the case, we would make every attempt to issue a death certificate promptly."

The lady pursed her lips. "No," she said reluctantly. "It would not."

"It's not a question of financial difficulties, Lieutenant," the judge intervened. "But Manuel's estate should not be neglected. It includes some significant investments which should be overseen by an experienced money manager."

Tejada suppressed a flicker of surprise—he had only thought of Arroyo as a petitioner, and not as a rich man. An aristocrat, perhaps, but one who had definitively thrown in his lot with the masses. He wondered if Arroyo's fortune amounted to a sum that men would kill for. "What investments would these be?" he asked baldly.

Otero hesitated. Then he said slowly, "Large amounts of stock in Banco Bilbao Vizcaya. And smaller holdings in several foreign companies."

"Also banks?"

The judge shook his head. "Pharmaceuticals, I believe. They're German firms, not ones I'm familiar with. Manuel probably bought them on the advice of his medical colleagues."

Tejada had been doing rapid mental arithmetic. Depending on the number of shares involved, Arroyo's estate could well be worth murderering for. And the immediate beneficiaries of the lawyer's death were sitting comfortably in front of him, probably the least arrestable people in all of Salamanca. He remembered that

Señora de Arroyo had not reported her husband's absence to the Guardia. But that doesn't make sense, he thought. Not if she killed him for his money. She'd want everyone to know he was dead. And she wants a death certificate as soon as possible. So she'd want him to be easily identifiable. Unless she simply gave instructions and whoever carried them out got a little rough. But if she was involved she'd still come forward and report him missing. He dismissed the train of thought, and focused on the judge's last words. "His medical colleagues?" he repeated. "Was your brother-in-law friendly with any doctors, Your Honor?"

There was a tense silence. It was broken, oddly enough, by Judge Otero's wife. "I imagine you'd know more about them than we would, Lieutenant." Her voice dripped malice.

Judge Otero seemed to think that the remark had been unnecessarily vehement. He turned reprovingly to his wife. "Really, dear. Poor Manuel is dead."

"Only to be expected, given the sort he was mixed up with," she retorted.

"Are you referring to these gentlemen's political sympathies?" Tejada asked smoothly.

"Of course." Señora de Otero jerked her head. "I imagine you've seen his file. He was mixed up with Reds. And Reds killed him."

"My husband was never a Red," Señora de Arroyo snapped.

"I suppose he signed that petition with a gun held to his head?" her sister-in-law retorted.

The judge and the lieutenant exchanged swift and silent glances. One looked rueful, and the other compassionate. Tejada's sympathy for the judge increased. Dealing with two venomous women was more than any man deserved, especially when one was his wife and the other his sister. "Were you referring to Doctor Velázquez or Doctor Rivera, Your Honor?"

Judge Otero cast a slightly apprehensive look at his sister before replying. "I suppose I might have been thinking of them. But Manuel's association with those two was years ago. Before the war."

"Your brother-in-law's stock holdings date from before the war, then?"

"Yes, he made almost no acquisitions during the war. The markets were disrupted, you know. In fact it's only recently that he—" The judge stopped himself. "Started buying again," he finished after an almost imperceptible pause.

Tejada noted the pause, but could think of no graceful way to pursue it. Instead, he turned to Señora de Otero. "You say that Reds killed Professor Arroyo, Señora. May I ask why you think that?"

"Because he was bound to end up making a public show of himself somehow," the lady replied, with more annoyance than logic.

"How you can blame a man for being martyred by those bloodsuckers?" Señora de Arroyo began fiercely.

"Pepa! Margarita! I'm sure we don't want to bore the lieutenant with this!" Judge Otero's voice could have cleared a noisy courtroom. Both women fell silent, and the judge turned apologetically to Tejada. "Do you have any further questions?"

Tejada turned back to Arroyo's widow. "You say you've been prepared for the worst since your husband disappeared, Señora. Could you tell me exactly when this was?"

Señora de Arroyo looked reluctant, but her voice was steady as she said, "I haven't seen Manuel in over two weeks."

"Then your husband disappeared sometime before. . . ." Tejada frowned a moment, calculating. "Saturday, the fifteenth? Is that correct? Can you give me an exact date?"

Señora de Arroyo put her fingers to her lips, a gesture of contemplation rather than silencing. "Yes, I think so. It was in the evening . . . Wednesday? Yes, Wednesday." She looked apologetic at her own hesitation. "I do remember that it was exactly six o'clock, because the radio was on, and they announced the hour."

A complication presented itself to Tejada. "It might have been Thursday?" he suggested, without offering a reason.

She shook her head decidedly. "No, it must have been Wednesday. Or . . . no, it wasn't Friday."

"You weren't sure before," the lieutenant pressed gently. "Why couldn't it have been Thursday?"

Señora de Arroyo looked annoyed, and for a moment Tejada thought that she would refuse to answer. Then she said a little sharply, "Because Manuel was on his way to his . . . job." She cast a glance at her sister-in-law, and then continued defiantly, "And that was Mondays, Wednesdays, and Fridays."

"I see." In fact, Tejada did not see at all. Señora de Arroyo had given an absolutely plausible account of her husband's movements, except for one trifling detail: according to his file, Manuel Arroyo Díaz had presented himself, alive and in good health, at the Guardia Civil post on the Thursday evening after his disappearance. Tejada could think of no reason why the lawyer would have avoided his home for twenty-four hours, shown up for his parole appointment, and then been murdered. He made a note to check with Eduardo Crespo as to whether the lawyer had in fact presented himself for work on the evening of Wednesday the thirteenth. And then, Tejada thought with distaste, I'll have to ask Rodríguez about his last parole appointment. And fat chance of getting anything reliable out of him about Arroyo's state of mind. Maybe Hernández will remember something. The lieutenant turned to Judge Otero and his wife. "Did either of you see or speak to Professor Arroyo later than his wife?"

Señora de Otero pursed her lips and did not reply. Judge Otero shook his head. "I'm afraid not."

"And none of you thought of reporting his absence to the Guardia Civil?"

"In my experience the Guardia are quite zealous enough without encouragement." Señora de Arroyo spoke with unmistakable significance.

"Fortunate for those of us who are law-abiding citizens," her sister-in-law added with deadly sweetness.

Señora de Arroyo turned on her, swift to avenge insult. "I notice that you never called them when—"

"Do you have any further questions, Lieutenant?" Judge Otero's voice cut across his sister's.

"Not at present." Tejada, who had been trying to think of a way to change the subject, gratefully seized the judge's opening. "Thank you for explaining the need for releasing a death certificate as soon as possible. I'll try to have one for you right away."

"You're most welcome, Lieutenant." The judge saw him out into the hallway. As they descended the stairs he said apologetically, "I'm sorry you were witness to that little scene. My wife is naturally quite upset."

Tejada, who could scarcely remember a time when his mother had been on speaking terms with all of his aunts at once, nodded understandingly. "Shock sometimes has that effect," he said.

"Poor Manuel." Otero's voice was reflective. "I suppose in some ways his death was a blessed release."

"Your Honor?" Tejada's voice was respectful, although it occurred to him that the phrase "blessed release" was generally not applied to crushed skulls.

"He couldn't work anymore. Well, you know what he was doing. He'd lost his friends, his career, everything really. And he lived with the knowledge that he was an embarrassment to his family. A sort of millstone around their necks. All the same," the judge sighed, "I imagine that he wouldn't have wished for an end like this."

"Probably not," Tejada agreed.

Otero smiled a little. "I trust you won't find this callous, but Manuel always had the most fatal sense of timing. My wife was planning a little party for our granddaughter's birthday next weekend, and now it will have to be curtailed, of course. That may be part of the reason for her distress."

"Very unfortunate for the young lady as well," Tejada said sympathetically, as they reached the door.

"Oh, Eugenia was never close to Manuel." The judge's voice was dismissive. At the doorway he paused. "I suppose, having mentioned Eugenia's party I should issue an invitation. Naturally, the officers of the Guardia will receive formal invitations as well, but may I offer a personal one, Lieutenant?"

"I would be delighted." Tejada knew that this response was mandatory, but it was not completely untruthful. He was still not sure of the motive behind Judge Otero's graciousness. But he would have been foolish to waste it. The Oteros' party was sure to include a vast number of people who had known Manuel Arroyo Díaz well. The lieutenant intended to take every opportunity to observe them while they were at ease, and off guard.

# Chapter 11

"Really, dear, it's not as if you're going to a party," María reminded her daughter, a few days after Judge Otero's invitation to the lieutenant.

Elena nodded, and made a disgusted noise. "Just as well. Honestly, who could possibly *wear* these things?" She held out the magazine she had been reading for her mother's inspection.

María glanced at the picture Elena was pointing to. "Which one? The beach pajamas or the winter underwear?"

Elena laughed. "That's a bathing suit, Mama."

Her mother looked startled. "You mean it's to wear on the beach? My goodness, I can't imagine who would wear it anything so dowdy."

"Just as well we aren't ordering new suits then. All the patterns are along these lines 'to oprotect our Christian morality!'." Elena cast another glance at the penciled illustration. The black bathing suit had caused her initial exclamation, but she secretly thought the lean silhouette of the beach pajamas, with their flared legs and high-waisted belt, looked rather elegant. Pale blue, she thought. With white trimming, maybe . . . not that I'd ever actually *wear* it but. . . .

"I don't think we need to attract any more attention than absolutely necessary." Her mother's dry voice interrupted her thoughts. "And regardless of the opinions of *Blanco y negro*, I do *not* think that the standard dress in San Sebastián this summer will resemble those drawings."

"I doubt His Holiness, Bishop Eijo Garay, will be policing the beach," Elena agreed. She stood up, dropping the magazine as she did so, and her mother swung open the dark trunk she had been sitting on, releasing a strong smell of mothballs.

The Fernández family had decided, after a nerve-wracking family conference, that their obligation to Joseph Meyer must be honored. Guillermo had sent a return wire, bearing the words, "MESSAGE RECEIVED. STOP. WILL CONTACT SOON," and had written to several hotels in San Sebastián, asking about the possibility of rooms for his wife and daughter. The family had agreed that it would be best for María and Elena to arrive in San Sebastián as tourists, explaining simply that Guillermo had been detained in Salamanca on business. Guillermo had initially suggested that Professor Meyer join them and masquerade as "Señor Fernández," but Elena had pointed out that even if they had been able to provide the necessary papers, the Guardia Civil in San Sebastián were quite capable of telephoning their counterparts in Salamanca to verify Señor Fernández's identity. "And it would be very awkward to have you in two places at once," she'd said.

"Besides," María had added, "Meyer's practically a caricature of a German. And even if his appearance could pass for Spanish, he'd be recognized as a foreigner as soon as he opened his mouth."

After some further argument, pending a better idea, the family had decided that Joseph Meyer would have to pose as a distant relative of María's. "Deaf!" Elena had suggested with sudden inspiration. "So no one will think it's odd if he has trouble understanding, or sounds a little strange."

Guillermo had laughed a little at the idea of his colleague posing as an afflicted relation, but he had approved the scheme. He had retreated to his study to write another careful letter to his son, asking if Hipólito could arrange to book a passage for Joseph Meyer. Meanwhile, María and Elena, determined to act as normally as possible, having consulted a magazine devoted to summer fashions, were carefully assembling clothing to pack for a few weeks at the seashore.

The Fernández's had not taken a family vacation in over four years. The battered, metal-hinged trunks that María and Guillermo had used since their honeymoon were buried in back of the attic, amid yellowing piles of Guillermo's old manuscripts, dust-laden games and toys (some of them broken) from Elena and Hipólito's childhood, and other miscellaneous residue of a more prosperous era. The two women braved the forgotten corners of the attic one evening, after the worst of the day's heat. María occupied herself searching out long-neglected bathing suits and sandals. Elena perched herself on one of the black trunks and leafed through the magazine, allowing her fancy to roam over new fashions, before turning once more to the faded reality, stiffened by salt and musty with the odor of the long-forgotten sea.

María carefully began to unpack the trunk. "These will be no use. They're all your father's. Except for the hats." She gently laid the old summer suits to one side, and lifted out an eggshell-shaped hat, once white but now slightly yellowed, trimmed with lace.

Elena smiled. "I remember that one. You wore it the year we did the play in school."

"You're right." Her mother laughed. "I'd forgotten."

"The year after Professor Meyer visited us." Elena was thoughtful.

"I'm afraid wearing it again would attract as much extra attention as one of those bathing suits." Her mother smiled slightly. "It's not exactly in style."

"No," Elena agreed, shaking off her memories. "But maybe we could bring along a few of papa's old suits for Professor Meyer. They're out of fashion, but they're local at least, and they might make him a bit less conspicuous."

"Good idea," her mother agreed.

The two women made several trips from the attic, bearing old bathing suits, sandals, parasols, and all the paraphernalia of barely remembered trips to the seashore, into the living room. Following Elena's suggestion, they also brought along an old suit of Guillermo's as a possible disguise for their guest.

Guillermo, poking his head into the living room that evening, gave a startled exclamation. "You're not planning to take all of this?"

"It does seem like a lot," Elena admitted, observing the miscellaneous objects strewn over couches and tables. "But it's no more than we used to take with us. Less, really, since you and Hipólito aren't coming."

"Most of it should fit in the trunk," María confirmed. "And then there are the two little suitcases."

The professor's private opinion was that he and his son together had contributed less than a tenth to the family packing in the past, but he contented himself with saying mildly, "Are the bags still up in the attic? I'll give you a hand bringing them down."

María accepted her husband's help with a gratitude that turned out to have far-reaching consequences. Had she thanked him with a little less alacrity, and had she been more successfully furtive as she wiped sweat from her face, Elena would not have realized the extent of her mother's exhaustion. And had Elena not realized, she would not have insisted on helping her father carry the bulky trunk downstairs. And had Elena and Guillermo not been fully occupied with the black trunk, María would not have returned upstairs alone to drag down the two "little" suitcases.

Father and daughter had just set down the trunk in the living room and swung open its top, when they heard a muffled crash, and then a cry of distress. "María! Are you all right?" Guillermo ran for the stairs with Elena one step behind him.

"Mama?"

They found María lying on the first landing, surrounded by the two hard-sided suitcases that had been her downfall, holding back tears. "It's nothing. I tripped over the bags. I'm an *idiot*. It's nothing." María's little gasps of pain belied her words.

"You could have been killed!" Guillermo knelt by his wife, tried to pull her upright, and was interrupted by an involuntary cry of pain.

"My hip! Don't, Guillermo. I'll be fine in a few minutes, honestly. Ow! No, I really can't sit up."

The professor looked up at his daughter, white-faced. "Call Doctor Velázquez, Elena!" he ordered, and then returned his attention to María. "What happened? Did you fall from the top of the stairs? Are you *certain* you can't move?"

In spite of the urgency of the situation, Elena hesitated. "Doctor Velázquez? Are you sure? I mean, the Guardia Civil questioned both of you so recently—"

"Don't argue, damn it!" Fear made Guillermo's voice sharp.

María spoke at the same moment. "No, don't call Velázquez. It'll only bring the Guardia down on us."

"Who then?"

María's breath hissed between her teeth. "Antonia Santana has mentioned a Doctor Ferrer. Call her, and see if you can get his number."

Elena ran for the phone, more frightened by her mother's willingness to see a doctor than by the sight of her lying on the landing apparently unable to move. Fortunately, Doña Antonia, a garrulous former baby-sitter of the professor's daughter, was at home and only too happy to provide Doctor Ferrer's telephone number, though not before she had wrung the details of Señora de Fernández's accident out of Elena. Although Elena had not issued an invitation, Doña Antonia arrived within a few minutes to soothe the professor and "his little girl," and to fuss over the invalid. Her exclamations were little appreciated by any of the Fernándezes, but her assistance in carrying María to bed when the doctor arrived was helpful.

Doctor Ferrer, who arrived half an hour after Doña Antonia, heard the details of the accident, made a cursory examination, and delivered his verdict. "You may well have fractured the hip, Señora. It's impossible to tell without X-rays. But in any case, the treatment is simple: rest and complete immobilization."

"For how long?" María's voice was low. She was in considerable pain, and the effort to remain conscious without crying left her little energy for speech.

"Difficult to say. Two to three months, probably."

María's breath hissed between her teeth. Doctor Ferrer drew the professor aside. "I'll prescribe an opiate if you wish, Señor. It may help some of her pain. But medicines have been in short supply since the war. And they're expensive."

Professor Fernández glanced over his shoulder at his wife. She was crying silently. "There are no coupons for them in the ration books, I suppose," he said, resignedly.

The doctor snorted. "Keep dreaming."

Guillermo sighed. "Write the prescription. We'll fill it somehow."

Elena was kept fully occupied by the intrusive benevolence of her old baby-sitter, the grave instructions of Doctor Ferrer, and the suppressed panic of her father until quite late that evening. Guillermo flatly refused to leave his wife's side until she finally fell into an exhausted sleep, without the aid of narcotics, a little after two in the morning. His daughter, who had been waiting in the hall outside his room, firmly steered him downstairs to the kitchen. "Doña Antonia left soup," she said, in a tone of voice she had developed for the benefit of her elementary school students. "And we have some old bread left."

"I'm not hungry." Guillermo sank limply into a chair without bothering to turn on a light.

Elena ignored his words, lit the lamp, and brought him a bowl of soup and a spoon. "Eat. You won't do Mama any good by starving yourself."

He obediently picked up the bowl, but stood. "I'll take it upstairs in case she wakes."

His daughter blocked the doorway. "What she needs now is rest. You'll do more good by leaving her alone."

Guillermo ate in silence for a little while. Then he said, in a slightly choked voice, "This is all my fault."

"How's that?" Elena demanded gently, feeling as she did when she escorted her father to the Guardia Civil on Friday afternoons: strong and competent, and maternal and resentful.

"She wouldn't have been getting out the suitcases if it wasn't for me." The professor spoke bitterly. "A fine head of the family I am, risking you and María, for the sake of some foreigner."

Elena had almost forgotten the trip to San Sebastián and its ultimate purpose in the tumult of the afternoon. "We agreed to the risk," she said slowly. "Because it was the right thing to do. Because we'd want someone to do it for us."

"Because we thought Meyer was at greater risk than we were," Guillermo finished dryly. "And I don't *know* if that's true. I got a feeling of urgency from his letters. But it's hard to tell. He could just have been dramatizing."

"It would have to be urgent for anyone to want to get *into* Spain, now," Elena remarked with a slight twist to her mouth.

"Well, it looks as though we'll have to let him down, doesn't it?" Guillermo said. "I can't leave Salamanca, and even if I could, I wouldn't with your mother like this. The only question is how to let him know."

"There's no need to do that," Elena said slowly, aware that she was committing herself. "I can go to San Sebastián on my own."

# Chapter 12

"**Y**ou can't just go off to San Sebastián for a holiday by the sea!" Captain Rodríguez exclaimed.

Tejada, who had expected this reaction, was prepared. "I've worked out the patrol schedules for the following week," he said. "Betances can keep the files organized, and Hernández has agreed to see the parolees in my absence, if I'm gone for the entire week, which isn't likely. And with respect, sir, I think it may be vital to the Arroyo case."

"Ahh. You mean you think Arroyo's murderer is taking a vacation there?" The captain's voice dripped sarcasm.

Tejada, standing at attention in front of the captain's desk, gritted his teeth and reflected how much he disliked Rodríguez's particular brand of jovial mockery. "I spoke to Eduardo Crespo again yesterday, sir," he said, carefully. "According to Crespo, Arroyo was preoccupied and nervous for some time before his disappearance. He was following the news of the war in France with anxiety."

"Well, of course he was," the captain snapped. "He was a Red. He probably didn't like the German victories."

"Arroyo had an account at Banco Bilbao Vizcaya," Tejada continued, ignoring the interruption. "I've looked at his bank statement. He had about ten thousand pesetas in the account."

"So? He was well-to-do."

"That's just the point, Captain." Tejada was unable to

suppress a flicker of annoyance at his commanding officer's naïveté. "Señora de Arroyo has been pressing us for a death certificate because she wants control of his estate. I doubt that she'd be that urgent for just a pittance."

Rodríguez snorted. "You call ten thousand pesetas a pittance? You move in exalted circles, Lieutenant!"

"*I* call ten thousand pesetas more than my annual salary," Tejada retorted, finally goaded. "But Arroyo's investments probably brought him over twice that in interest. And I'm sure he had savings as well, plus a pension, and a salary, although that probably *was* a pittance. The point is, where are the rest of his assets?"

Like many people, Captain Rodríguez was made slightly uncomfortable by the casual discussion of great wealth. He shifted a little in his chair and said truculently, "Lots of people don't trust banks. Maybe he kept his money at home."

*Peasant!* Tejada thought with disgust, holding on to his temper with some difficulty. What do you think he did, stuff it into a mattress like an old woman? He made sure that his voice was under control before he said, "I've spoken to the branch manager, Captain. At the end of the war Arroyo had just under two hundred thousand pesetas in his account." The captain made a strangled noise, and Tejada watched the clockwork in Rodríguez's brain attempt to translate the amount into something comprehensible. "He's been steadily withdrawing significant sums for the last eight months," the lieutenant continued. "If one puts that together with Crespo's information about Arroyo's recent behavior, there's a strong suggestion that he was planning to flee the country, with as much cash as possible."

"But he was murdered before he got the chance to flee," Rodríguez finished, apparently relieved to be back on solid ground.

"We don't know that," Tejada replied carefully. He took a deep breath, and prayed that Rodríguez would be able to follow his hypothesis without too much difficulty. "We know that an

unidentifiable body with his wallet was found last week. Crespo
says he last saw Arroyo on June tenth. His wife last saw him on
June twelfth. And he showed up for his last parole date on June
thirteenth. That's a very gradual disappearance for a man who's
been murdered. But for a man who's planning to slowly fade
out of the picture it's very clever. Crespo didn't look for Arroyo
because he thought that Señora Otero would be sure to know if
something was wrong. And she didn't look for him because she
thought the Guardia were following his movements anyway. And
we didn't look for him because he'd made his last parole date.
Everyone assumed that someone else knew where he was."

"I don't see what this has to do with going to San Sebastián."
Rodríguez's voice was still aggressive, but there was a note of
uncertainty as well.

Tejada took a deep breath. The next part was tricky. It
involved a hunch—a hunch based on information that he pre-
ferred to withhold from the captain. That morning, as he
reviewed the weekly surveillance reports of Arroyo's fellow petitioners, Guardia Estrada's report on Guillermo Fernández had
caught his eye:

> **Wednesday 3/7/40:** Subject went to railway station with
> daughter and wife. Purchased tickets. (Subject has been pro-
> hibited from leaving Salamanca. Suspicious behavior???)

> **Thursday 4/7/40:** House visited by unknown woman at 19:00,
> by a doctor at 19:30. Subject emerged to walk doctor to his car
> at 20:15. Subject's daughter saw off female visitor at 21:00.
> Both appeared healthy. Possible some accident/illness has
> affected subject's wife???

Tejada's first casual thought had been that he hoped that
Elena's vacation with her mother was not spoiled. She was
unlikely to go without Señora de Fernández. Then it had

occurred to him that it was a bit odd for her to want to go without the professor. He had offered the permission to travel as a courtesy, because there was nothing else that he could do for her. But now that he thought about the matter, it was strange that a girl who faithfully accompanied her father to his parole appointments every week was willing to leave him to take a vacation just when the Guardia Civil had become more suspicious of his behavior. It did not fit with what he knew of her.

Unless she has some other reason for going to San Sebastián, Tejada thought, and reluctantly recalled his interview with Eduardo Crespo a day earlier. "A terrible business," the lawyer had said, shaking his head, his voice as loud in grief as it had been in jovial welcome. "You may not believe this, but Professor Arroyo wasn't a bad man before he got mixed up with the Reds. And now, honestly, I don't know whether to hope that he's dead or has fled. At least if that body you've found is his, there's no disgrace. Surely it's better to remember the professor as he used to be: a fine scholar, teacher, and athlete."

"Athlete?" Tejada had asked with some interest.

"Oh, not so much lately," the lawyer had replied. "But he used to be quite a notable swimmer and sailor. He and his wife have, oh God, *had* a house in San Sebastián and a little yacht. My family and I visited them one summer when the kids were small and I remember the professor taking the boys out on the bay for entire days."

Tejada had not particularly noted the words at the time. But pondering Elena Fernández's mysterious determination to go north to San Sebastián for the summer, Crespo's words struck an ominous chord. *"A house in San Sebastián. And a little yacht."*

It was, Tejada thought, ridiculous to imagine that Elena might be mixed up in Arroyo's disappearance, much less his murder—if it was a murder. She hadn't even recognized the man's name. There was absolutely no evidence linking her or her father to the former professor of law. And yet . . . and yet,

Guillermo Fernández had asked for permission to travel immediately after the discovery of the body that might or might not be Arroyo's. To San Sebastián, where Arroyo had owned a house. And a boat that would certainly be capable of making the brief trip up the coast to France.

Elena had nothing to do with any of this, the lieutenant decided. But if another man were in charge of the investigation, he might accidentally misread the evidence and waste valuable time focusing on her. This would allow Arroyo (or, if the corpse proved to be his, Arroyo's murderers) to slip away, and would also spoil Elena's vacation. Therefore, Tejada felt, it was in everyone's best interest for him to go to San Sebastián to search for clues to Arroyo's disappearance personally. "Dr. Crespo mentioned that Arroyo owned property in San Sebastián," Tejada said carefully. "Apparently he also owned a boat there. If he were thinking of leaving the country, it would be a logical place for him to go."

To Tejada's relief, the captain seemed willing to accept this line of reasoning. Unfortunately, Rodríguez showed an unexpected flash of intelligence. "If he did go there, he has a week's start," he pointed out. "Wouldn't it be faster to call the post in San Sebastián and ask them for any information?"

"Yes, sir," Tejada admitted. "But they've never had any dealings with him and he'd be hard to describe. I thought it would be better if someone who could recognize him went in search of him."

"It'd make more sense to send Hernández then," commented Rodríguez, still showing regrettable acuity. "Or one of the guardias who tailed him. You've never met the man."

"Actually, I have, sir." Tejada spoke in an expressionless monotone. "I was a student of Arroyo's."

Rodríguez's head jerked up to look at his lieutenant with something like disbelief. "A student? When?"

"Spring of 1929, sir." Tejada stared straight ahead, avoiding Rodríguez's eyes.

The captain's eyes narrowed. "Did you also meet Judge Otero then, Tejada?"

"No, sir."

"I see." Rodríguez spoke slowly, and Tejada had the impression that the captain was attempting to use caution. "Are you aware that His Honor has invited you to a gathering at his home tomorrow evening?"

"Yes, sir," Tejada said quietly. "He extended an invitation to me when I spoke to him last week. I believe it includes all the officers at the post."

"The letter was addressed to me." Captain Rodríguez's mouth twisted slightly. "And the exact wording, Lieutenant, was '*We wish to invite you, Lieutenant Tejada, and your other officers.*' You seem to have made a good impression on the judge."

"Captain?"

Rodríguez drummed his fingers on his desk for a moment. Then he said, "You'll attend the Oteros' party, Lieutenant. You can leave Sunday morning. I'll send a wire to San Sebastián, so they'll expect you."

"Thank you, sir." Tejada relaxed imperceptibly. Rodríguez, the lieutenant thought, was an idiot, but an idiot who respected the Oteros. As long as Tejada enjoyed the Oteros' patronage he would be relatively safe from interference.

Which brought Tejada back to the question of the Oteros' patronage. Was Judge Otero merely being gracious because of an old family connection? Or did the judge have information about Manuel Arroyo that he wished to conceal? Tejada remembered the pause when the judge had spoken of Arroyo's finances: "It's only since the war that he . . ." Tejada was now fairly sure of what Otero had originally intended to say. But if the judge knew that his brother-in-law was withdrawing funds, he might well know a good deal about Arroyo's disappearance as well. Keep an open mind, Tejada reminded himself. Maybe Arroyo really is dead. In that case, if Otero knew that he was withdrawing funds, would that be a motive for murder? To prevent Arroyo from fleeing, and leaving his wife penniless? Would Arroyo have left his wife like that? That might give *her* a motive for murder . . . if she knew about it. But she had money of her own, didn't she? All in all, Tejada looked forward to his next meeting with the Oteros with interest.

That Saturday evening, when the guardias civiles entered the Otero home, however, he realized that any chance of personal conversation would be remote. No one in Salamanca had entertained on a grand scale since the war, but the Otero family had come closer to full-scale balls than anyone else in the city. The party, given by Jorge Otero in honor of his oldest daughter's birthday, was lavish by postwar standards, even allowing for the hasty cancellation of the orchestra in consideration of Manuel Arroyo's presumed demise. There were, in the lieutenant's quick estimate, already over fifty people in the grand salon when the officers of the Guardia Civil made their entrance.

Their party numbered six in total: Captain Rodríguez and his wife, Sergeant Betances, Corporals Méndez and Jiménez, and the lieutenant. (Sergeant Hernández was nursing a toothache. Rodríguez had refused the sergeant's mumbled pleas to be excused, but Tejada had compassionately suggested that it would be better to leave one officer at the post in case of emergencies.) The guardias were by no means the only uniformed men in the room. The party was sprinkled with young men in the uniforms of cadets and of the fascist volunteers, and older ones wearing the ceremonial dress of colonels and brigadier generals.

On the whole, Tejada thought, the guardias showed up well compared with the other military men. True, Captain Rodríguez was a bit overweight, but the same could have been said of almost all the senior officers. And Corporal Jiménez's tendency to clamp his tricorn under his elbow as if he expected it to make a break for freedom at any moment was remedied as soon as they surrendered their hats in the hallway. If Corporal

Jiménez's tricorn was slightly the worse for wear at least the cloakroom gave it decent anonymity. As he handed over his own hat, Tejada caught a glimpse of the outerwear of his fellow guests. War had touched them as well. It was difficult to date the cloaks and gabardines of the men, but the women's furs followed the fashions of the early thirties. The set of tricorns took their places alongside a profusion of top hats, red berets, and (the lieutenant noted with amusement) at least half a dozen silver-handled walking sticks. Judge Otero had apparently started a fashion trend.

The guardias were greeted by Judge Otero, who presented them as a group to his son and granddaughter. Having observed the formalities, they melted into the crowd. The captain and his wife spotted acquaintances and went to speak to them. Sergeant Betances and Corporal Jiménez remained in a knot of people near Señorita Otero. Corporal Méndez was rapidly absorbed by a group of young soldiers who were dissecting the latest match of Madrid's soccer club.

Lieutenant Tejada slowly circled the room, moving inconspicuously from one chatting group to another, occasionally exchanging tentative greetings with people who encountered his cool stare and wondered with embarrassment if they had met the officer somewhere before and were unintentionally snubbing him. Halfway through his circuit of the room he acquired a champagne glass and noted absently that the champagne was excellent. Snatches of conversation swirled around him. "... I told her it was impossible, but you know girls today...." "... believe he scored an own goal! I was nearly sick on the floor!...." "... Thank you, I bought it in Lisbon, last summer...." "... No, we reopened the branch in Barcelona in October, but it's not a good time to expand...."

"... won't last six weeks!" In the shadow of the double doors leading to the dining room, Tejada at last heard a voice he recognized, raised just a hair more loudly than necessary to drown out the other conversations. Eduardo Crespo was standing in a little knot of men, waving patterns in the swirls of cigar smoke to emphasize his point. The lieutenant wordlessly joined the group. Most of them were of Crespo's generation, and all but one wore civilian evening dress. They moved aside amicably to give him room, each assuming that he knew one of the others. "The English don't have a hope," the lawyer continued. "They couldn't pull out fast enough."

There was a murmur of amused agreement, and then a slender, bearded man said with considerable belligerence, "I'm not disagreeing! I'm just saying that it's naive to think we'll get Gibraltar out of it."

"Why not?" A balding man with glasses seemed to take the second speaker's statement as a personal affront. "If they sign an armistice with Germany—" All of the men were now speaking as loudly as Crespo. Tejada wondered if they were slightly drunk or simply all lawyers.

"Why should the Germans do us any favors?" Another man spoke up to defend his bearded colleague.

"Any *more* favors, you mean." The white-haired man whose uniform proclaimed him a colonel gave voice to Tejada's thought.

"At any rate, it's the end of the British Empire." Crespo raised his voice again. "The Germans are invincible." He caught sight of Tejada, and nodded sociably. "Good evening, Lieutenant. Nice to see you again."

After waiting to see if Tejada wished to speak or was going to move away, Crespo began a hasty round of introductions. "I don't believe you know Colonel Alarcón? And this is Señor Romero," (nodding to the balding man), "Doctor Blanco," (with a nod at the bearded man), "and Don Gabriel, Marqués de Torrenegra. This is Lieutenant Tejada."

"A pleasure to meet you, gentlemen," Tejada said, inspecting Crespo's companions with interest. Those who were lawyers, he thought, might well have known Arroyo.

After a brief round of hand shaking and conventional nothings, the colonel smiled paternally at Tejada. "You must find our political debates rather dull."

"Not at all." Tejada was polite.

"But too much like business for a social occasion," Señor Romero suggested with a smile.

Tejada smiled back, and deliberately misunderstood the statement. "Are you in politics?" he asked innocently.

"Me? Oh, no," Romero looked half horrified and half embarrassed. "Nothing so important. I'm just a businessman, I'm afraid."

"Not *just* a businessman." Crespo was jovial. "One of our finest, Lieutenant. And one of my best clients."

Señor Romero's smile might have been false modesty or concealed fear. "No one with any right to express opinions about politics, I'm afraid."

"If lawyers have the right to opinions, I agree with Crespo," the marqués spoke up. "Germany must triumph."

"Hear, hear." The echoes of Doctor Blanco's voice bounced off of the glass doors. "But I don't know if the English—"

"England will surrender in six weeks," Crespo repeated loudly, and Tejada noted that an empty glass was leaving a ring on the handsome sideboard beside the lawyer. "The Germans are invincible. Don't you think so, Lieutenant?"

A strange trick of memory reminded Tejada of his boyhood when a serious young tutor had taught him the meaning of the word *invincible*. Don Leonardo's real passion had been sixteenth-century history and he had done his best to impart his interest to Tejada and his older brother. But he had also been a conscientious and creative teacher, and had encouraged his charges to decipher newspaper headlines as reading exercises. The German troops Tejada had encountered during the war were still fresh in his memory. They had been well trained, well equipped, and well commanded. But the painfully decoded headlines of his childhood had left a deep impression. "*No, Carlito, Portugal hasn't sunk. Lusitania is the name of a ship.*" "I think," he said slowly, "that the Germans are a good ally and a bad enemy. And that it's bad luck to call any invader of England invincible," he added.

Colonel Alarcón laughed. "How cautious! I don't need to ask if you're a betting man, Lieutenant!"

"I prefer sure things," Tejada admitted. "It's why I've never invested in stocks," he added casually.

Señor Romero shook his head. "Another one! This is why it's impossible to raise capital in Spain."

"The Castilian temperament isn't suited to finance," the marqués reminded him, absentmindedly drawing a cigar case from his pocket and opening it. "Would anyone like one?" The invitation was clearly addressed to Tejada and Blanco. The others were already smoking. The lieutenant, who pre-ferred cigarettes, declined politely, but Doctor Blanco leaned forward with alacrity.

"I've always heard that Castilians weren't fiscally minded," Tejada agreed as the lawyer struck a match. "But now and then I find myself proven wrong." He turned to Eduardo Crespo. "Professor Arroyo, for instance. Did you know that he held shares in Banco Bilbao Vizcaya?"

"No, really?" Crespo was politely interested. "He dealt with the Basques? Typical of him, I suppose."

Doctor Blanco blew a reproving smoke ring. "Come, now. *Nil nisi de mortuis bene.* After all, the poor man didn't deserve to be murdered."

"Did you know him?" Tejada asked.

The lieutenant had tried to keep his voice casual, but there was a brief, tight silence after his words. Blanco's voice was a lit-tle too careful as he answered, "Not well."

"We were classmates," Crespo amplified. "I told you no one who ever had Arroyo as a teacher ever forgot him."

"Very true." Don Gabriel raised one hand to signal one of the waiters bearing trays of hors d'oeuvres. As he did so, Tejada noticed that the ring on his smallest finger looked like a match to Doctor Crespo's. For the first time, the lieutenant regretted that he had ignored the multiple fraternal societies that flourished at the university. An experienced fraternity man could probably identify the ring at a glance, he thought ruefully. Or a classics scholar, like Fernández, I suppose.

There was an awkward pause, as the marqués nibbled at a sliver of cheese. Then Doctor Blanco, with a gesture that spilled a few ashes from his cigar, said loudly, "These are excellent, Don Gabriel."

The marqués swallowed. "Havanas." He was succinct.

"Of course."

There was another pause during which Tejada considered whether and how to ask Don Gabriel what he thought of Manuel Arroyo's writings on Cuba. Before he could frame a suitable question, a lady in black silk appeared beside Colonel Alarcón and tapped him on the arm with her fan. "There you are, dear. Señora Díaz has been asking to meet you."

"I wouldn't wish to snub her," the colonel replied. He turned apologetically to the little group. "If you'll excuse me. . . ."

The colonel's departure sent little eddies through the group. Shortly afterwards Señor Romero murmured an excuse and drifted away and the remaining men soon followed his example. Tejada strolled aimlessly, reflecting as he did so that one of the drawbacks of his job was that it was impossible for him to socialize with most of the people who he met in a professional capacity, and that he had precious little time for unrelated social events.

The rest of the evening passed uneventfully, and from Tejada's point of view, unprofitably. He met no one else who had known Manuel Arroyo, or at least no one else who admitted to knowing him. The food was good, and the company polite enough, but the lieutenant was relieved when the guardias finally took their leave and he stepped out into the cool, quiet stillness of Salamanca after midnight. Captain Rodríguez and his wife had left somewhat earlier, sharing a cab with friends. The remaining guardias walked down the Calle San Pablo toward the post, automatically falling into patrol formation as they trod the silent streets.

Tejada drew a long breath and expelled it upwards, clearing his lungs of the heat and smoke of the Oteros' party. He could just make out the stars of Orion's belt rising behind the buildings. Somewhere, several streets over, a horse-drawn carriage clattered along, the clop of the horse's hooves loud in the silence.

"Well," said Sergeant Betances, "that was a very pleasant evening."

Betances's voice was still pitched to carry above the constant hum of conversation at the party, and it grated on the lieutenant's nerves. He said nothing, hoping for silence. His wish was not granted.

"Wonderful!" Jiménez agreed fervently. "I mean, that elegant house, and meeting everybody who's anybody in Salamanca, and Judge Otero being so gracious and everything."

Tejada felt a flicker of interest. "Did you speak much to Judge Otero?" he asked. "I only did when he presented us to his granddaughter."

"Well," Jiménez flushed, but the dim light protected him from discovery, "so did I. But such a gesture of trust, to introduce us to Señorita Otero! I mean bringing up a young lady like that, her family must be very careful about who she meets."

Only everybody who's anybody in Salamanca, Tejada thought. Jiménez might well be slightly drunk, or sleepy, or both; it would have been unfair to mock his befuddlement in such a condition.

Corporal Méndez laughed. "Forget it, son," he advised Jiménez. "Eugenia Otero's not for the likes of us."

"More's the pity," Betances agreed, good-natured but rueful. "She's a real beauty."

"She is, isn't she?" There was a certain rapt note in Jiménez's voice. "Don't you think so, sir?" He had intended to ask for confirmation from Tejada, but the lieutenant was pondering his conversation with Crespo and his associates, and did not immediately reply.

Sergeant Betances filled the silence. "Yeah. A Velázquez," he said, nodding.

Tejada blinked at the name, and remembered that he had not asked Arturo Velázquez anything about Arroyo's holdings in pharmaceutical companies. "Do you think foreign companies pay dividends in pesetas?" he murmured, wondering if the doctor might also hold shares.

"I don't think so," Corporal Méndez said at the same time. "Not if Velázquez is the one with the long necks."

"That's El Greco," Betances informed him loftily.

The sergeant's emphatic correction put a damper on conversation and Tejada, who was tired, allowed his thoughts to skitter randomly, like waterflies on the surface of a pond. The cliché was truer in Eugenia Otero's case than in most, he thought. The judge's granddaughter did have something of the polished, photographic beauty of Velázquez's *meninas*. He wondered idly what painter's work Elena Fernández might be compared to. Not a Murillo: although she did have something of his Madonnas' dark beauty, she lacked their softness. Not Zubarán. *Goya*, Tejada decided with satisfaction. Proud, and secret, and completely composed, no matter what.

"But it's not just that she's pretty." Jiménez broke in on Tejada's reverie, sounding a little defensive. "She's very . . . very gentle, and innocent. Young," he added, from the lofty height of his two decades.

"Unlike you?" Méndez challenged good-naturedly.

"She hasn't seen much of the world." Jiménez was painfully

serious. Flushing half with embarrassment and half with pleasure he added, "She asked me if I'd ever killed anyone. I didn't know what to say."

"I've found saying 'no' usually ends those discussions fairly quickly," Tejada commented dryly. "It's always interesting to see how well they control their disappointment. Or how badly, as the case may be."

Jiménez was shocked. "Disappointment! How can you think that a young lady would *want*—" He broke off suddenly. "Wait a minute, *you* tell them no?"

"They're like cats," Tejada said, ignoring the second half of the corporal's statement. "Beautiful, fluffy, and cruel beyond belief."

Jiménez undoubtedly would have argued the point but a train whistle echoed out of the night, distracting him. Betances glanced toward the sound, which heralded the chug of a locomotive, and then turned to the lieutenant. "You're going north in the morning, then, sir?"

"Yes. Just for a few days. I want to check on some property of Arroyo's," Tejada explained.

There were only a few hours left before dawn when they finally reached the post. The other officers went straight to bed. Tejada was about to undress when he remembered that he had left his notebook in his office and that he wished to take it with him to San Sebastián. He headed toward that room, crossing the post's main waiting area on the way. As he was returning the door opened, and Guardia Gómez entered, looking slightly worried. He relaxed when he saw the lieutenant. "Sir! You're still up!"

"What is it?" Tejada asked, surprised.

"I was assigned to the Fernández surveillance this evening, sir," Gómez explained hastily. "And Fernández and his daughter headed for the train station at around ten o'clock. Fernández put her on the night train north. Then he went home. You said she had permission to travel, so I suppose it was all right, but I thought you might like to know."

"Thank you, Gómez. Good job." Tejada spoke automatically, wondering if the whistle in the night had come from the train carrying Elena to San Sebastián. What is she up to? he thought uneasily. And then, with a flash of annoyance, and hasn't she learned any better than to travel alone?

# Chapter 13

E lena looked out over the sweep of the wrought-iron promenade and sighed. The trip from Salamanca had been
remarkably smooth and uneventful. She had even managed to
get some sleep on the train. There had been cabs at the station
and she had easily found her way to the hotel where her father
had reserved rooms. Paying the cab had been her first worry.
The driver had demanded what seemed an exorbitant amount,
and Elena had remembered her mother saying, many years ago,
*"The prices are outrageous at all these resort places!"* She paid, uncomfortably aware that if all the prices in San Sebastián were equally
inflated she would have no money left for the bribes that
inevitably would be needed.

Her misgivings had not been soothed by the hotel manager.
He had been dubious about a young lady traveling alone, but
when Elena explained her mother's unfortunate accident, and
added that she hoped to be joined soon by family, he relaxed
somewhat and offered to show her to the rooms Señor Fernández
had reserved. Elena, who knew that her father had exclaimed
over their cost, was distressed when the manager showed her to a
suite on the top floor, at the back of the hotel, overlooking the
street instead of the ocean. They were clearly the cheapest rooms
the hotel offered. And if this is cheap, I'll be bankrupt within a
week, the professor's daughter thought grimly.

She declined the manager's suggestion that she go down to

breakfast, fearing the expense, and claimed great weariness from the journey. She unpacked, ignoring her stomach's treacherous pangs, and considered what to do next. Given the cost involved in staying in San Sebastián, the obvious course of action was to contact Meyer as quickly as possible. After some hesitation, she decided a telegram might be worth the money. Unfortunately, it was Sunday. She would be unable to contact Meyer—or anyone else—until tomorrow.

After a brief rest, which did not really make up for the breakfast she had missed, Elena headed downstairs, determined to act normally. She walked out into the town, noting absently that the fashions of the dresses around her seemed to mimic *Blanco y negro* far more closely than her mother had predicted. Long experience with hunger had taught her that unnecessary walking was unwise, but she had the feeling that spending the entire day in her hotel room would be conspicuous. She was unwilling to part with more of her dwindling funds for the sake of a movie theater's anonymity, and so, with a slight sense of distaste, she entered the cathedral and played at devotion. The markets were closed so she was forced to spend more money than she would have wished at a restaurant that afternoon.

She rose early Monday morning, glad to have something definite to do, and asked for directions to the telegraph office. "I would like to wire my parents, to tell them that I made the trip safely," she explained. She sent two telegrams, despite the expense. One went to Salamanca, to make good her excuse to the manager. "ARRIVED. STOP. AM WELL." The other went to the Poste Centrale in Biarritz care of Jean Samuels with the carefully chosen words: "IN SAN SEBASTIAN. STOP. HOTEL MARIA CRISTINA. STOP. WOULD LOVE TO SEE YOU." Then, made reckless by the expenditure, she had sacrificed even more money for a croissant and coffee at a nearby bakery.

The food had warmed her, but now, standing on the promenade overlooking San Sebastián's main beach, she was not feeling hopeful. Professor Meyer would need one vital thing to cross the border: money. And she was not able to provide that. Even if he did manage to slip through the mountains and make his way to San Sebastián, providing an explanation for his presence would be difficult. Guillermo had scoffed at the idea of Meyer needing a "chaperon." The hotel manager's polite incredulity had reminded Elena that her own unchaperoned state was likely to occasion more comment than an elderly foreigner's. In Madrid it didn't matter, Elena thought resentfully, leaning against the wedding-cake swirls of the white-painted iron promenade and staring out to sea so that she would not need to make eye contact with any of the passersby. No one thought it was strange that I lived alone there. She knew it was not the place that mattered so much as the time. In the here and now, a young woman unaccompanied by her husband or parents was an oddity.

As if in response to her thoughts, a young man raised his hat as he passed her. "Good morning, Señorita."

"Good morning." Elena turned to face the young man unwillingly. He was her own age, or perhaps a few years younger, and looked like one of the pictures in a fashion magazine: tanned, handsome, impeccably dressed in tennis whites, with a racquet tucked under one arm.

"Smile," he suggested, suiting his action to his word. "It's a beautiful day." Elena obligingly moved her lips, but said nothing. "That's better." He lounged against the railing beside her. "I don't think I've seen you here before. Is this your first time in San Sebastián?"

"Yes." Elena hoped that the monosyllable would discourage him.

"It's a beautiful place." The young man spoke with obvious enthusiasm. "We came here every summer until the war."

Elena nodded coldly, but he seemed impervious to snubs. He was bubbling with good humor, and ready to share it. "We have a house on Monte Igueldo," he explained. "Or we did. The Reds vandalized it, of course. Pigs! They'd destroy anything beautiful. But we've spent the last two weeks cleaning it up and now it's starting to get back into shape."

"How nice," Elena said acidly, since it was no longer possible to say nothing.

"You can say that again. It's great just being back here. And really, little has changed."

"That must be a comfort to you." The wind from the sea whipped Elena's dress around her legs, emphasizing her still-ness. Not changed! she thought, too stunned to be disgusted. He can't have fought. No soldier could say that, even one of *Them*. A guardia wouldn't say that. Tejada wouldn't say that.

"Yes. For instance, there's a little café up the street that's been there forever. Not many tourists know it but they serve the best pastries in the province. Would you like to come and have a cup of coffee?"

"No, thank you." Elena's voice was courteous, but final. "I'm waiting for someone."

"Don't say your husband!" he exclaimed with comical distress. "No, you don't have a ring. Tell me that you're waiting for a female friend."

Elena bowed her head without speaking, annoyed at the idea of having to invent a male protector, but unwilling to offer any encouragement. Her unknown suitor took the dismissal with good grace. "Some other time then." He bowed to her, waving the tennis racquet with a flourish. "Welcome to San Sebastián, *bonita*. Enjoy your stay."

Elena watched him out of sight with relief, and then she set off for the hotel. Drab and cheerless as her room was, it was at least private. She spent the better part of the day there, evolving hopeless and fantastic schemes for sneaking across the border and spiriting Dr. Meyer away, while doing her best to ignore her increasing hunger. The thought of food reminded her that the waiters at lunch yesterday had been politely amazed by her solitude, and that dining alone again was likely to attract unwanted attention. Hating herself for the subterfuge, she unpacked her bag and opened the small jewelry box she had almost decided against bringing. Elena seldom wore jewelry, and only at her mother's insistence did she bring along a formal dress and some things to wear with it. The little jewelry box was nearly empty. It contained an extra pair of earrings, a chain with a small gold cross hanging from it ("In case you go to Mass," María had suggested), and a small pewter ring set with rhinestones. "Take it for good luck," Elena's mother had said, smiling slightly from her sickbed, as Elena reviewed her packing arrangements with her. "You always wanted to wear it as a child."

This was true. The ring had been Elena's favorite piece among all of her mother's jewelry. She loved the way the glittering stones caught the light and still remembered her shocked disappointment when she learned that they were not really diamonds. The ring was of no great value and María had frequently allowed her daughter to use it to play dress up. Elena picked up the ring and slid it onto the fourth finger of her right hand with the bitter sense that she was committing sacrilege. The ring had belonged to her childhood fantasies, to the world before the war, when anything had been possible. Using it now was a desecration. But the glitter of false diamonds might at least keep unwelcome cavaliers at bay.

Armed against further attentions, she set off into the town again, in search of an only slightly overpriced place in which to eat lunch. She ate peacefully and without interruption, either due to the costume jewelry, or to her grave expression. Afterward she returned to the hotel, relieved but also somewhat woebegone. It was difficult having no one to talk to. Elena had lived alone in Madrid, but she had acquaintances and colleagues there, and the war years had fostered a fatalistic camaraderie that made friends even of strangers. She felt very solitary surrounded by the crowds of brightly dressed tourists, calling and laughing to each other.

The siesta passed quietly and Elena was just debating whether her pose as a light-hearted vacationer required her to go and sit in the hotel lounge in the evening when there was a knock at her door. She felt her stomach clench and wondered automatically if there was anything incriminating in the room. I've done nothing wrong, she reminded herself. I have permission to travel. I haven't broken any laws. And even that telegram. . . . She pulled the door open, and gave a silent gasp of relief to see one of the hotel porters standing in front of the door. "There's a telegram for you, Señorita," he said politely.

Elena took the message eagerly, and tipped the porter reluctantly, when she realized that he would wait for a reply until he received some money. It was an international wire. The knot in her stomach was from excitement as well as fear now. He's responded fast, she thought. Oh, good. If we can just get this over with. . . . As she looked at the message, her heart sank. Professor Meyer had written in French: "SEE TELEMACHUS BOOK XVI. STOP. EUMAIOS AT PENSION D'OR. STOP. DON'T WRITE. STOP. HURRY." The bald command—or was it a plea?—shocked her a little. Why is it so urgent? she thought. What's *happening* in France that he's so frightened? And why shouldn't I write? Although Elena knew the *Odyssey* well, she was uncertain what happened in Book XVI, and she had not thought to bring along a copy. Exhaustion forgotten, she hurried out in search of a bookstore, realizing as she did so that many stores would be closing, and also that Meyer would undoubtedly have a Greek edition in mind, and that another translation might well break up the text slightly differently.

The streets were crowded in the evening. The sandy sports clothes of the morning had given way to a general air of cool, freshly bathed elegance. Families strolled together, blocking the sidewalks, and beggars and hawkers of souvenirs took up strategic positions in doorways and on corners. Elena, who had idled away the morning hours that should have been devoted to physical activity, found herself once more out of step with the crowd. She forced herself to stroll although she dearly wanted to hurry. The seemingly unbroken line of cafés and souvenir and clothing stores irritated her. Surely there must be a bookstore somewhere in San Sebastián.

Elena crossed the river and wandered inland, away from the more fashionable parts of town. She finally found a bookstore in the sedate little Plaza de Cataluña across the street from a red stone church. There was a grille across the display window, but a sign proclaimed that it was open from 10 A.M. to 2 P.M. and from 5 P.M. to 8 P.M., Monday through Friday, and on Saturday mornings. There was a light on inside the store, and she could just make out a figure moving among the shelves, but when she tried the door it was locked. Just as she was resolving to return the following morning, the figure made its way toward the front and there was the sound of bolts rattling. Then the door opened and a white-mustached man said, "Can I help you, Señora?"

"Errr . . . no, thank you. That is, I only wondered if the store was open." Elena floundered, unhappily realizing that she had made herself conspicuous.

The old man consulted a pocket watch. "Come in." He pulled the door open wider. "I was closing up early. But since you're here . . ."

"I don't want to trouble you."

"It's no trouble." The man bowed her toward the towering stacks. "It's not quite eight yet, after all. Were you looking for something specific, Señora?"

Elena swallowed, realizing that to ask for a specific book would oblige her to buy it, and worried whether she had enough money. "I'm looking for a copy of the *Odyssey*."

The bookseller laughed. "That's some light beach reading!" He headed for the back of the shop and clambered up a ladder that was leaning against the shelves. "Here, I have two editions actually."

Elena looked at the books that he was holding out. She would have liked to inspect Book XVI in both of them at leisure, but she did not feel equal to reading them under the gaze of the store owner. She quietly asked the prices of the books and then bought the cheaper edition. It was, in fact, no more expensive than her breakfast had been, although the slick paper had all the durability of newsprint, and she was not surprised to find, when she returned to her hotel room, that the spine cracked as soon as she opened the volume to Book XVI.

She skimmed the beginning, and was relieved to see that Telemachus appeared almost immediately. The passage the professor had referred to dealt with Telemachus's visit to Eumaios. Elena chewed the inside of her lip thoughtfully, considering the poem. "*Telemachus put on his fair sandals . . . and went with measured pace towards the stockade. . . .*" She inspected Meyer's telegram again: "Eumaios at Pension d'Or. Don't write. Hurry." With some dismay, Elena realized that Meyer was demanding—or begging—that she cross the border. Two border crossings, she thought, one there and one to accompany him into Spain. Damn. I wish someone was here to help . . . Or to talk me out of this.

She went to bed early, uncertain what else to do, and hopeful that sleeping on the problem might provide a solution. But falling asleep presented some difficulty. It occurred to Elena, as she tossed uncomfortably in the unfamiliar hotel bed, that Lieutenant Tejada's permission for her to travel, given with the kindest of intentions, had placed her in an incredibly dangerous position. Not his fault, she reminded herself. And then, with a certain grim humor, she thought, he certainly would have stopped me if he'd known this was going to happen. Then she resolutely returned to the business of trying to fall asleep.

Nervousness woke her at dawn the following morning. She was up and dressed by seven, uncomfortably aware that the night had presented no answer to her problems and that it was several hours before she would even be able to leave her room without causing comment. She would have liked to write to her parents, or simply to write down her thoughts to organize them, but she was aware that putting too much into writing was dangerous. After pacing her room for twenty minutes, Elena cast caution into the wind, slipped her ring onto her finger, and headed downstairs.

The hotel lobby was empty except for a few maids and the night clerk. All of them were too well trained to show any surprise at the eccentricity of a guest who was awake so early in the morning. The clerk contented himself with saying, "Good morning, Señora. Do you need a cab?"

"No, thank you." Elena deposited her keys at the front desk as she spoke. "I'm just going out for a walk."

She turned away from the elegance of the casino and the promenade instinctively, and headed for the river. Cool wind struck her as she crossed the bridge, raising goosebumps on her bare arms. She shivered slightly, and suddenly remembered the freezing mornings in Madrid, when she had risen at first light to get to school early to prepare for the children's arrival. She had hated actually rising so early. But she had enjoyed the good-natured greetings and sleepy complaints she had shared with the icemen and milkmen and others whose profession required an early start. *Madrid* . . . for a moment Elena felt a lump in her throat. She turned away from the sleepy streets of San Sebastián, pale mockeries of the capital that she had loved, and found a stairway down to the beach.

The long strip of sand on this side of the river belonged to the townsfolk. Unlike the horseshoe crescent of the Playa de la Concha, which was almost completely blocked by the isle of Santa Clara, where the water was nearly as flat as a lake, this part of the coast was unprotected by breakwaters and the beach was steadily pounded by long, rolling waves. The surf left arches of foamy bubbles on the sand, evidence of the contamination the river carried down from the paper factories to the south. The martial rows of furled umbrellas and neatly folded deck chairs that lined La Concha were absent here. A few soggy and sand-logged beach towels were the only evidence that anyone used the beach for swimming.

In her unsuitable footwear, Elena tottered along the sand near the seawall, far from the water, pondering whether to take off her shoes, and suffer from sandy feet for the rest of the day, or risk ruining her shoes. The wind wrinkled the sea, giving it the texture of crushed silk. Clouds scudded rapidly across the sky—huge, ragged parodies of the gulls. A few pieces of garbage blew across the sand, which were idly chased by gray gulls. Cinderella, the morning after the ball, Elena thought, watching the stray wrappers, still soaked with the oil stains of hot french fries, or sticky with the syrup of lemon ices. All the ball gowns turned to rags, like Odysseus's rags when he returned to Ithaca. . . . Odysseus goes to Eumaios when he returns, to avoid the suit-ors and meets up with Telemachus there. . . . I'm supposed to be Telemachus . . . but how I am supposed to get to Biarritz? And if I do get there how will I find the Pension d'Or?"

As Elena made her way toward the rocks at the far end of the beach, the smell of salt air was gradually overwhelmed by a fishy odor. A huge collection of gulls congregated just ahead of her. A pair of fishing boats pulled well up from the water explained both phenomena. Four men were sorting their catch into buck-ets, occasionally tossing away a minnow, which was instantly fought over by the crowd of gulls.

Elena's immediate impulse was to withdraw and leave the fish-ermen to their work. But as she hesitated one of them glanced up and saw her, and turning away from him seemed discourteous. She continued toward them, nodding as she did so to the one who had made eye contact with her. "Good morning."

"Good morning, Señorita." It was the oldest of the men who spoke to her. "You're up early." His accent was unfamiliar to Elena and she guessed him to be a Basque.

Elena smiled. "It looks like a cloudy day."

The old man squinted at the sky, deepening the crow's-feet around his eyes. "Don't worry, Señorita. It won't rain. You'll have nice weather for your holiday."

His voice was kindly but Elena winced. It was not right for him to be so deferential. *What about* your *work day?* she wanted to ask. *Isn't that important?* Instead, she found herself saying awkwardly, "Thank you. This is my first time in the Basque country. It's very beautiful here."

"Yes, Señorita." One of the other men spoke. His voice was polite; the voice one would use for a pretty, spoiled child. "You should see Irún, where I'm from."

Elena smiled, and then, perhaps because she was tired, or because her memories of Madrid had made her nostalgic, or simply through carelessness, she said absently, "I remember the broadcasts about the defense of Irún."

There was a sudden fraught silence and Elena tensed as she realized what she had said. All of the men had looked up to stare at her, and she got the impression for the first time that they were looking at *her*, instead of at yet another tourist. Then one of them said in a carefully casual tone, "You're from Madrid, Señorita?"

"No . . . I . . ." Elena tried to meet the blank stares. They were wary, but not hostile. "I lived there until the end of the war though."

"Until Madrid was 'liberated,' you mean." It was the old man again, his eyes twinkling with amusement under raised brows.

"Yes." Elena smiled back, relaxed, and wondered why the men trusted her. It did not occur to her that most tourists would not have stayed to talk to them, much less that her own face was as communicative as the fishermen's raised eyebrows. "I suppose I must mean that."

One of the men grunted, a sound somehow conveying amusement. Another turned, and made a remark to his companions in a language completely unfamiliar to Elena. Another replied, laughing, and Elena realized that they were speaking Basque. The man who had first spoken to Elena turned back to her. "You enjoy your stay here, dear," he said.

When he had first spoken Elena had suspected that his courtesy was false. Listening now, she realized that her suspicion had been the merest shadow of the truth. "Thanks," she said, knowing that the word couldn't convey her gratitude for the men's unexpected warmth. "Thanks a lot."

The fishermen nodded and returned their attention to their nets. Elena, looking at the boats, and then out to sea, had a sudden idea. She did not think that they would betray her, but to trust them further was dangerous. Exchanging pleasantries was one thing but to ask them to risk prison. . . . What choice do I have? she thought wryly, and then said quickly, before fear closed her throat, "Do you go out fishing every morning?"

"Just about." One of the younger men looked back at her.

"You couldn't . . . take a passenger, could you?" Elena had the miserable feeling that she was not handling the conversation with any grace, but at least she had managed to frame the question.

"Fishing's a boring sport for a young lady." The man did not answer directly.

"I'd like to see more of the coast." Elena's voice was quiet.

Once again, there was a conversation between the fishermen that Elena could not understand. She held her breath. Finally, the oldest of them turned back to her. "Whereabouts along the coast would you like to see most?" he asked.

The time for seemingly innocent conversation was past. "Biarritz," Elena said flatly.

The intricacies of the Basque language fluttered around her like the cries of the gulls. "We can take you," the old man said finally. "But it's putting our boat at risk. And our lives."

"I can't pay very much," she said, opening negotiations.

"Two hundred pesetas."

Elena hesitated, heartily regretting the cheap edition of the *Odyssey* and the overpriced breakfast that she had been weak enough to buy. Still, she had budgetted for a ten-day stay in the hotel and had thus far only passed two nights. Very carefully, she said. "I need to return also—"

"No," he interrupted her bluntly. "We can drop you off, but we can't hang around in French waters waiting for a rendezvous. It's too dangerous."

"Not even for two hundred pesetas?"

"'Not even for four hundred." One of the old man's companions made a quick comment in Basque. Another seemed to concur. The old man turned back to Elena. "Jorge says he has a cousin on the French side. We'll give you his name, and tell you where to find him if you like, and he can take you back."

"For the same fee?" Elena inquired softly.

The fisherman laughed. "Two hundred pesetas will take you safely to Biarritz and get you the name and contacts you need there, sweetheart. You work out the price of your return trip once you get there."

"When can we go?" Elena asked, rapidly calculating whether three nights of saved hotel fees would leave her with sufficient funds to get back from France.

"Tonight, if you like. Daytime's too dangerous."

Elena nodded. "All right. Tonight then." She held out her hand. "For two hundred pesetas."

There was a glimmer of amusement in the fisherman's eyes but he took Elena's hand gravely and shook it. "Meet us here at midnight," he said.

"Here?" Elena asked, with some surprise.

"It's as good a place as any, and we don't have to give you directions," he explained.

"All right. And thanks." Elena hurried away, almost afraid to believe that she had achieved her goal.

She spent much of the day sleeping, trying to make up for

the previous night's lack of rest, and for the probable disruption of her sleep the following evening. Shortly before dinnertime she left the hotel, hoping that her departure would not be remarked upon amid the flow of guests leaving to search for restaurants. Once more she wandered through town and then headed down to the beach, this time posing more carefully as a stroller, enjoying the cool of the evening, with her face turned as much as possible toward the fading sunset.

The beach was empty when she returned to the spot where she had earlier encountered the fishermen. She sat on the sand, arms wrapped around her knees, and stared at the darkening water for as long as she could see it, hoping that if anyone noticed her they would think she was merely lost in contemplation. There was no sound except for the endless thud and swish of waves against the shore. She could make out few stars. Low, fast-moving clouds skated across the moon, blocking and then uncovering the pale light. She wondered, a little nervously, if it was going to rain. How long do I stay here? she thought, anxiously. What if it's past midnight? What if they don't come? Or if they alert the Guardia? I haven't done anything wrong yet. . . . but if they arrest me for plotting to cross the border. . . . I wish Tejada was here instead of in Salamanca. She shuddered slightly, knowing that whatever feeling of benevolence the lieutenant might have toward her would not survive if she were arrested.

Waiting alone in the dark was maddening. They may have decided not to come. Or else they've been caught by the Guardia. Or maybe I'm in the wrong place. Or they've forgotten. Finally, after what seemed like decades, but was in fact less than half an hour, a dark shape appeared on the water, and the crunch of a keel on sand distinguished itself from the slap of the waves. Elena pushed herself to her feet and hurried down to the water's edge. The moon was behind a cloud again, and she could make out no more than dark shapes, and an overwhelming smell of fish. "All safe and sound, Señorita?" She recognized the voice of one of the men she had spoken to earlier.

"Yes."

"Come on, then." A hand cupped her elbow and she felt the waves soak her shoes and skirt as she clambered into the boat. Another dark shape filled the back of the boat.

"Sit on the nets," one of the men ordered her. "It's safer, and you won't throw off our balance. Come on, Jorge."

The man who had helped her shoved the boat out into the water as the one sitting above her seemed to lever with the oars and the little craft took float. Jorge took a running leap, and landed on the other bench, splashing her slightly.

The oarsman rapidly rowed out past the breaking waves and then, when they were merely drifting on swells, slowed his pace. Elena, who had obediently crouched on the fishing nets, risked sitting up, and hoped that her far from full stomach was not about to betray her. "Payment?" It was Jorge again. "Two hundred pesetas."

Elena nodded, and reached for her pocketbook. She handed over the money in silence.

A lantern flared briefly as Jorge took the bills and carefully counted them. Then he put out the lamp once more. "No sense attracting attention," he explained. "We have a right to have a lantern in Spanish waters, but there's no need to advertise that we're here either."

Elena nodded. "How long will it take?" she asked, trying to distract herself from an increasingly nauseous feeling.

"A few hours. We'll get you there and be away before dawn."

"Good." Elena forced herself to reply although she found herself wondering how she would be able to stand the bobbing of the boat for a few hours. She slumped, leaning her forehead against the edge of the gunwale, swallowing rapidly.

It was a smooth trip, although it did not seem so to Elena.

She did not vomit, although she would have liked to, in order to relieve her agonizing seasickness. She felt as if days, if not weeks, had passed by the time the crash of breakers made the little boat pitch even more wildly, announcing the end of their journey. She stumbled out of the boat, into knee-deep water, and very nearly lost one of her shoes in the darkness.

"Look," said Jorge, as he guided her up onto the shore. "There's a bar on the Rue Gambetta called the Magdalene. You go there, and tell the owner you're looking for Jorge's cousin Daniel. And tell Daniel that I said Conchita's gone to the dogs. He'll help you, if he can."

"Thanks." The feel of solid beach under her feet had done wonders, and she spoke with real gratitude.

"We've put you down a little distance from the town. If you walk that way," the fisherman gestured with his right arm, "you should start seeing houses within a couple of miles. There's a road inland that runs parallel to the coast, too. You've got about two hours before dawn." Jorge held out his hand. "Good luck."

"Thanks. And you." They shook hands.

Then the boat ground over the pebbles and pulled out to sea again, and Elena found herself alone on French soil.

# Chapter 14

The summer home of Manuel Arroyo Díaz and his wife was set high on Monte Igueldo, on a rocky outcropping overlooking the sea. A broad porch at the back of the house led into what had once been a elaborate flower garden. Straight ahead there was only the endless blue of the Bay of Biscay. To the right lay the golden horseshoe of the Playa de la Concha and the green bulk of the Isle of Santa Clara, so far below the garden that the lighthouse on Santa Clara looked like a white sheep on a green field. The patio and garden faced northeast, and received breezes from the sea, making them pleasantly cool, even in the full heat of a July noon. Tejada paused a moment on the threshold of the patio to admire the view and render a silent homage to his former professor's good taste in real estate. It was a beautiful spot.

Glass crunched underfoot as he stepped onto the balcony. The garden had grown wild in the last four years, the more delicate plants dying and the hardier weeds spreading their tendrils onto the porch, climbing the foundation and sinking their roots into the stone, as if determined to finish the destruction that the Reds had begun. The lieutenant took a deep breath, and tasted the salt air with relief. An acrid smell of smoke still clung to the inside of the house.

Captain Alfanador, who headed the Guardia in San Sebastián, had readily supplied Tejada with the address of the Arroyo

property, and offered an escort to assist the lieutenant in entering, if necessary. As it had turned out, the two guardias who
accompanied the lieutenant were superfluous. Every pane of
glass in the window had been smashed, and the door, half ripped
off its hinges, had creaked open without the pressure of rifle
butts. The three men had found themselves inside an empty hallway, thick with dust, and rancid with the stench of old fire.
"Search the bedrooms," Tejada had ordered. "You're looking for
any signs of recent habitation. And for any papers or documents,"
he had added, although the hope seemed a faint one in view of
the ashes that mingled with the dust in the ruined hallway.

The guardias had obediently tramped up the stairs and
fanned out. Tejada had made his way through what he guessed
to have been the parlor and dining room, and found a long,
narrow chamber with one wall looking out over the sea, filled
with overturned bookcases and the remains of a rolltop desk.
With distaste he picked over the remnants of what seemed likely
to have been Arroyo's study. Charred lumps of twisted leather,
which might have once been the covers of legal tomes, were all
that he found. The mob—or subsequent thieves—had taken
everything of value. He searched with increasing haste and
impatience, more and more convinced that Arroyo's house had
stood empty since its destruction at the beginning of the war. It
was too difficult to imagine anyone breathing the air of this
sooty ruin for long.

The clean smell of the ocean and the rhythmic thump of
breakers was a relief to the lieutenant. He moved out across the
patio, eyes fixed firmly on the distant view, trying to ignore the
broken glass and weeds underfoot. This was what Arroyo
believed in, he thought with an admixture of pity and anger that
was infinitely worse than disgust. The Republic! The People!
The people, who had destroyed his home because they were too
stupid to realize that he was one of them. God, if the poor bastard was here to see this it'd almost be punishment enough.

Tejada stepped into the garden and accidentally kicked something half-hidden in the tall grass. As it rolled away, he saw that it was an old soccer ball, half-flat and stained with time. He wondered idly if Arroyo had played ball as well as been a sailor. It was a shame, in a way, that the professor and his wife had not had children. This garden would have been a paradise for them. If Elena saw this, the lieutenant thought, she'd understand why the war was necessary. Why the Movement is necessary. But she hasn't, thank God, because it doesn't look as if Arroyo has been here recently, and she has nothing to do with him anyway, except for being in San Sebastián now. Purely a coincidence.

He had received almost immediate confirmation of Elena's arrival in San Sebastián without even asking. Captain Alfanador, with an efficiency that Tejada envied, had pointed him to the records of summer arrivals in San Sebastián, neatly catalogued by province of origin. About fifteen Salmantinos had checked into hotels in San Sebastián in the last month. The most recent arrival was listed as "Fernández Ríos, Elena. HOTEL MARIA CRISTINA." Tejada had noted the name with inexplicable anxiety and had similarly noted the absence of Arroyo's. "Of course, that's just the hotels," Alfanador had said, a little apologetically. "It's harder to keep tabs on people if they're visiting friends or if they own property here. But if you want, take a look at Arroyo's house."

Now Arroyo's house appeared to be a dead end also. Tejada wondered if it would be worthwhile to try to find out if Arroyo had friends in San Sebastián, when he heard footsteps behind him and turned. "There's no sign of life upstairs, Lieutenant. But Espinal found this." One of the guardias held out a scarred metal strongbox with a rusty lock.

Tejada took the box and tested its weight. It was light, so light that it might well have been empty. But why bother to lock an empty box? "Where was it?" he asked.

"Back of the closet, sir. Top shelf."

The lieutenant gave the box a thoughtful shake. Something

rattled within. "Let's go," he ordered, tucking the box under one arm.

Tejada left the ruined house with a strong sense of relief. As he and his escort headed down the mountain toward the post, there was a shout above their heads. "Guardia!"

The lieutenant looked upward, shading his eyes with one hand. He located a man standing on the ornamental front balcony of a neighboring house, leaning down toward him with one hand raised to wave. He felt a flicker of interest. "Can we help you, Señor?"

"I wondered about the house you just left." The man's voice was a little hesitant. "Do you know if it will stay vacant long?"

"Very likely," Tejada said.

"I see," the man frowned. "Will it be up for sale, do you think?"

"I really couldn't say," Tejada replied, with perfect honesty.

The man on the balcony seemed annoyed. "It's been vacant for some time, and it's becoming a nuisance," he explained. "My caretaker has been complaining about rats. We share a wall, and if the building's structurally unsound we could be affected. Besides, it's unsightly. Everyone else has been at least making some attempt to refurbish their houses." He waved an expansive arm at the row of summerhouses along the street. Most of them did show evidence of recent repair; fresh whitewash, or newly fitted windowpanes to replace shattered ones.

As far as Tejada was concerned, one of the advantages of his job was that it spared him the headaches of home ownership. But faced with an irate property holder, he did his best to be soothing. "Would you wish to be informed if the property is put on the market, Señor?" he asked, recklessly committing his colleagues in San Sebastián to acting as brokers.

"No, that isn't necessary." The man was still peeved. "I'll write to Arroyo myself. But I must say it's damn inconsiderate of him to not tell us a thing."

"You're acquainted with Arroyo?" Tejada asked with interest,

taking a few steps closer to the house, and wishing that he did
not have to interrogate this unexpected witness while craning
his neck upward like an idiot.

"Not well. I was. A little." The professor's neighbor knew
when to backpedal. "Everyone in this neighborhood has been
coming here for years. We all knew each other slightly. But of
course we lost touch when the war broke out." He recollected
himself. "I do hope nothing's happened to Arroyo or his wife,
Guardia? I understood they were in Salamanca, so I assumed
they'd be safe."

"Yes, they survived the war," said Tejada truthfully. After a
moment's thought he added, "But some questions have arisen
with regard to their house here, and also a boat. I wonder if I
could ask you a few questions about that, Señor . . . ?"

"Ruíz. Ruíz Vanegas. Of course, Guardia. When is convenient?"

"Now," Tejada suggested promptly.

Señor Ruíz assented courteously and withdrew from the balcony, calling to someone inside to open the door for the guardia.
Tejada turned to one of his subordinates. "Take this," he ordered,
holding out the metal box. "Get someone to pry the lock off, and
have it ready for me when I get back. This shouldn't take long."

"Yes, sir." The pair of guardias saluted and headed down the
street, and Tejada walked up the steps to the door of Señor
Ruíz's house.

Ruíz Vanegas, Tejada found, was courteous, helpful, and
(except when the conversation strayed to the problems of own-
ing summer real estate) to the point. He was a banker and a
native of Madrid who had passed the war in exile in Lisbon. He
had purchased the house in San Sebastián in the spring of 1926
(here the lieutenant was treated to a lengthy analysis of the condition of housing prices relative to the stock market in '26 and
the reasons why the investment had been a good one). The
Arroyos had already owned the property next door. They had,
until the war, been good neighbors. (Ruíz paused to animadvert

about various other supposedly solid citizens who managed their houses with criminal recklessness or violated all-known noise statutes and boundaries of good taste. Tejada felt obliged to agree that leaving sharp roofing tiles where children could run across them was probably slightly worse than anarchism.) Ruíz had known that Arroyo was some sort of lawyer but they had never discussed business. There was no point in dragging your work with you on vacation. Yes, he remembered Arroyo's yacht quite well. A nice little craft, and Arroyo had been a good sailor. It was probably still rotting in storage at the yacht club if the Reds hadn't destroyed it. Yes, of course he could give the lieutenant the yacht club's address. "A real shame," Ruíz repeated meditatively, as he showed Tejada out. "I remember Arroyo was planning to race that yacht in '36. He and his wife were delayed for a few weeks that summer—some social function, I think—and then after the uprising they decided not to come."

Tejada reflected that by the end of 1936 Arroyo had been in imminent danger of arrest, but he kept his thoughts to himself. "Did the boat require a crew?" he asked mildly.

"If you were sailing her, of course." Ruíz seemed startled by the question. "But she had a little outboard motor as well, and I've known Arroyo to take her out alone."

Damn. Arroyo could have reached France in a couple of hours, if he had the gasoline, thought Tejada. "Thank you very much for your time, Señor Ruíz," he said. "I will try to make sure that Arroyo's property is properly cared for."

As he had expected, the last comment assured him of the banker's effusive good will, and they parted on a friendly note. When he reached the post, he found Guardia Espinal waiting for him. "We got that strongbox from Arroyo's open, sir," Espinal reported. "But there's nothing much in it."

Tejada raised his eyebrows. "Nothing much?"

"Well, nothing at all, except an old address book. A miracle it wasn't burned really, but the metal must have protected it."

"Any addresses?" Tejada asked, restraining his eagerness.

"I haven't looked, Lieutenant. I thought you might like to inspect it personally." The guardia opened a drawer, and drew out the battered metal box. The cover was sitting loosely on top now, and as Tejada lifted it he saw a fat address book, the leather cracked and gray with age, lying against the rusted metal. He picked it up and opened it eagerly. The edges of the paper flaked away in his hand, and he hastily shifted his grip to protect the fragile pages.

The book was only about half-filled, but Tejada quickly saw that inspecting it would take some time. Most of the names and addresses were organized alphabetically, without any indication of whether they were friends, family, or professional acquaintances. Tejada recognized Eduardo Crespo's name and address, neatly listed under C, along with someone named Alejandro Colón, also in Salamanca. Eleuterio Blanes, identified as Arroyo's banker, was also listed in the book. There were a long list of Díazes, whom Tejada guessed to be the professor's maternal connections, and several other names that were unfamiliar to him. Otero Martínez was listed both at his home and work addresses. Most of the addresses were in Salamanca. A few, including Ruíz Vanegas's, were San Sebastián addresses, all in the immediate vicinity of Arroyo's house. Sometimes a phone number was jotted down beneath the address and sometimes not. Tejada painstakingly read each entry, looking for a pattern without much hope.

His persistence finally paid off when he got to the letter V. Arturo Velázquez was listed, as was someone named Enrique Villamán, also in Salamanca. And then, in the same precise script: "*Vogel, Adolf. 42 Gelt Strasse. Zurich. 09928394038, 27364939921.*" Tejada carefully copied the entry, doing his best to control his excitement. It's not Geneva, he reminded himself. Arroyo had connections in Geneva, not Zurich. But it's close.

He flipped hastily through the remaining pages of the

address book in such a hurry that he almost missed what he was looking for: "*Yves, Alain. 18 Avenue de l'Impératrice. Biarritz.*" He copied the French address out next to the Swiss one, and for a moment everything looked crystal clear: Arroyo had staged his own death, and had disappeared to the north, taking his yacht to the relative safety of Biarritz, staying there with a friend until he could make the trip to Switzerland—either Geneva to visit old colleagues, or Zurich, where the mysterious Vogel lived.

Then the lieutenant sighed. It was a pretty theory, but it didn't completely make sense. He looked again at the entries he had copied, wishing that Sergeant Hernández, or someone else whose judgment he trusted, was around to discuss the odd clue. He quickly discounted the idea that Arroyo had used the address book recently to contact Yves or Vogel or anyone else. He was sure that the lawyer had not been near the house in San Sebastián since 1936. If Arroyo *had* contacted someone in France or Switzerland, he had used a different source for the address. Which is odd, Tejada thought. The point of an address book is to be easily at hand to refer to it. Arroyo might have accidentally left the book behind the last time he was here. But why would he put it in a locked box, and store it at the back of his closet, as if it were something vitally important? Carefully, Tejada inspected the book again. It seemed quite ordinary. The addresses and telephone numbers in it seemed ordinary as well. He could positively identify some of them as friends or family of Arroyo's, and verify both the addresses and phone numbers from personal experience. It was hardly the sort of thing a man would feel the need to hide.

The only anomalies were the Swiss and French entries. But why would he hide that in '35, Tejada wondered. He couldn't have foreseen the business with Unamuno, and the war, and everything. Why would he care? The string of numbers below the Swiss address caught his attention. Idly, he counted the digits, and tried to see patterns in them. None appeared. But presumably they were not merely random. Tejada was no cryptographer, and he felt reasonably sure that if the numbers were a code they were a code that would defeat him. But there was no reason to suppose that Arroyo was a cryptographer either. He looked through the rest of the address book again, confirming what he already knew: the Swiss entry was the only one with a long list of digits below it. They were too long for phone numbers. Perhaps, Tejada speculated, they were the number of some kind of identity card. The Swiss did everything by numbers, didn't they? Even bank accounts. . . . Another piece of the puzzle clicked. Bank accounts! Tejada thought. That's where his money went. And I'll bet that's what Otero meant when he said, "It's only since the war that he started—" Arroyo wasn't withdrawing money from his accounts in Spain to accumulate cash. He was illegally transferring it abroad. And that's why he hid the address book. It had his account numbers in it. My God! Two hundred thousand pesetas moved into Switzerland in the last year alone. And who knows how much before the war! And Otero knew about it! But did he know Arroyo was planning to flee?

The lieutenant closed the address book with a snap, and rose quickly. He paused to ask Guardia Espinal for directions, and then headed for the San Sebastián yacht club almost at a run. It was imperative to know whether Manuel Arroyo's boat was still "rotting in storage."

It was just before five when he reached the club. Siesta had just ended and the few members, festively dressed in blue and white, cast curious glances at Tejada's uniform as he presented himself to the secretary at the main desk. The secretary was courteous. Yes, the club kept membership records, and yes, naturally there were records of whose boats remained in the marina, and in dry dock. Yes, the war had disrupted the usual activities somewhat, although this year the members were coming back. Yes, a few boats had been left in storage since before the war. The club had continued their upkeep, assuming that their owners remained members in good standing. Yes, it would be possible to check the club's records for a specific ship. Did the Señor Guardia know her name? The name of the owner, then? Tejada gave Arroyo Díaz's name with barely controlled impatience, and waited eagerly for the reply.

The secretary seemed to be taking her time among the records. A quarter of an hour passed before she returned. "Yes, Señor Guardia, you're correct. Manuel Arroyo Díaz is listed as the owner of the *Santa Justicia*. She's a yacht, put in dry dock on August 28, 1935."

"And?" Tejada demanded.

The secretary looked puzzled. "And what?"

"When was she taken out of dry dock?" he asked.

"I'm sorry. We have no record that she was."

For a moment Tejada was struck dumb. Then his need to verify information reasserted itself. "In that case I'd like to inspect the *Santa Justicia*," he said firmly.

The secretary looked nervous. "Under normal circumstances—" she began.

"I'd like to make sure that the *Santa Justicia* is in fact in dry dock," Tejada interrupted bluntly. "I'm investigating a felony, and I will consider any individual or organization—including this yacht club—which hinders my investigation as an accessory to subversion."

The secretary blinked. "I'll speak to Señor Montero," she managed. "He's the only one who can approve your request."

"Good," Tejada said grimly, and settled down to wait.

Señor Montero, when he appeared, was inclined to demur. But Tejada was insistent and Montero finally became aware that antagonizing the Guardia was stupid. Somewhat nervously, he led Tejada past the marina to a large hangar, where boats of various sizes and shapes sat propped on huge blocks, covered by canvas tarpaulins. "Here," Montero said, reluctantly gesturing to a canvas-draped shape. "This is the *Justicia*."

He made an unhappy noise as Tejada stepped forward and lifted the tarp. The lieutenant ignored him. "*Santa Justicia, San Sebastián,*" read the lettering on the boat's prow.

Damn, thought the lieutenant. Damn, damn, *damn.* Why can't anything be simple?

Tejada returned to the post discouraged. Gold-edged clouds were floating across the sky, as if echoing the stately promenade of the tourists enjoying the rain-scented evening breeze. Why is it, he thought with disgust, that as soon as I've figured out one thing in this case, something else turns up to contradict it? At the moment I don't even know whether Arroyo's alive. I suppose he could have slipped across the border some other way, especially if he was known at the yacht club and wanted to avoid attention. And he must have realized that we'd find out about the boat. But why stage his own death, if not to gain time? And who did he stage it with? Did he murder someone else whose family haven't bothered to report *him* missing yet? Or is he actually lying in the morgue in Salamanca, and I'm on a wild-goose chase!

When he reached the post, the guardia on duty told him that Captain Alfanador wanted to see him.

"Was your search productive, Lieutenant?" the captain asked courteously, when Tejada reported to him.

"Yes and no, sir," Tejada said. Seeing that the captain looked quizzical, he added, "Well, it was productive, sir, but not exactly enlightening."

"Ahh." Alfanador made a sympathetic noise. "Well, I'm sorry to add my mite to your frustration, but there's been a development that I thought you might be interested in. Perhaps it will clarify things."

"Sir?" Tejada could not imagine anything, short of a positive identification of Manuel Arroyo, which would simplify his life.

"The manager of the Hotel María Cristina reported a guest missing this afternoon," the captain said. "He said she was a young lady, traveling without family. She stayed for two nights and then walked out yesterday evening and didn't return. Her bed hadn't been slept in. I thought you might be interested, because she was a recent arrival from Salamanca." He picked up a piece of paper on his desk and held it out. "Here's the report filed. The woman's name is Fernández. Elena Fernández."

Tejada felt a knot in his stomach. A frustrating day had just gotten dramatically worse. "Is he . . . worried about the young lady's safety, sir?" Tejada asked, although his lips did not appear to be working too well.

The captain laughed. "Actually, Tejada, I suspect he's worried about getting paid. She left without settling her bill. But her things are all still in the hotel, so it's possible that she simply ran into friends and has decided to stay with them for a few days. As I said, I wouldn't have mentioned it if she hadn't come from Salamanca. Does the name ring a bell?"

"I doubt that she has anything to do with the Arroyo case," Tejada lied. (I gave her permission to travel. Rodríguez is going to have my head on a plate. Damnit, how could she be so stupid?) He took a deep breath. "But I do think it's possible that Arroyo may have crossed into France from here, sir. With your permission I'd like to make some inquiries across the border."

"You're not under my command," Alfanador pointed out. "And I assume your own captain trusts your discretion enough to let you make whatever inquiries you think necessary."

Tejada did not challenge this assumption. "I'd like to borrow a truck, sir," he said. "I'll try to return it within forty-eight hours."

Alfanador responded readily enough. "I'll see what we can do tomorrow, Tejada. The problem is really the gasoline. The war in France hasn't made getting supplies any easier."

Tejada considered the prospect of a sleepless night, turning over the day's various revelations. Arroyo probably had a week's start already. But Elena had only left the previous evening. Time was of the essence in catching up to her if she was going to meet Arroyo in France. "Tonight, sir," he said, as firmly as possible. "I don't want to waste any more time than necessary."

"If Arroyo's already in France, he's out of our jurisdiction, Tejada," the captain pointed out mildly.

"I know, sir." Tejada swallowed. "I give you my word, I won't make a scene, sir. But I'd like to go as quickly as possible."

The captain considered for a moment. "It's probably a wild-goose chase, you know," he said.

"I know, sir."

Alfanador tapped the report of Elena Fernández's disappearance thoughtfully against his desk. "All right," he said finally. "We can spare a truck and a tank of gasoline, I suppose. And I can phone the border and let them know you're coming, so they don't make a fuss over visas. Give me an hour."

For a moment Tejada was wildly relieved. Then he remembered the dual purpose of his errand, and his stomach clenched again. "Thank you, sir," he said quietly. "I'll go and get my things together."

# Chapter 15

Like San Sebastián and most other summer resorts, Biarritz took its life from the crowds of transients who descended on it in the summertime. The town gained color from the bright clothing of the strolling tourists, and gained prosperity from the money they spent on ice creams, parasols, and all the protection against the sun and heat that they had forgotten to bring from home. It was easy to be a stranger in Biarritz.

This year most of the summer visitors had worn uniforms, but the town was beginning to return to normal. The flood of desperate refugees had slowed to a trickle, and those few who still came had the decency to attempt to blend in. Of course, even among the tourists, there were eccentrics. No sane tourist, for instance, would wear a heavy wool suit in July, or read incomprehensible Greek texts on vacation. But the gentleman with reading glasses and a white mustache, sitting alone at a table overlooking the sea on the terrace of the Café Lyon, was wearing a musty gray worsted suit and had buried his nose in a book whose title Louis, his waiter, could not make out.

The gentleman had been sitting in the Café Lyon for some time, and although he always nodded amicably when someone expressed a wish to share his table, he seemed to have attention for nothing but his book. He had successfully made two cups of coffee last for three hours and Louis and his colleagues were getting used to avoiding the table.

So it was something of a surprise to Louis when a dark-haired young woman headed for the reader's table and greeted him. She could have done better, Louis thought. There were other tables available, with more agreeable clients, and she was a good-looking woman. Perhaps the eccentric gentleman noticed this. In any case, he emerged from his book long enough to begin what seemed to be a friendly chat. When Louis approached to take the young woman's order (and inspect her more closely), she asked for coffee. Her voice held the faintest hint of an accent, but her words were too few for the waiter to be sure. He withdrew, wondering where she was from. Her clothing was not local, he was sure. Spain or Italy, he decided finally, and turned his attention to other, more demanding, clients.

When the waiter had departed, the gentleman with the reading glasses smiled. "So, Helenka," he said, in thickly accented French. "You have grown. A foolish remark, but true."

Elena looked embarrassed by this comment, a normal reaction for anyone over the age of sixteen. "I'm glad you recognized me," she temporized.

"You have not changed so much. And I am glad that I have not changed so much either, so that you could recognize me."

"It was your book," the young woman admitted. "My father has the same edition."

"I have always found Homer reliable." The old man smiled again, and patted the battered hardcover fondly. "But this is unexpected, that you are alone. Were your parents unable to cross the border?"

"Actually, I came north alone," she admitted.

The professor looked surprised. "But why?"

Elena rapidly summarized the chain of events that had led to her traveling to San Sebastián without her parents. Professor Meyer was frowning when she finished. "I am sorry," he said. "I add to your trouble at a bad time, it seems. Forgive me."

Elena shook her head. "It's not your fault."

"No." Meyer's face twisted briefly into a humorless grin. "And you will note that I do not offer to release you from your offer to help. I have spent several weeks here avoiding the German troops in the town. The presence of so many Germans makes me uncomfortable."

"We'll leave tonight," Elena promised.

"How?" the professor demanded reasonably. "How did you come? You do not have a passport?"

"No. A pair of fishermen took me along the coast last night, and set me down on the beach at around four o'clock this morning," Elena explained. "After that, I just had to follow the inland road as far as the town."

"You came alone? In a fishing boat?" The professor was shocked.

Elena thought it was a little ungracious of him to exclaim at her lack of a chaperone. She smiled, but her voice was not as light as it might have been as she said, "It was nothing. But I wish you had been more specific about our meeting place."

"Telegrams are expensive." Meyer spoke apologetically.

"I know. Actually, I didn't have trouble getting directions. It was knowing how to ask for you when I got there that was the challenge." Elena's annoyance subsided, although her experience at the Pension d'Or had not been pleasant. It had been quite awkward appearing at an unknown pension, and facing the landlady's wary hostility as she asked hesitantly to speak to a guest she was afraid to name for fear that he was using an alias. Fortunately, her stumbling description of "a German gentleman, a colleague of my father's" had been instantly recognized by the landlady, and she had been directed to the Café Lyon without further difficulty.

"I'm sorry." Meyer's regret was genuine. "But you speak French very well."

"I wish it were true!" Elena laughed. "We'll need it, before the day's out."

"Oh?" the professor asked.

"We need to make contact with our transportation out of here," Elena explained, quickly relating what Jorge had told her on the beach that morning. "So the next thing to do is to find the Magdalene," she finished. "Do you want to wait here, or should we meet back at the pension?"

"No!" Meyer looked aghast. "I will go, of course. You cannot enter a strange bar called the Magdalene by yourself!"

"I'm not going to drink there," Elena pointed out.

"That does not matter." The German was inflexible. "You will go back to the pension and I will find this Daniel and give him the password he asks for."

For a moment, Elena was tempted to agree. She was exhausted, hungry, and frightened, and the thought of letting someone else do a little work was extremely appealing. Then certain practicalities presented themselves. "No," she said firmly. "You can't go. At least not alone. Daniel wouldn't talk to you."

"And he will talk to you? Why?" the professor retorted.

"Because . . ." Elena hesitated, unsure how to explain without hurting his feelings. "Because I'm a Spaniard, and so's his cousin."

"He knows this?" Meyer protested.

Elena sighed. "It's the accent. You sound very German. And . . . well, would you talk to a mysterious stranger who sounded like a German, in Biarritz now?"

Elena had avoided the explanation merely because she did not want to seem to boast of her own mastery of French. But as she spoke, she realized that even her gentle comment had hurt Meyer more deeply than she had imagined. He looked haggard. "You are right." His voice was humble. "I had not thought that it could ever hurt to be mistaken for a German but you are right. But I will come with you. I will not speak, I promise."

Elena, who was in fact a bit uncomfortable with the idea of seeking out a strange fisherman in a bar of unknown reputation on her own, accepted his offer with relief. At her suggestion, she and Meyer returned to the pension where he collected his suitcases, and settled his bill. "You can leave them at the station," Elena said. "That way you won't have to worry about an inconspicuous departure this evening. No one will care if you redeem the claim ticket at an odd time."

Once the professor's luggage was safely stowed, he and Elena started up the Rue Gambetta, doing their best to look like casual strollers as they searched for the Magdalene. They spoke little. Just as well, Elena thought. If no one overhears us we might be mistaken for relatives, I suppose. She wondered if Meyer was silent because he was still brooding on her comment about his accent, and for the first time it occurred to her to puzzle over his phrase "be *mistaken* for a German." Perhaps he had become a naturalized citizen. "Do you have a French passport?" she asked, when she was fairly sure they would not be overheard.

"If I did, I would not impose on your kindness." Meyer spoke with a trace of bitterness.

"But surely Germans can enter Spain?" Elena's puzzlement grew. "It's a friendly country."

"I imagine they can. But my passport is a Jewish passport. It has a . . . what is the word? . . . a stamp on it."

Elena bit her lip, aware that discussing the subject in the street was unwise, but she was too curious to let it go. "Is it so hard for Jews in Germany, now?"

The professor cast a furtive glance around the street. His voice, when he spoke, was so low that Elena could hardly hear it. "Yes. In Germany now, I cannot walk certain streets, enter certain shops. This is by law, you understand." He glanced around again, to make sure that they were not being overheard, and then continued. "And always there are the deportations, of course."

"Deportations?"

"To the work camps. They will put up a notice, telling all Jews to meet at the train station on a certain day. And then they are taken to the camps. And no one hears from them again."

Elena shuddered slightly, remembering the posters plastered across Madrid at the end of the war. "*All members of the Red Army are to report to Chamartín Stadium to surrender their weapons. No reprisals will be taken against common soldiers . . .*" Machine gun fire had sounded to the north of the city all day. "Was that why you left?" she asked.

"Not exactly. It is difficult to explain. They took my work from me four years ago. But I had in 1937 a student, a former student rather, who came to see me. A fine boy. He was translating *Oedipus at Colonnus.* After our visit, they called him a Jew-lover and beat him to death in the street. That was when I decided to leave."

Meyer's voice was calm as well as quiet; almost emotionless. But Elena found herself listening with the horrified fascination of a child picking at a scab to make it bleed. "What will happen if they find you?" she asked, her voice as soft as his own.

He shrugged. "I will be deported and sent to one of their work camps. I will die, probably. I am old. I will die soon anyway. But we are all like Admetus; we want to live on, even if it is only for a short while longer."

Elena began looking for the Magdalene with renewed determination. She found herself shuddering at the sight of a German soldier, obviously off duty, strolling by on the other side of the street. Her overwhelming desire was to be safely back home. She had forgotten that she was hungry and tired. Adrenalin kept her muscles clenched, and her eyes darted from side to side in a constant quest for the bar Jorge had named. Clouds had been gathering all day, and Elena jumped, nervous as a cat, as the first drop struck her cheek.

"It's raining," she said, and then wondered with sudden fear if bad weather might prevent their crossing.

"Look." Meyer ignored her comment and jerked his chin in the direction of a bar across the street. A grimy wooden sign with a woman's profile painted on it proclaimed the single word "Magdalene."

Elena gulped. "All right," she said softly. "We need to talk to the owner."

Meyer took her arm as she crossed the street and Elena was glad of the gesture. As she pushed open the door of the bar, she realized that he had been right to insist on coming with her. The Magdalene was not only a bar avoided by ladies of good reputation, it was a place completely devoid of female presence. The dim room reeked of liquor, cheap cigarettes, and unwashed bodies. Men were sprawled at tables in darkened corners she preferred not to examine too closely, and a few were hunched over the bar. Her entry attracted the same amount of attention as a small explosion.

She forced herself to run the gauntlet of eyes all the way to the counter. She wondered if Meyer's German accent if he spoke would really be as noticeable as she had thought. He tagged behind her now, silently. The barman was staring at her with unconcealed curiosity. "Can I help you, Miss?" As soon as he spoke she knew that Meyer's accent would have been as damaging as she had suspected. Her own would be remarked upon. She might pass, for a sentence or two, as Parisian. But there was no way that she could imitate the thick patois of the barman.

Elena swallowed, feeling gauche. "I am looking for the owner of the Magdalene." She pronounced each word carefully and quietly, wishing that the bar had not gone dead silent at her arrival. She was convinced that her carefully lowered voice echoed in the farthest corners of the smoky room, and was certain that every man there was hanging on her words.

"You've found him. What do you want?"

It occurred to Elena that she had no idea whether the

barman was telling the truth. But there was no alternative to trusting him. "I was told you could help me find a fisherman named Daniel," she said.

"I don't know any Daniel. Sorry."

"I have a message from his cousin," Elena said, a little desperately, wondering if there could possibly be two bars named Magdalene.

"Sorry," the barman repeated.

"About Conchita," Elena persisted.

The barman stooped below the counter, emerged with two shot glasses, and poured an infinitesimal amount of brandy into them. "Here you are, Miss," he said, slightly more loudly than necessary.

Meyer took the drink gratefully, and downed it, apparently without ill effect, although a careful observer might have noticed that his eyes watered slightly. Elena sipped, choked, and hastily set the glass down again. "Thank you," Elena said. "You're sure you don't—"

"Positive." The barman's tone was final.

"Oh. Well, then . . ." The interview had not gone as Elena expected. "How much do we owe you?"

"On the house, Miss. Good-bye."

The farewell was too pointed to ignore. Elena escaped from the Magdalene uncertain whether to be relieved or despondent. "So, we're leaving tonight?" Meyer said dryly.

"Look, I followed the directions," Elena snapped, out of patience. She had passed a sleepless night, and eaten nothing in twenty-four hours, and the rain, which had changed to a light mist, was making her shiver.

Meyer shook his head. "Sorry. What do we do now?"

*I don't know!* Elena wanted to cry. I want to go home, and have done with you, and war, and always being responsible for everything! I'm scared and hungry and tired and you're not helping! She clamped her lips firmly over this reply, but she was unable to repress a little shriek of alarm as someone lurched out of an alleyway and grabbed her elbow, dragging her backward. She whirled, breaking free as she did so, and found herself looking at a tall stooping man in a dirty overcoat. He looked vaguely familiar.

"The Gestapo picked up Daniel this morning," the man said, without preamble. "If I were you, I'd tell his cousin to lie low. And don't go near the bar again. The place is probably watched."

He melted into the alley again. Beside her, Elena heard the professor mutter something in German. "What?" she asked, irritated.

"Pardon." Meyer sounded weary.

"The Gestapo are the German police?" Elena asked.

The professor nodded. "Your Daniel was perhaps of the Left."

Elena felt a slight chill. Meyer's voice had the resignation of one who no longer fears the worst because it has already happened. She accepted his use of the past tense calmly, wondering briefly if she would ever be able to report back to the fishermen she had met in San Sebastián. Her memories of Madrid saved her from total lethargy. Three years earlier she had been in the midst of teaching her class a lesson when a bomb hit the neighboring building. When the planes had gone and the students had emerged from under their desks, she had been faced with fifteen frightened seven-year-olds who had looked to her for cues. She had astonished herself by saying calmly, "Carolina, get the broom out of the closet and sweep up that glass. Ramón, hold the dustpan for her and be careful not to cut your fingers. Antonio, pick up the reading from where Maribel left off, please." It's the same thing, Elena thought. Don't worry about making plans. Just take care of whatever seems most urgent first, and you'll get through the day. She considered what the most urgent thing might be. "I'm hungry," she said aloud. "And it's starting to rain harder. Let's find a place to eat."

Amazingly, the technique worked. "There's a nice little restaurant near the station where I've eaten once or twice," Meyer volunteered. "It's not too expensive, and there's a back door that looks like it might provide a good escape route, if we need one."

Elena enthusiastically approved the suggestion, and the restaurant turned out to be as convenient as the professor had boasted. Elena ate a large lunch on the premise that it was useless to save money now. Meyer also ate as heartily as he could. They eked out the meatless cuisine with anecdotes of obscenely huge dinners they had eaten in the past, and did their best to rival each other in description of the succulent details.

The meal was a respite and they lingered over it as long as they could. Finally, when Elena's stomach was as full as it had been any time in the last four years, she turned her attention to the next immediate problem. "Do you want to try an overland crossing?" she asked quietly.

Meyer nodded. "It seems the only way," he sighed. "I am sorry that I brought you here. I imagined, when I wrote, that your father would come. I thought that perhaps it would be possible for him to purchase backpacks and a tent, perhaps even a mule. I cannot, because I have no valid papers, but I thought perhaps a Spaniard . . . And I used to be something of a hiker. A pair of men, with backpacks, might be mistaken for tourists. But I am afraid that you and I make an odd pair."

Elena blinked. "You were planning to cross the Pyrenees on _foot?_ Without even a guide?"

"My wife and I vacationed in Austria for many years." Meyer added, a little apologetically, "In the Tyrol. And I have bought some maps."

Elena held the basic Castilian opinion that any land fit for human habitation was flat. "I'm not dressed for hiking," she pointed out.

The professor looked at her with some amusement. "No, you are not," he agreed. "Which is why I am afraid that we will not be able to pose simply as tourists. It would perhaps be better to travel by night, at least until we reach less-inhabited country. Fortunately, the weather is good."

"It's raining!" Elena pointed out, again with the natural distaste of a desert dweller.

"But the weather is warm." Meyer spoke reassuringly.

Elena opened her mouth, but the professor's next statement effectively silenced her objections. "It will not be a pleasure journey," he said quietly. "But it is preferable to staying here and finding out if the Gestapo are in fact watching the Magdalene."

Elena closed her mouth. When she opened it again, she spoke very carefully. "Professor, I didn't sleep at all last night. If we are going to start a lengthy journey tonight, I would like a rest."

"Reasonable," Meyer agreed, nodding. "But you cannot check into a hotel without papers. And even if you could, to stay for only an afternoon would arouse suspicion."

Elena nodded. "I know." Her days of enforced idleness in San Sebastián came to her aid. "But what about a hotel lounge? People sit in them for hours at a time, and no one seems to mind if they doze off."

"It is a good idea," the professor said, after some consideration. "Perhaps you will have just arrived in Biarritz, and be very weary?"

"There'll be some mix-up with the luggage," Elena suggested, inspired. "And I can't check in until it's settled . . . no, better, until my husband arrives. He'll be detained at the train station, sorting out the search for our lost suitcases."

"Good," the professor approved. He smiled slightly. "But although you are very kind, Helenka, I think I am more convincing as your father."

"Not when you talk," Elena reminded him bluntly. She hesitated, and then advanced the suggestion she and her family had decided on in Salamanca. "Do you suppose you could be deaf?"

Professor Meyer was inclined to object to this proposal, but after some argument Elena was able to convince him. And so, a little before four o'clock that afternoon, a young Spanish lady and her invalid father entered the chandeliered lobby of the Hotel Miramar. When a porter intercepted the pair, the lady, who leaned heavily on her father's arm, explained that she had missed a train connection, been delayed for several hours, and was now utterly exhausted. To cap off her misfortunes, her baggage had been mislaid, doubtless as a result of the missed connection. Her husband was at the station, dealing with the confusion, but he had thought it best for her to come ahead, as she was so tired. Would be possible for her to wait for him here?

The porter was certain that it would be possible. He bowed the young lady to one of the large and comfortable armchairs in a secluded corner of the lounge, and assured her that she was unlikely to be disturbed. She sank into it with obvious relief, and asked hesitantly if it would be possible for her father to look at a Spanish paper. He disliked speaking, because of his disability. The porter bowed again, and reappeared shortly with a paper for the gentleman, who grunted his thanks, and immediately seemed to become absorbed in the news. The young lady leaned back and closed her eyes.

Elena's exhaustion had begun to tell on her, and the large lunch helped to play its part. After a short while, she fell into an uneasy doze, frequently starting awake and shifting position, but studiously keeping her eyes closed. Finally, the sound of a newspaper rattling as if it were hastily and clumsily being folded brought her awake again. She shifted position, aware that her back hurt. "Helena!" Meyer's voice hissed in her ear. "Wake up! No one from Spain could know you are here?"

Elena raised her head with relief, and put one hand to the back of her neck, blinking slightly. "I don't think so. Why?"

"Because there's a man in a uniform I don't recognize," Meyer began, and broke off suddenly, as a deferential voice became audible saying, "*Alors, Monsieur. Elle est là.*"

Foolishly, Elena leaned foward out of the protection of the arm-chair's wings and found herself looking up at Lieutenant Tejada.

# Chapter 16

The road from San Sebastián to the French border followed the railroad tracks, sandwiched between the river and the green mountains that blocked it from the sea. It twisted through pine forests, and over and under innumerable streams and waterfalls. Many would have found it idyllic. Tejada had driven along it blind to its beauties, with near-suicidal disregard for its many hairpin turns, and for the sheep who frequently ambled across it in search of greener pastures.

He had been hardly aware of the small, canvas-roofed truck's lurching progress. His mind had been devoted to a problem which became more depressing on every review of it: what was he going to do if he found Elena Fernández? He still could see no logical link between Elena and Arroyo. But Elena's trip to San Sebastián, and her subsequent disappearance, was too strange a coincidence to ignore. She was certainly up to something, and it was almost certainly illegal. Logically, that meant arresting her if he found her. (A cow stepped into the road, and Tejada leaned on the horn, barely lifting his foot from the accelerator.) But the time to arrest Elena had come and gone a year ago in Madrid, when she had first identified herself to him as a Socialist. He was the only one of the Guardia who knew, perhaps the only one who cared. He had known for a year, and done nothing.

The rain that had threatened for several hours finally began, and Tejada was glad of the tarpaulin Guardia López had thoughtfully provided. He flicked on the windshield wipers and rolled up the side window as the rain hit his face, reflecting miserably that it would have been easier if Elena had at least tried to seduce him. He would have felt less guilty about his vivid memory of the taste of her tears if she had used feminine wiles. He also would have felt less haunted by an opportunity missed, although he never would have admitted it. Arresting her now would be a betrayal of the night in Madrid when he had held her, and reassured her, and promised that no guardia would ever harm her.

Of course, if he didn't find her in Biarritz, then it would be impossible to apprehend her. The problem was that if she was *not* in Biarritz, and had *not* disappeared for some illicit reason, then she was in trouble. And if she's been hurt, or kidnapped, or something, then no one will know if I don't look for her, Tejada thought. Her parents can't make inquiries, and Alfanador thinks she's staying with friends. And if she needs help—

The truck skidded on the wet road, nearly ending up in a ditch, and Tejada forced himself to concentrate on driving for a moment. He would have to look for Elena, to make sure that she was not in any kind of trouble. That was his job: to protect innocent citizens. And if she was not an innocent citizen, he would have to do his job anyway. Regardless of the fact that she was brave and generous, and that her hair was long enough for a lover to tangle his hands in it and . . . Tejada was grateful to see a roadblock up ahead, flanked by guardhouses on either side.

As he approached the barrier, two men emerged from the guardhouse. Both wore raincoats and carried electric lanterns, but Tejada was surprised to see that only one of the men wore the blue uniform of the French gendarmes. The other was dressed in the dark khaki of the Germans. "Your papers?" The question was in French, but it was the German who spoke, and Tejada again felt a flicker of surprise. They're not just guests here, he reminded himself. France is occupied. But for the French just to tag along at their heels! Petain is a military man, after all. So much for the *Zone libre*.

"Here." Tejada handed over his identity card.

The rain had made darkness come early and the German trained his lamp on the document to read it. "Passport?"

Tejada had carefully thought out the necessary phrase while the man read. "I'm chasing someone we think crossed the border. In a hurry. My captain called already."

The border guard blinked. "You speak German?"

"I knew German troops during the war," Tejada replied diplomatically, suppressing several years of university instruction focusing on foreign jurisprudence.

The German laughed. "So did this one." He gestured to his French colleague with some contempt. "And he doesn't know a word." As if to illustrate his point, he switched to clumsy, schoolboy French. "He says his captain calls the border. You go and see if it's true."

The Frenchman cast a look of dislike at both men, and then crossed the road to the opposite guardhouse, pounded on the door, and disappeared inside. He returned a few minutes later, and delivered a confirmation of Captain Alfanador's call as rapidly and idiomatically as possible, to avenge himself. He had the satisfaction of seeing both of his counterparts look utterly bewildered. Finally, the Spaniard apologetically asked for a clarification. *"J'ai dit que c'est vrai."* The Frenchman rolled his eyes as if this was exactly what he had said the first time, and he could not understand why he had to deal with such idiots.

"All right, then." The German returned Tejada's identity card, just as the lieutenant swung himself out of the truck, regardless of the rain.

"I'd like to report to my own men," he explained, retrieving his papers and then hurrying across the road.

A bored pair of guardias occupied the other guardhouse. Judging from the half-empty bottle of wine and the pack of cards on the table, they had decided that few people would attempt to cross into Spain this evening. They straightened at the sight of Tejada, and saluted in a manner that managed to be both respectful and sociable. "Lieutenant Tejada?" the more senior spoke.

"Yes. You received a call from Captain Alfanador?"

"Yes, sir. And that Frog across the way just came in and said something about a Spaniard crossing."

"Fine." Tejada allowed himself to relax slightly among his countrymen. "I just wanted to identify myself. I'll be crossing back within a few days at the outer limit and I don't want to have to put in another call to Alfanador then."

"Very good, Lieutenant." The guardia spoke with gratifying promptness. "I'll tell Alberto, when he comes on duty. At your orders."

"Thanks." Tejada hesitated. It was pleasant in the guard-house—dry and comfortable, and familiar feeling. It was pleasant to speak his own language to men whom he knew would obey him. Guard duty wasn't so bad, he thought.

His subordinate sensed his hesitation. "Anything we can do for you, Lieutenant? Glass of wine?"

Tejada sighed, and turned toward the door, putting on his hat and hoping that the rain would not come down any harder. "No, thanks. I'm in a hurry. As you were, Guardia. See you soon."

"Good hunting," the German called, as he raised the barrier.

"Thanks," Tejada said absently in his native language. The friendly wish had returned him to his doubts about whether he really wanted to find his quarry.

Tejada forced himself to drive more carefully on the French side of the border, and scrupulously follow the road signs to

Biarritz, although in fact the road simply continued along the coast. It was past eight o'clock when he reached the outskirts of the town. He slowed the truck further, and considered what to do next. Officially, I'm here to find Arroyo, he reminded himself. So, start with Arroyo. That address: 18 Avenue de l'Impératrice. Alain Yves.

Finding the address presented a reasonable challenge for the evening. Tejada began to look for the Avenue de l'Impératrice, carefully avoiding the fact that the address was probably at least four years old, and that even if he found it he was unlikely to find the man Arroyo had listed as Yves. He drove slowly through wet, empty streets, searching for the center of the town, preferably for a police station where he could ask for directions.

Tejada had not been north of the Pyrenees since his adolescence, and had forgotten that French towns could not be relied on to have a central plaza where government and commerce were centered. He drove at a crawl past nineteenth-century mansions and modern shops, all with their shutters tightly closed against the night rain. The road he had been following seemed to be a central artery, but it did not lead to any recognizable public space, and he began to be frustrated. Even Madrid had more logically placed plazas than Biarritz. He wondered how the French found the authorities in an emergency and where politicians made speeches. Perhaps even priests had to give directions to their cathedrals. How was anything ever organized if the town randomly spilled all over the landscape like this? It occurred to him that he did not yet have a place to spend the night, and that finding one would probably be difficult.

A roadblock stopped his uncertain progress. Once again, electric flashlights bobbed, illuminating dark khaki raincoats. Tejada came to a halt with relief. "Your papers?" Once again, the question was asked in badly accented French. "Officer," the German added, taking in the military vehicle and the uniform.

Tejada handed over his papers and rapidly explained his difficulty. The soldier was apologetic. He knew nothing of Biarritz. But, he regretted, the lieutenant's vehicle could not proceed further. This area of the town was cordoned off. Mustering his long disused German, Tejada asked if perhaps the soldier could ask his companions about the whereabouts of Avenue de l'Impératrice. There was a rapid discussion that Tejada was unable to follow and then a gendarme spoke up. The Avenue de l'Impératrice was over toward the waterfront where all the fashionable hotels were. The most direct route was along the barricaded street, but the lieutenant could go three streets over and continue straight until the square and then turn right.

Tejada offered his thanks and was already letting out the clutch when one of the Germans spoke up again. "*Herr Offizier!* There is a roadblock past the plaza too." To Tejada's surprise, the words were in halting Spanish. "You will have to walk."

"Thank you." The friendly advice gave him the heart to ask, "You were in Spain?"

"*Sí, mi teniente.*" The German saluted.

"Then I owe you a double thanks." Tejada smiled, and backed up the truck, feeling happier than he had since crossing the border.

He managed to find a boulevard wide enough to allow him to park the vehicle without obstructing traffic. After a moment's thought, he lifted the tarp that covered his kit, and dug out the regulation rain cloak that he had, for a wonder, remembered to bring. Naturally, it was impossible to hold the tarp over his kit while searching for the cloak, and naturally the cloak was at the bottom of his pack, so his belongings were nicely damp by the time he was finished. He hurried toward the Avenue de l'Impératrice, head bent against the rain, and began to climb up its long slope. The soldiers had told the truth when they said the elegant hotels were here. Slanting streams of rain were visible in pools of light spreading out from broad windows and the sidewalk was frequently broken by wide driveways between wrought-iron gates. The road had apparently only been blocked from the south, and he saw taxis sitting outside the hotels, waiting hopefully for customers. A few automobiles passed him, spraying water from the gutters, and thoroughly drenching him anew.

After his second soaking, Tejada lost patience. He stepped into one of the hotels and marched up to the reception desk. The clerk was mysteriously blind to him, until he allowed his cloak to fall open, revealing his uniform. Under normal circumstances, the clerk would have continued to ignore him. But it was wartime, even in Biarritz, and even the most exclusive hotels had learned that it was wise to extend courtesy to men carrying side arms. "May I help you, Monsieur?" The question was frosty.

"I am looking for number eighteen, Avenue de l'Impératrice." Tejada's accent was far from perfect, but his tone was at least equally frosty.

"A moment." The clerk consulted a directory, relieved that the dripping military gentleman did not require a room. "That is the Hotel Miramar, Monsieur. About two blocks from here."

"Thank you. I would also like to borrow an umbrella."

The clerk's nostrils flared, but he agreed to send one of the porters to accompany the officer with an umbrella. Tejada's entrance to the Hotel Miramar was therefore somewhat more dignified. He was glad of this. The chandeliers in the lobby were lit, and the sound of a piano tinkling came from within the hotel's restaurant. The lobby was crowded. People were already coming down for dinner, a fair number of them in evening dress. Tejada slung his cloak over his arm, took off his tricorn, and approached the main desk. He was met not by a mere clerk this time but by a slightly more senior personage. "Good evening, Monsieur." (The Hotel Miramar had also learned the value of courtesy toward uniforms. Moreover, Spaniards were frequent guests there, and the uniform of the Guardia was recognized.) "How may I help you?"

Tejada was too tired to overtax his French. He decided on the simplest phrase possible. "I am looking for a man named Alain Yves."

"At your service, Monsieur. How may I help you?"

For a moment, Tejada thought that the man had misunderstood his request. "Alain Yves?" he repeated.

"Yes, Monsieur. I am the manager of the hotel." The man produced a card from his breast pocket.

Tejada read it, feeling stupid. He had not really believed that he would find Yves, much less that Yves would smile and identify himself as soon as Tejada asked for him. Faced with the totally unexpected, he flailed about for something to say. "I obtained your name from a man called Manuel Arroyo," he managed. "Perhaps you recall him?"

"Arroyo? A Spanish gentleman?" The manager thought for a moment. "Arroyo? Ah, yes, I know the name. An older gentleman, a professor, no? He and his wife have been our guests several times. Not, alas, recently. The recent disturbances in Spain, you understand."

"Yes," Tejada said, disappointed. He had, he realized, been foolish to think that simply because an address was foreign it connoted something sinister. Yves had probably provided Arroyo with a card during his last vacation in France, and the lawyer had happened to copy down the name and address.

"It is always an honor to receive a new guest recommended by a former patron," Yves continued, smiling. "I do hope you will remember the Hotel Miramar kindly to Monsieur Arroyo."

"Yes, certainly." Tejada's mind had been occupied, and he had only followed the manager's speech with difficulty. He appeared to have hit a dead end in the Arroyo case and there was nothing more he could do that night. He was tempted to turn around and go back to the border. He was sick of speaking foreign languages, and sick of things that made no sense. But having come this far, it would be lax to ignore the other part of his mission. Once again, he fell back on a simple phrase. "Also, I am looking for a woman. A brunette, with long hair."

He was expecting a denial, or at best a demand for more particulars. Once again, Yves surprised him. "The Spanish lady? Whose luggage was mislaid at the station? But yes, she is in the lounge, with her father. A shame their bags have not arrived yet."

Tejada felt slightly dizzy. "Oh. Good," he managed. "Could you show me where, please?"

"But of course." The manager led Tejada across the parquet floor and into the lounge. Tejada followed, hardly knowing what to expect. It was possible, and even likely, that the Spanish lady Yves had referred to was *not* Elena. After all, there were lots of women with long dark hair. And "with her father" was puzzling. Tejada was fairly sure that Professor Fernández was still in Salamanca. An unpleasant thought occurred, that Arroyo might be masquerading as Elena's father. But *why?* Tejada thought. It doesn't make sense.

The lieutenant reflected unhappily that if Professor Fernández or Professor Arroyo were in Elena's company he would be obliged to arrest both of them and Elena as well if he wanted to avoid Rodríguez court-martialing him for incompetence or worse. He was still pondering what to do or say when Yves gestured to a secluded corner of the lounge, where a white-mustached man whom Tejada had never seen before sat staring at them from over the top of a Spanish newspaper. He certainly was not Guillermo Fernández and even allowing for ten years and a disguise Tejada did not think that he could be Manuel Arroyo. He heaved a sigh of relief. It was merely a question of mistaken identity. Some compatriot, traveling with her father, who had lost her luggage at the train station. He was already framing a civil apology for intruding when Yves spoke again. The woman who had been half hidden in a wing chair started forward.

Elena looked up at him. There were smudges under her eyes and her lips were trembling slightly. Tejada stared down at her, stricken, horribly aware of what he should do, and of his own reluctance to do it. He almost missed the import of the hotel manager's cheerful salutation. "*Voilà, Madame. Votre mari est arrivé.*"

# Chapter 17

E lena was the first to break the tense silence. "What are you doing here?" Her voice had the deceptive quietness that Tejada knew was her particular prelude to hysteria. But since she had spoken in their native language, neither Yves nor Meyer understood her.

"I might ask you the same question," Tejada replied. He became aware that the hotel manager was hovering at his elbow, turned, and added firmly, "*Merci bien de votre assistance.*"

There was little the manager could do in the face of Tejada's determined politeness but bow and move away. Elena started to rise. The lieutenant seized her elbow, and pressed her back into the chair. "Don't move," he ordered. "You either," he added to Elena's unknown "father." He glanced around. It was past the hour for evening drinks and the only people lingering in the lounge were in the far corner. There was another set of vacant chairs nearby, set around a low glass table. He seized one of the empty chairs, and dragged it over to face Elena's. Then he dropped into it, and said quietly, in Spanish, "Now suppose you tell me just what the hell is going on?"

Elena chewed her lip for a few seconds. Then her mouth opened and closed several times, silently. "I . . ." she began finally. "I thought you were in Salamanca."

"I'm sure you'd rather I was," Tejada retorted with considerable anger. "But as I recall I gave you permission to travel to San

Sebastián, not outside the country. Monsieur Yves informs me that you're here with your *father*, which this gentleman manifestly is not, and he seems to have mistaken me for your husband, who as far as I know doesn't exist, unless I owe you congratulations?"

"No," Elena flushed. "That is I . . . I mean . . ."

Tejada turned his attention to the unknown gentleman. "Perhaps you're a little less tongue-tied, Señor?" he suggested. And then, as he received no reply except an anguished stare, "Answer me, damnit!"

Elena got a grip on herself. "He can't . . . He doesn't speak . . . he doesn't hear."

"Deaf?" Tejada thoughtfully picked up an ashtray that was resting on the low table in front of him, and turned it between his fingers. "He doesn't read lips?"

"Not well," Elena said with tremendous relief.

"Interesting." Tejada hurled the ashtray to the ground with as much force as he could muster. Elena, whose nerves were already on edge, started violently at the thud. So did Meyer. Tejada smiled, a little grimly. "You heard that," he said to Meyer. "And something tells me you're hearing me perfectly now. So let's stop playing games, shall we? Who are you? And what are you doing here?"

"*Pourquoi demandez-vous comment il s'appelle?*" Elena demanded, desperately switching to French. "*Vous n'avez pas le droit, ici. . . .*"

Tejada, who had been narrowly watching Meyer, blinked suddenly. "Jesus, Elena, doesn't he even speak Spanish?" he exclaimed. "Who is he? What is he doing with you?"

Elena did not reply. Tejada shrugged and turned back to Meyer. "I'm sure you don't want to get the young lady in trouble," he said in French. "Tell me who you are, and what you're doing, or I promise you, she leaves here as a prisoner."

To the lieutenant's relief, the unknown man did not call his bluff. He sighed, and then said slowly, in heavily accented French, "Helena has broken no laws. She was helping me."

"Professor—" Elena began.

He gestured her to silence. "Let be, Helena. I am tired. Perhaps I am not so much like Admetus after all." He turned back to Tejada. "My name is Joseph Meyer."

Tejada had already realized that the white-mustached man spoke with the same guttural consonants as the soldiers who had directed him, so his surname did not come as a surprise. But the information puzzled him all the more. "You're a German?" he asked, pitching his voice low to match Meyer's, and wondering why Elena was involved with a foreigner from a country which—it occurred to him for the first time—she would probably regard with hostility.

"Not exactly." The old man smiled, a little bitterly. "I was born there. But I have no country now."

Tejada thought over the statement for a moment. Then he put his head in his hands and groaned. "Elena! Tell me he's not a Communist. *Please* tell me you haven't mixed yourself up with a Red."

"I am not a Communist." To his surprise, the answer came from the man who had identified himself as Joseph Meyer.

"Merely an internationalist?" Tejada asked sarcastically.

"Merely a Jew."

The lieutenant gaped, and then felt a sudden rush of hope. Perhaps Elena was not really helping a Red after all. It was almost too good to be true. He inspected the man before him more closely: a full head of white hair, completely uncovered; a neatly trimmed white mustache; a dark suit that was a few years out of fashion, but in no way remarkable. He did not look anything like the portraits of Maimonides and Abravanel that the lieutenant had seen. "You're sure?" he demanded suspiciously.

It was Meyer's turn to look surprised. "Sure? Why . . . yes."

"And that's all?"

"It's usually enough."

"Prove it."

"What?"

"Prove you're a Jew," Tejada commanded. "Or I'll assume you're a Communist and act on that assumption."

There was a brief, tense silence. Then Meyer began to laugh. It was a high, wheezing, choking sound and it went on for too long. Elena leaned forward, concerned, and placed one hand on his arm. "Professor. . . ."

Meyer took a handkerchief from his pocket, mopped his streaming eyes, and murmured a few unintelligible sentences, still chortling slightly. Tejada's eyes narrowed. "You'll have to do better than mumbling Hebrew."

"That was Greek." Meyer gave a final wheeze, and then dug inside his coat. He handed over a rumpled traveler's wallet to the lieutenant, translating into French as he did so. *"Why ask my birth? Very like leaves upon the earth are the generations of men. . . ."*

Elena mentally translated the French into Spanish as Tejada opened the wallet. "Is that the *Odyssey*?" she hazarded, smiling a little at the professor.

He shook his head. "The *Iliad*, actually."

Tejada stared down at the passport in his hand. It had been issued only two years previously. The photograph unquestionably matched the man in front of him, and the name given was Joseph Meyer. Stamped across the place and date of birth was a yellow J in gothic script, and the bearer of the passport was clearly identified as a Jew. He folded the passport shut, and handed Meyer's wallet back to him. "All right," he said to Elena. "He's a Jew, even if he doesn't look like one. Now how does he know you?"

Elena looked at her hands. "He's a colleague of my father's."

"You traveled north to meet him?"

The lieutenant's voice was almost gentle. Elena felt a strong urge to cry. She thought she had done so well. Perhaps the fishermen had betrayed her. But at least it was Carlos who had found her, and not some stranger. She nodded slowly, without raising her eyes, wondering what he would do. Make a quiet phone call from the hotel, probably. And sit with her until the police came to pick up Professor Meyer. And then he would take her arm, as courteously as if he were helping her across a street, and escort her back over the border, to await trial and sentencing.

"Why?"

Both Elena and Meyer looked at the lieutenant in surprise. This was not the question he was supposed to ask. *How did you expect to get away with it?* or *Do you know what the penalties are?* would have been reasonable questions. But he seemed to be conducting the interview along unique lines. Elena glanced at the professor. "I've told him you're a friend of papa's," she said, in French. "And that I came here to meet you. He wants to know why."

The Jew turned to Tejada. "I hoped to cross into Spain," he said quietly. "To avoid deportation to Germany."

Tejada was torn between relief at the plausibility of the explanation, and annoyance at the kind of man who would involve a misguided and quixotic young woman in a fatally reckless enterprise. "What were you doing here?" he asked softly.

"Helena wished to find some place to rest until—" Meyer stopped abruptly, discovering too late that evasion and prevarication are difficult in a foreign language.

Tejada was grateful for the pause. "Never mind," he said. "I don't want to know how you planned to cross the border. The question is—"

Elena, who had been listening intently, suddenly coughed and said loudly in Spanish, "But I am so tired of sitting here *in public.*"

Tejada and Meyer both took warning from her tone, and neither was startled when, glancing around, they saw Alain Yves approaching their corner. "May I be of assistance?" he asked smoothly, when he reached them. "Madame informed me that your baggage was lost due to a faulty train connection. I take it that you still have not found your suitcases, Monsieur?"

Suddenly it seemed as if the three people in the armchairs were sitting inside a little circle of silence where the sounds of the lobby and the rest of the lounge reached them only as distant cries. Meyer sat quietly, his hands resting on his knees. His face reminded Tejada of the face of a man facing a firing squad; a man to whom the worst has already happened, and who merely waits for the physical execution of an irrevocable sentence. Elena leaned forward and took one of the professor's immobile hands between her own, chafing it slightly as if to keep it warm. But she turned her face towards the lieutenant. "Carlos?"

Tejada pushed himself to his feet. "Unfortunately not," he said. "But my wife is exhausted, and I doubt that anything more will be achieved tonight. If one of the porters could show her and my father-in-law to their rooms, I'll come and register."

"Of course, Monsieur." The manager bowed again, and Elena found herself following a bellboy up the sweeping marble staircase on Meyer's arm before she had fully realized what had happened. It was impossible to discuss the strange turn of events with the German as long as the bellboy was present, and Elena was not sure what she would have said in any case. Her strongest feeling was a wish that the lieutenant, who had remained at the reception desk filling out the necessary papers, would rejoin them as soon as possible.

The bellboy led them to the third floor, and unlocked a door at the end of one corridor. He glanced a little uncertainly between the two guests, and finally decided that since the gentleman was deaf, the key should be presented to the lady. "It's a suite, Madame," he explained, stepping through the door, and flicking a light switch as he did so. The glow of a lamp with a Tiffany-glass shade illuminated a small foyer with two doors, each ajar, leading to a bedroom. Elena, comparing the suite with her room in San Sebastián, ruefully thought that the uniform of the Guardia Civil insured better service, even in a foreign country. The bellboy stepped into each of the bedrooms and turned on the lights, to allow the guests a view of their surroundings. Heavy drapes hung to the floor at the far wall of both rooms. "You have views of the ocean," the bellboy explained. "And the master bedroom has a little terrace. Perhaps if the rain has stopped tomorrow you may use it."

He left, and Meyer and Elena stood alone in the foyer. Automatically, Elena moved toward one of the bedrooms, and sank into the first available chair. The professor followed her, looking slightly stunned. He was the first one to recover his voice. "Are all Spaniards like that?" he demanded.

"No. Lieutenant Tejada is exceptional." Elena found that she was grinning foolishly.

"You know him?"

"He's . . ." Elena considered. "He's my father's parole officer," she explained finally, feeling vaguely dissatisfied with the designation, but unable to think of a better one.

"How did he find you?"

"I don't know." Elena frowned. "He looked surprised to see me."

The sound of a key in the lock prevented further discussion. A moment later, Tejada entered. He hung up his cloak and took off his holster and jacket in silence. Elena reflected irrelevantly that it was the first time she had seen him unarmed. He sank onto a corner of the bed and rubbed his eyes. "I hope you're happy," he commented.

"Lieutenant." Meyer's voice was awkward, and slightly choked. "I-I cannot thank you enough. . . ."

"Don't try," Tejada interrupted wearily. "I still haven't decided what to do after tonight. By the way, I told the manager we'd be staying for two days, but that I might send you two on ahead early." He grimaced slightly as he added, "I assume I was correct when I said that my father-in-law was most anxious to return to Spain?"

"I . . . yes." The professor smiled weakly.

There was an awkward silence. Then Elena said. "How did you find me?"

"Partly by accident," Tejada admitted. He flashed her a brief smile. "I don't spend *all* my time chasing after you to make sure you don't get into hot water."

Elena blushed and fell silent. "What *were* you looking for then?" she demanded, to cover her confusion.

Tejada hastily summarized his search for Manuel Arroyo, speaking in a mixture of Spanish and French for Meyer's benefit. "I'm tempted to have the French arrest both of you," he said. "I could say you were accessories to Arroyo's flight, or to his murder. But extradition of foreign nationals is tricky, and it's not a strong case. And, of course, the Germans might want to take Professor Meyer into custody. I'm not sure of their status here, but there does seem to be one next to every French policeman."

Meyer had gone white. "If I am arrested," he interjected, "I will be deported as a Jew. I beg you to believe this."

The lieutenant shook his head. "It was just an idea. Alternatively, we can separate tomorrow. You can pursue whatever arrangements you had made." As Meyer opened his mouth to speak again the Spaniard added, "Don't tell me. I don't want to know."

"What do we do now?" Elena asked, to break the silence that followed.

Tejada shrugged. "Would you like to go down to dinner?"

"No!" The professor and his presumed daughter spoke at the same time.

"Me either," Tejada agreed. "And due to our lost luggage we don't have the clothing for it. We could have a tray sent up."

"I'm not really hungry," Meyer said dryly.

Tejada shot him a sharp look. "Do you not eat pork, and all that?" he asked, half suspicious and half curious.

"I'm not worrying about keeping kosher." The classics professor spoke with some amusement. "But Helena and I had a large lunch."

"I didn't," Tejada said flatly. He turned to Elena. "Do you want anything?"

Elena knew that she ought to feel a horrible sense of obligation. The lieutenant had done so much already. It would be only courteous to refuse this further favor. She was not particularly hungry. But she found herself smiling and saying easily, "Thanks. Maybe tapas or something light. We did eat a lot earlier."

In the end, Tejada ordered enough tapas for three. After the tray had been delivered, and the door had closed behind the waiters, Meyer stood up, shaking off the attitude of age and infirmity he had assumed for their benefit. "How much do I owe you?" He reached into his jacket.

"Nothing. You didn't want any, remember."

"I insist, Lieutenant. It's a small price to pay for your kindness."

Elena picked at a piece of bread, and listened to the men argue with the vague feeling that she should be taking part. She was, she knew, as much in Tejada's debt as Meyer, and she was probably less impoverished than the professor. But it was an incredible relief to not feel responsible for once.

It was not a disagreeable meal, although conversation was minimal. All three were too tired to easily speak a foreign language, and all three appreciated the chance for quiet thought. But as the little plates were emptied, most of them by Tejada, the silence became oppressive. Finally, Meyer gave voice to their common thought: "Are we planning to get an early start tomorrow, then?"

Tejada frowned. "I'd hoped to pursue Arroyo further. If I take the two of you into the countryside, will you be able to get across?"

"Of course." Elena spoke with forced cheerfulness.

"The less I know, the better," the lieutenant said frankly. "But yes, we probably should get an early start tomorrow."

There was another long pause, as each one thought, *If we want an early start, it makes sense to turn in now*, and waited for someone else to say it. Finally, Tejada stacked the empty plates on the tray, and carried it to the door which he opened. He set the tray down in the hall, and then closed the door. "I suppose you'd better pick which room you want," he said as he carefully locked the door.

Only the doorjamb got the full benefit of his mumble, but he had spoken in Spanish, and Elena accurately guessed that the question was aimed at her. "What was that?"

He started slightly to hear her voice directly behind him. Meyer stood behind her, in the doorway of their improvised "dining room" with the slightly anxious look he always had when they spoke Spanish together. "Which bedroom do you want?" Tejada repeated, acutely embarrassed.

"I don't really care." She was obviously embarrassed also. "They're the same, aren't they?"

"I guess. I haven't really looked at the other one." He headed for the unused room with a rush of relief, and inspected it minutely. Elena trailed behind him. Meyer, unable to follow their conversation and assuming that it did not concern him, retreated to the other bedroom. "Oh, look," Tejeda swept aside the curtains. "This one has a balcony."

"How nice! A sea view, the bellboy said." Elena's voice was determinedly bright.

"You should definitely take this one then." Tejada spoke as if a balcony overlooking the sea was of the utmost importance for sleeping on a rainy night.

"You're sure? If you and Professor Meyer would like it . . . ?"

"We'll be fine," Tejada assured her.

"Oh. Well, then—"

"Well . . ." Tejada echoed, acutely aware that she was standing between him and the door. "Well, good night, then."

"Good night." She moved aside to let him pass. His hand was on the doorknob when he heard her voice again. "Carlos."

He froze. "Yes?"

"Why did you decide to help us?"

Tejada turned around and inspected her: a slender woman, not quite starving thin as she had been when he had first known her, but still giving the impression of an alley cat rather than a spoiled pet. Her shoes and the hem of her skirt were stained and muddy, perhaps from the rain. She was a woman who would never think to ask a guardia if he had ever killed but who would risk her life to help a man who was no kith or kin of hers. He thought of many answers, some of them having to do with Meyer, some with Germans he had met, and some even with his duties as a guardia civil. But this was Elena, and for Elena only total honesty would do. "Because you've got guts," he said. "And I'd hate to see them eviscerated."

Elena laughed, shakily. "Seriously."

"Seriously," Tejada said quietly. "You're the bravest woman I've known. And most women wouldn't take that as a compliment."

"They don't take courage as a compliment?"

Tejada smiled. "I could tell many women that they were *courageous*. Most of them wouldn't appreciate being told that they had guts."

"Well, I do. But it isn't true you know." Elena laughed again, but this time the laugh ended on a choke. "I'm scared all the time . . . no, not even scared exactly, just incredibly *tired* of having to be the one with guts all the time. Tired of having to be the one who knows the answers and carries out the plans and . . ." She choked again, without even the pretense of a laugh this time.

"And takes the responsibility," Tejada finished. "And is always the grown-up."

"Yes." Elena looked at him, wondering. "Exactly."

"We call it command responsibility," the lieutenant said gently. "And if you were one of my men, I'd say that you handle it well enough to be officer material."

"Thanks." Elena was once more in control of herself, but she took a hesitant step toward him. "I suppose it's not living up to my reputation, but I'd like a break now."

"I know. That was why I helped out."

She was chewing her lip nervously. He waited for her to

speak, knowing that the wisest—and also the cruelest and most difficult—thing to do would be to end the discussion. Elena stared down at the carpet. It was a blue Persian, and she would remember the shapes of the shadows cast by the lamplight until her dying day. "Would you stay, for a little while? Just until I fall asleep? I don't want to be alone."

Tejada drew a ragged breath. "I'm not superhuman, Elena."

"I know."

There was a pattern of green leaves and cream-colored buds on the border of the carpet, and an ink stain near one of them. Elena memorized the shape of the ink stain in the moments while she waited for the sound of the lieutenant's voice, or for the handle turning as he let himself out of the room, or for a cough, or for footsteps. There was utter silence and then a new shadow fell across the carpet, and Tejada's arm slid around her waist. Elena raised her head and kissed him. And then the sequence of events became unclear. She was never sure afterward if she began inexpertly unbuttoning his shirt before or after he found the zipper at her waist.

Several hours later, Elena started out of an uneasy doze, choked by a fear that she could not immediately place. She forced herself to lie quietly, and did her best not to think about how she and the professor were going to make it back to San Sebastián. After a few moments, she closed her eyes and tried to steady her breathing. But she remained resolutely awake. She inched a little closer to the warm, breathing bulk beside her, hoping that some of Carlos's calm would rub off. To her immense relief, he stretched out one arm, and pulled her into an embrace.

"You're not sleepy, love?" The voice was a warm, deep murmur, soothing in and of itself. It did not occur to Elena that he had not been asleep either.

"No," she admitted. "I'm scared. Do you think we can really get away with this?"

"I don't see why not." The lieutenant forced himself to speak lightly. "I'll tell my mother we eloped because my captain is a vulgar peasant and I couldn't bear to have him play any role at my wedding, which is true, and I'll tell my father and brother we eloped because I couldn't bear to have my mother arrange everything, which is also true."

"I didn't mean . . . Wedding?" Elena's tone changed abruptly as his meaning sank in.

"You've spent too much time among the Reds." Tejada's amusement was less forced now. "It'd be a nice thing if I didn't intend to marry you now, wouldn't it? Besides . . ." he ran a meditative thumb along the curve of her shoulder blade.

"Besides?"

"I think I'd like to marry you. Because . . ." The caress became less thoughtful and more definite.

Elena laughed in the darkness. "What are you doing?"

"What do you think?"

Professor Meyer was embarrassed. His friendship with Guillermo Fernández was basically professional. He respected Fernández's work, and he knew from their years of correspondence that Dr. Fernández was a man of liberal sympathies and considerable humor. Fernández's response to his plea for help had shown him to be both generous and loyal. But Meyer knew nothing of his colleague's religious convictions or opinions about the upbringing of children. Professor Meyer felt that fate had placed him *in loco parentis* to his colleague's daughter and it seemed like an ill return for Fernández's kindness to throw her into the arms of a Fascist policeman. On the other hand, there was absolutely nothing he could do about it. At least, Meyer thought glumly, shortly after the pair disappeared into one of the bedrooms, it did not seem to be against Elena's will. Still, he was sure that her father would disapprove, and for the sake of his own peace of mind he wished that the wall between their rooms was considerably thicker.

The professor made a conscientious effort to lie down but he was too anxious to sleep, even after all the noise from the next room had died away. Fear magnified the patter of rain against the window and the occasional footstep in the hallway or overhead. He heard the murmur of voices when Elena woke, and heard her sudden laughter. Oh, no, he thought, despairing. Can't they at least sleep through the night? He remained in his room for a few more minutes, with a pillow clamped firmly over burning ears. Then his embarrassment finally won out over fear and caution.

He stood up, flicked on a light switch, and then carefully made his way down the hall to the bathroom. As he had expected, it was deserted. He locked himself inside and waited. If Elena Fernández and her lieutenant did not have the common decency to be asleep at such an ungodly hour, he was not going to lie awake and listen to them. And that was why Joseph Meyer, German citizen of Jewish extraction, was not in his hotel room at the fatal hour of four in the morning.

# Chapter 18

All in all, Tejada looked back on it as one of the more unpleasant moments of his life. But perhaps it was only the severe contrast. One minute he was sleepily nuzzling Elena's shoulder, completely relaxed, and the next the door banged open, the light went on, and an excited voice shouted "*Raus! Raus!*"

He sat up, grabbing at the sheet. "What the *hell?*" he began, rapidly repeating the question in French and then in German as his brain started working. "What gives you the right to come barging in—"

"Never mind that." Meyer was too excited to abandon his native language. "Get up! Get up, now! They're coming."

"*Qui arrive?*" Tejada demanded, aware of Elena's fingernails digging into his arm, and determined to force the Jew to use a language that she would understand.

"The Gestapo." Meyer got a grip on himself, and switched to French. "They are accompanying the gendarmes. They are searching the floor below, demanding papers. I heard them in the bathroom. The noise carries there because of the. . . ."

"Oh." Without completely sharing Meyer's panic, Tejada saw why he was upset. "Get out of here, and let Elena get dressed. And take off your jacket, and unbutton your collar."

Meyer blinked. "But why?"

"*Jetzt!*" snapped Tejada, borrowing both the word and the tone from a drill sergeant he had met during the war.

The professor blinked and retreated. Tejada began to dress rapidly. Elena, he noted with approval, did the same thing. "It's no use fleeing," he explained quickly. "They'll have men on the exits, unless they're total incompetents, and trying to sneak away is asking for trouble. We need an excuse to leave. Your father's been taken suddenly ill in the night. We need a taxi to his doctor in Biarritz. Understand?"

"Yes."

"Good. Never mind all those damn buttons, just fasten your coat over it. Oh, and try to cry a little. Crying women tend to be distracting."

Tejada headed for the next room and rapidly repeated his explanation to the professor while Elena fumbled with her shoes. "Your chest hurts, and you have shooting pains in your left arm," he added. "You've had this before, understand? And you're stone deaf and semiconscious. The feebler the better and *for God's sake don't talk!*"

"Yes, Lieutenant," Meyer nodded. "And thank you."

"Thank me when we're out of here," Tejada said tersely. "Let's go."

The two Spaniards took up their places on either side of the professor, each supporting him under an elbow, and hurried him out of the room and down the corridor. "Elevator," Tejada murmured urgently. "Can't take a sick man down the stairs." He leaned on the bell intently and repeatedly, and was rewarded a moment later by the creaking of slow gears. At least, Elena thought, Meyer looks plausibly sick. He was pale and sweating and she could feel his arm trembling.

The elevator seemed to take forever. Was it her imagination, or were there noises in the corridor below? At last, there was a light from the elevator shaft, and the cage came rattling into sight, just as Elena realized that the tramping of boots on the stairs beside the elevator was becoming more distinct.

"Hurry up, damnit!" Tejada's French accent deteriorated

under the stress. "My father-in-law is ill. He needs to be taken to a doctor immediately! Where have you been?"

As the door to the cage opened, Elena realized that a man in a dark trench coat was standing in the elevator beside the sleepy porter. "Come on, come on. Take us down as fast as you can," Tejada continued, pulling Meyer (and incidentally Elena) into the elevator without seeming to see the other occupant.

"*C'est que vous êtes malade?*" The man in the trench coat's accent was far less obvious than Meyer's. He could almost have passed for French.

Elena could feel Meyer shaking. Now, she knew, would be an opportune time for tears, but she was stuck in dry-eyed, dry-mouthed terror. "My father has a weak heart," she managed. "He had a sudden . . ." She looked over at Tejada, and switched to Spanish. "How do you say a sudden attack?"

Tejada turned back to the unknown occupant. "It's not the first time this has happened. We even have the name of a doctor in Biarritz. But it's upsetting for my wife." He rolled his eyes. "This was *not* how I wanted to spend my leave."

"You are a soldier?"

The elevator reached the ground floor. "A guardia civil," Tejada flung over his shoulder as the porter opened the gate.

As Tejada had predicted, there were uniformed soldiers standing at the foot of each stairwell in the lobby. A man with a gun was stationed by the reception desk, next to two gendarmes. Tejada and Elena levered Meyer into an armchair, and Elena leaned over him, concerned, while the lieutenant headed for the desk. "Call a cab," he ordered the night clerk, ignoring the man beside the desk. "My father-in-law is ill. We must get him to the doctor."

"*Oui, Monsieur.*" The clerk looked relieved at such an ordinary request. He reached for the telephone.

"A moment," the Gestapo officer interjected. The clerk froze.

Tejada glared. "I apologize, Officer, but this is an emergency."

"Your papers?"

"Of course." Tejada knew that this was the tricky part. Surprise, and a little reserve were important, because most honest people seemed to resent the demand a little. But not too much surprise or reluctance. It was important not to seem too eager either. Men tended to thrust forgeries rapidly under the noses of the Guardia, trusting that their eagerness to seem cooperative would prevent the guardias from reading their documents too closely. The lieutenant handed over his identity card readily, but fidgeted a little as the German looked at it. "I'm sorry to be difficult, but we really do need a cab."

"Call a taxi," the German ordered the clerk, and then turned his attention back to Tejada. "You are on leave?"

"Yes. This was *supposed* to be a vacation." Tejada cast a worried glance over his shoulder at where Elena was still bending over Meyer. "But between the troubles we've had with the trains, and now Don José's heart . . . I'll be relieved to get back to work." He shook his head and then looked at the men waiting at the stairwells and on guard in the elevator. "Although it seems work is following me."

"There is a Communist cell here, we think," the German admitted. "We picked up one of them this morning."

"And this is the mopping up?" Tejada asked with interest. "It looks like a very efficient operation."

"Thank you."

Tejada felt the beginnings of nervousness. He would have been annoyed by a civilian who had attempted to engage him in any more conversation. The natural thing was to move away toward Elena and the professor. But he was afraid that any movement in their direction would result in a demand for their papers as well. He turned back toward the clerk. "How long until the taxi gets here?" he demanded, with real and urgent interest.

"A few more minutes at most, Monsieur. Do you require the name and address of a doctor as well?"

"No, thank you," Tejada replied, grateful for the additional subject of conversation. "My wife received a referral from my father-in-law's doctor before we left."

The awkward silence descended again for what was one of the longest minutes of the lieutenant's life. It was broken when the front door opened, and a bearded man entered. "Someone called for a cab?"

"Yes." There was nothing feigned about the relief in Tejada's voice. Elena had also started up, gesturing the man towards where Meyer lay slumped in the chair, and explaining, in a voluble mixture of Spanish and French the nature of his malady and the need for haste.

Tejada suppressed the urge to hurry toward his little "family" and rush them out the door. "Elena," he called in Spanish. "Wait a minute." Elena turned and Tejada hoped that her horrified look was read only as concern for her father. He turned back to the silent man by the desk who had been watching the charade with interest. "With your permission, Officer?"

The German nodded. "Fine. But it's good you asked."

"Professional courtesy," Tejada replied wryly. "Good hunting."

"Thank you."

Tejada advanced on Elena, who had enlisted the taxi driver's aid in supporting Meyer down the hotel steps. The professor was certainly playing his part well. "All right," he said to her, taking the driver's place. "Slow and steady, remember."

Elena smiled at him briefly, and he knew that she had understood the message. "At least he hasn't had too much excitement lately." There was a quaver in her voice that could have been mistaken for tears, although Tejada suspected it was a suppression of a hysterical giggle.

"Real guts," he murmured appreciatively, as they maneuvered Meyer down the stairs and into the cab.

Somewhat to Elena's surprise, Tejada immediately gave the driver an address. Meyer, who knew Biarritz after several weeks' stay, was startled to recognize their destination as only a few blocks away. They remained in suspense for only a few minutes. Tejada paid the driver, tipped him profusely, and assured him that they did not need his further assistance. Then he ushered Elena and the professor toward a random doorway, until the cab was out of sight. "All right," he said, dropping Meyer's arm. "Down that way, and make the first right. *Run.*" Meyer, who needed no encouragement, ran. Elena managed a stumbling trot, head bent against the rain. Tejada, aware that her shoes and not her spirit were at fault, resisted the urge to drag her by the arm.

Elena had never thought that she would ever greet the sight of one of the Guardia Civil's vehicles with positive joy. But she laughed for sheer relief when she saw the canvas-roofed truck, parked where Tejada had left it. "Into the back, both of you," he commanded, relief surging in his voice as well. "And get under the tarpaulin. We'll probably meet roadblocks."

Meyer helped Elena into the back of the truck, and then clambered in after her. "Bless you!" His voice was fervent. "If you can take us as far as the hiker's trails—"

"Forget that," Tejada interrupted, swinging himself into the driver's seat and turning the key in the ignition. "I want to be over the border before someone bawls out those Germans for the incompetents they are. Now get under the damn tarp!"

Elena never forgot the ride to the border. The rain spattered heavily on the rough cloth above her for the first few minutes, but soon lightened so that she was no longer able to feel the impact of the drops. But it was difficult to keep her balance on the floor of the truck. Tejada was driving fast and the roads were not smooth. After a few bruising minutes, she managed to cling to one side of the vehicle, half lying down, knees curled to her chest. Meyer, who had been having similar difficulties, clung to the other side in a similar position. Tejada's kit lay between them, wedging them in as well as giving them some protection against being shaken loose. Elena's left leg and arm began to fall asleep, and she longed to stretch, or at least to be free of the bumping for a while, but each time the vehicle slowed to go around a curve her heart leapt into her mouth, afraid that they had hit a roadblock and were about to be stopped. Nearly blind in the darkness, and afraid to speak, she could only hope that the professor was surviving the trip.

The jolting ride seemed to go on forever, but in fact it was only just over forty minutes later that Elena felt the truck rattle to a stop. In the sudden silence, she heard the unmistakable voice of a Spaniard. "Lieutenant!"

"Good morning, Guardia." Tejada's voice was clear to the two people crouched in the back of the truck. "Here are my papers, if you need them."

"Yes, sir." There was a pause, which was agonizing to the lieutenant's hidden passengers, as the border guard smothered a jaw-splitting yawn. "You're back early, sir."

"I know. I found the address I was looking for but it turned out to be a false lead. I wanted to get back as quickly as possible and find the bastard. He's caused enough trouble."

"Yes, sir." The guardia yawned again. "At your orders."

"Go get some coffee." The lieutenant sounded amused. "You sound like you've had a tough night."

"Oh, no, sir. The border's been very quiet."

"Good. *Arriba España.*"

"*Arriba España*, Lieutenant. Welcome home."

"Thanks." The lieutenant's passengers, who had done their best to avoid breathing during his conversation with the border guard, let out simultaneous sighs of relief as the engine rumbled to life, and they began to move again. A few minutes later, the truck once more slowed and came to a halt. This time, they heard the sound of the door slamming, as Tejada climbed out. A moment later, the tarp that concealed them was pulled aside. "Everyone all right?" Tejada asked.

He had turned off the road just before one of its innumerable S-bends. A little clump of pine trees screened them from immediate view of the deserted highway. Leaning over the back of the truck, he looked genuinely worried about his passengers' comfort.

"Wonderful," said Meyer seriously, pushing himself into a sitting position with a slight groan. "If I haven't thanked you already, Lieutenant—"

"You have," Tejada interjected, pulling his kit out of the back, and helping the old man totter out of the jeep. "Elena? Are you all right?"

"Fine, thanks." Elena attempted to follow Meyer's example, but accidentally stepped out of the truck onto her left leg and nearly crumpled to the ground. "My foot's asleep," she explained as Tejada caught her. "I'll be fine in a minute."

"Good." He tightened his arms around her a little, in spite of the reassurance, and she leaned against him, content to be supported. He kissed her hair.

Meyer coughed pointedly. Tejada relaxed his grip, and Elena turned out of the circle of his arm, looking (in the professor's opinion) not nearly embarrassed enough. "Welcome to Spain," she said, smiling.

"Thank you." The Jew smiled back, unable to be seriously annoyed. He looked past Elena to the lieutenant. "And now the lieutenant will forbid me to thank you further, no doubt. Is this where we part ways?"

Meyer was not really surprised to see both Elena and her lover look distressed. Nor was he surprised when, after a rapid conversation that he only partially followed, the lieutenant said, "We're still some ways from San Sebastián, and Elena needs to return there to collect her luggage. I'll take you closer to the town, and drop you off where you'll have only a few miles to walk."

"You're very kind." The professor's voice was grave.

"I thought you might like to ride sitting up," Tejada explained. "That was why I stopped. No one will stop a Guardia

Civil vehicle here, and if you don't have papers . . . well, then I'm arresting you for not having papers."

"That sounds reasonable," Meyer agreed. He turned to Elena with a completely serious face and voice. "Would you like to ride in the front? Since your leg's asleep?"

"If you don't mind, thanks." Elena only blushed slightly.

Where Tejada had driven quickly before, he seemed to dawdle now. The sky was lightening rapidly in the east, and the clouds were lifting. As they came out of the trees into an open field beside the mountains, rays of gold shot out over the eastern hills with the intensity of spotlights at a movie's premiere. The clouds above them were pink tipped. Elena turned her head toward the rising sun. "Look!" she laughed, and pointed. "Rosy-fingered Dawn!"

The professor laughed also, but there was a hint of regret in his voice as he said, "I'm afraid I left all that remains of my library in the station in Biarritz."

"My father will know where to find new books," Elena consoled him.

"Are you planning to stay with the Fernández family for an extended period of time?" Tejada broke in.

"I don't know," Meyer hesitated, embarrassed. He did not begrudge the lieutenant the information but he had thought little beyond getting into Spain and had no answer ready.

"You won't be able to, without papers," Tejada said bluntly. "You'll be discovered within a fortnight, either because of routine surveillance, or because someone will pick up their dealings with the black market. Civilian ration books won't support more than one person."

Elena was glad of the opportunity to discuss the problem. "We were thinking my brother could help," she explained. "If he could get a passage to Mexico—"

"Mexico?" interrupted Meyer, who had not been able to follow.

"Sorry." Elena switched to French. "Hipólito is in Mexico,

and my parents thought you'd be safe from the war there. My brother has the money, and he could arrange the passage. It would just mean getting you a visa, and aboard a ship here."

"That's very kind of you." The professor spoke humbly. "I would pay back the passage, of course."

"If you can find work there," Tejada commented. "If I were you I'd try to head for the United States from there. At least they're not openly Socialist . . . yet."

Elena stiffened slightly, but the professor laughed. "*Doch es ängstet mich ein Land / Wo die Menschen Tabak Kauen / Wo sie ohne König kegeln / Wo sie ohne Spucknapf speien*" he quoted, and then, sensing bewilderment, continued, "I think the French translation is something like '*But I fear a land where men / Chew tobacco in platoons / There's no king among the pins / and they spit without spittoons.*'"

"Where is it from?" Elena asked.

"Heinrich Heine."

"Another Jew in exile," Elena commented.

"That's been our fate for centuries."

Something stirred in the depths of Tejada's memory. An exam paper . . . one of his finals at the university . . . old Professor Martínez Velez's . . . a pedantic old bastard, with something of Meyer's photographic memory and precision . . . Martínez Velez's snide comment at the top of an essay on immigration and naturalization that he had not had time to finish: "*Sr. Tejada: You show a regrettable ignorance of Primo de Rivera's policies for one who claims to admire his son. (Or else you failed to understand that the directions were to provide* three *examples.) Your first two examples of changes in immigration law are admirably supported. The third—which you appear to be unaware of—was promulgated by the Cortes of 1924.*" Tejada frowned suddenly. "Where are you from, Professor?" he demanded.

"I grew up in Danzig," Meyer replied, surprised.

"And your family, had they been settled there long?" Tejada persisted.

"No. My father moved the family there after the Franco-Prussian war," Meyer sighed. "Germany was better for Jews then."

"Your parents?"

"From Galicia. Why?"

"Galicia!" the lieutenant echoed eagerly. "They were Spanish?"

Meyer laughed. "It's a province in Poland, Lieutenant. Nothing to do with Spain."

"Oh." Tejada frowned for a moment. "What about farther back? How long had your family been in Poland? 1700s? 1600s?"

Meyer laughed again. "Genealogy has never been one of my interests, Lieutenant. I think my great-grandfather and grandfather grew up in the same town, but beyond that I really couldn't tell you."

"But you must have records?" Tejada protested, realizing even as he spoke that the permanent documents he thought of as normal—records of baptisms, marriages, funerals, and so on—would be foreign to the Jew. "How do you trace descent?"

"Jews were only allowed surnames at the end of the eighteenth century," the professor said quietly. With the teacher's instinct for when to clarify further he added, "My great-grandfather chose the name Meyer."

Tejada gasped, with the simple astonishment of a man who had grown up in a society where the titles to both rank and land had been fixed for centuries. "I've always thought of the Jews as a very ancient people," he said, feeling the inadequacy of the response, and suppressing an absurd desire to apologize.

"We are." The professor's voice was still quiet. "Ancient, and frequently scattered, and as frequently renamed."

"Oh." Tejada brought his mind back to the problem at hand. "I suppose there's no chance that your family were originally from Spain, then?"

"Sephardic?" There was a note of constraint in Meyer's voice, almost as if he resented the implication. "No, I'm afraid not."

"A shame," Tejada said. "But I suppose if you have no

records, then no one else can be expected to either. I suggest you start inventing a family tradition about being from Toledo."

"Why?" Meyer and Elena spoke at the same time.

"The Law of Return," Tejada explained. "Passed in 1924. Any Jew who can prove direct descent from those expelled from Spain by the Catholic monarchs is eligible for Spanish citizenship. If you're picked up without papers, claim Sephardic descent. You can't prove it, but we can't disprove it either."

"You mean I could stay here?" Meyer's voice was eager.

"I wouldn't bet on it for the long term," Tejada cautioned. "But it's better than being picked up as a German. That means instant deportation."

"You are a man of infinite resources, Lieutenant." Meyer smiled. "I would not like to have you as an enemy."

The professor's words reminded Tejada of Eduardo Crespo's, at the Otero's party a few days earlier. "Well," he said, with something approaching smugness, "the German army may well be invincible, but I'm damned if we can't match their police work." Meyer made no sound, and since he was sitting behind the lieutenant, Tejada could not see his amusement. Elena snickered.

Tejada felt the sun rising on his back, and was content. There was, he reflected, no real hurry to get to San Sebastián. In fact, Captain Alfanador would probably be surprised if he returned too early. The road swung out a little, to make room for a stream almost big enough to be called a river, which had hit a natural dam of fallen trees, and grown into a sluggish pool, several feet deep. In early spring the stream probably ran along below the road, but it had fallen already, leaving a few feet of grassy bank. Tejada glanced at his watch, and then pulled to a halt. "Why are we stopping?" Elena demanded.

"Because," Tejada said, "there's a path down to the water there, and I want to shave. I've spent too much time in the rain lately, and I feel scruffy."

He got out of the truck. "Pass me my kit, Professor."

"Here." The professor hesitated a moment, and then took the plunge. "Lieutenant! If we must stop . . ."

"Yes?" Tejada asked, surprised at the professor's diffidence, and half-suspicious. He tried to remember if he had heard anything about Jews praying in the morning. They had rules about bathing too. Perhaps Meyer wished to perform some ritual. Tejada was torn between a desire to shield Elena from any pagan rites and an overwhelming curiosity about witnessing them himself.

"May I borrow your razor?"

The lieutenant recognized his disappointment just in time to smother it, and feel embarrassed at being disappointed. He laughed. "Sure. Can you make it down to the water?"

"I think so. The rocks form a kind of stairway."

Meyer picked his way down the embankment with an ease that proved his claim of being a serious hiker. He was nearly at the pool by the time Tejada had dug his shaving equipment out of the pack. "Careful!" the professor called upward. "It is not difficult, but the way down is very dirty. I've stained my coat, I'm afraid."

"Thanks for the warning," Tejada replied, and unbuckled his holster. "Hold this," he said, handing the pistol to Elena. "If you hear anyone coming, put it under the seat, and hide. We'll be right back."

"All right." Elena looked dubiously at the gun and then placed it on the seat beside her.

Tejada shrugged off his coat and tossed it over the weapon. Then he kissed her lightly and followed Meyer down the cliff. Elena, left alone, collected her thoughts. She had gathered that both men wished for privacy in their toilette, and it seemed likely to take some time. She twisted in her seat to admire the rising sun, and then lowered her gaze to where Carlos had abandoned his coat. It was wrinkled and wet with rain. He was not likely to feel much less scruffy after putting it on again she thought. She picked up the coat and did her best to smooth away the wrinkles with her palm, aware as she did so that it had Carlos's distinctive smell and that the folds of khaki had molded themselves to the curve of his shoulders.

It was perhaps embarrassment about the possessive intimacy of the gesture that made Elena abandon her ineffectual attempts to press the coat and to give it a brisk shake by the shoulders. A folded paper fluttered from one pocket. Elena stooped to retrieve the paper and realized that it was covered with writing on both sides. Curious, she unfolded it, and read: "*Dear Carlos: Congratulations on your promotion! Mama has almost forgiven your decision to join the Guardia Civil. . . .*" She smiled, pleased with the deserved praise on Carlos's behalf, and kept reading.

When the two men made their way back up the incline, damp-faced and in a spirit of peaceable accord, they found Elena sitting in the front seat, staring straight ahead. Tejada retrieved his coat from where he had flung it, shook out the wrinkles as best he could, and put it on again. "What I wouldn't give for a hot bath and a cup of coffee!" he said cheerfully. "We've only got a few kilometers to go. You won't mind a bit of a walk, Meyer?"

"Not at all. It looks like it will be a beautiful day." The classics professor also seemed in a better mood. He leaned forward and tapped Elena on the shoulder. "Lieutenant Tejada has suggested that you tell the manager of your hotel that you met friends and have decided to stay with them," he said. "We can meet at the station then, and head south. And he thinks that you may change the francs I have brought. I cannot, without papers."

"How typical. Lieutenant Tejada thinks of everything." Elena had spoken in Spanish, and Meyer, only half understanding the words, assumed that the remark was not primarily addressed to him.

Tejada, who had no trouble with the language, was considerably surprised by Elena's tone of voice. He turned toward her in astonishment. "Are you—?" he began.

"Keep your eyes on the road," she snapped. "Do you want to send us into a ravine?"

Tejada scrupulously returned his eyes to the road, trying to figure out what was the matter with Elena. Had they been alone, he would have simply pulled to one side, and demanded an explanation, but it seemed discourteous to quarrel in front of Meyer. They drove in silence for perhaps ten more minutes. Then Tejada pulled off of the road for a final time. "All right," he said quietly as the professor scrambled out. "If I were you I'd keep off the road, Meyer. You're not likely to run into a patrol, but better safe than sorry. And there's no point in your being seen with Elena."

"Understood." The professor nodded and turned to Elena, who had climbed out of the truck unassisted, pointedly ignoring Tejada's outstretched hand. "We will meet at the station, then? Shall we say at one o'clock?"

"Yes," she agreed.

Meyer turned back to Tejada. "You are a good man, Lieutenant. Thank you."

Tejada gripped the professor's outstretched hand. "You've thanked me already, remember?"

"Yes," Meyer smiled. "But that was for my life. This was for your razor."

Tejada laughed. "Good luck, Meyer. And remember, if you're picked up: Law of Return."

"I will. Good-bye, Lieutenant Tejada. *Au revoir*, Helena." Meyer turned, and began heading up the slope away from the road.

Elena marched toward the highway without a word. Tejada took her arm. "I'm sorry I can't take you all the way," he said.

"That's all right."

She had stopped walking. "I'm afraid it will be better if we don't see each other too much until Meyer's safely away," he said apologetically. "It would be a bit embarrassing for me to not notice his presence in your house if I were a regular visitor there."

"It certainly would." Her tone was at odds with the growing warmth of the morning.

He raised one hand to touch her cheek, and she turned her head away. "It's only for a few weeks," he promised. "And then . . . well, Old Cathedral or New?"

"What about them?"

Tejada gave a somewhat forced laugh. "Did you think I wasn't serious when I said I wanted to marry you?"

She shrugged. "What for? You've already gotten what you wanted from me, haven't you?"

"Elena!" Tejada was shocked. "What's the matter with you?"

"Oh, nothing." Her voice was brittle. "I had hoped you'd spare me the humiliation of continuing with this affair when I returned home, but I suppose that's too much to ask from a guardia civil. I imagine rubbing my parents' noses in it will be your favorite part."

"What?" Shock was giving way to anger. "What are you talking about?"

"It must be very satisfying for you to have a Republican's daughter for your whore," Elena spat, all pretense at coolness gone. "Oh, that was very noble of you last night, to put us completely in your power! It would have been kinder to have just turned us over to the French!"

"Meyer wouldn't have thought so!" Tejada retorted.

"I know that! Why do you think I let you blackmail me like that?"

"You *asked* me to stay with you last night!"

"You knew I would!"

"No, I did not. Most women of my acquaintance are decent."

"Then marry one of them!" Elena cried. "And leave me alone!"

She pulled free of him, and plunged up the slope after Meyer, knowing that Tejada would have to leave the truck to pursue her, but suspecting that he was unlikely to do so. He could, she knew, overtake her on foot fairly easily. If he really wanted to, he would, she thought, and then struggled onward with even more speed, goaded by the fear—or hope—that he was pursuing her. She stopped, panting, when she reached the top of the ridge, and looked down at the road. It was empty, except for a single jeep, crawling carefully around the curves. Elena sank to her knees and sobbed. Then she wearily got to her feet, and began making her way back to the roadway. Meyer would be waiting for her in San Sebastián. It was time to start being a grown-up again.

## Chapter 19

The Guardia Civil post in San Sebastián was just beginning to stir to life when Tejada drove up and climbed shakily out of the borrowed truck. His brain was still numb but his body piloted itself towards the canteen for breakfast. He was intercepted. "Lieutenant Tejada?" A guardia saluted, looking both respectful and questioning.

"Yes?"

"Captain Alfanador wants to see you, sir. Immediately."

Tejada's first thought was that the Gestapo in Biarritz had been unexpectedly efficient. He followed the guardia to the captain's office, wearily reflecting that his career, and probably his life, was about to end ingloriously for the sake of an ungrateful little bitch who actually believed that he would stoop to forcing her into bed with him . . . He stopped. She had *not* believed that. She couldn't have believed it. This morning, when she had tottered out from under the ridiculous tarp, and into his arms, she had been . . . *frightened,* said a treacherous voice in his head. *Still in your power, and still afraid for Meyer. It got to be a strain for her, but she kept up the charade until he'd gotten away. She's not in love with you. How could she be? She fears you. And you took advantage of that. And now she hates you.* The fury and confusion that had left him speechless when Elena had fled were beginning to recede, leaving a dull, throbbing ache behind his eyelids.

"Lieutenant." Alfanador nodded at him when he came in. His

voice was not the voice of an officer who has discovered treason in one of his subordinates. "I'm glad you're back so quickly. There was a phone call for you from Salamanca, just after you left."

Tejada blinked. "Sir?"

"A Sergeant Hernández," the captain explained. "He asked you to call as soon as possible. I'll put the call through now, if you like, and you can make your report while we wait."

"Yes, sir," Tejada managed.

"Fine." The captain picked up the phone on his desk and spoke into it briefly. Then he signaled Tejada to go ahead. The lieutenant gave a carefully edited account of his hours in France, still half-wondering if his activities had been discovered and the invitation to make a report was designed as a trap. Alfanador listened without much interest. Tejada had just finished when the telephone rang again. The captain raised the receiver. "Yes? . . . Yes, thanks . . . Captain Alfanador, at San Sebastián. Your Sergeant Hernández put in a call yesterday . . . yes, to Lieutenant Tejada . . . Yes, he's here now." Alfanador held out the phone to Tejada.

The lieutenant took it, and was rewarded by the sound of Captain Rodríguez's voice, slightly tinny, and thoroughly annoyed. "Hope you're enjoying your vacation, Tejada! You've wasted enough time!"

Tejada gritted his teeth. It was too early in the morning. "At your orders, sir," he said, hoping that the phone disguised his tone of voice, and too tired to care if Captain Alfanador over-heard him.

"The orders are to return immediately, Lieutenant." Tejada suspected that Rodríguez would have dearly liked to slam down the phone at that point, but there was an indistinct noise on the other end of the line, and then the captain added, "And Hernández here can tell you why!"

"Sir?" It was a relief to hear Sergeant Hernández's voice, which was not only friendly, but even contented.

Tejada made an effort to match the sergeant's good humor. "Good morning, Hernández. What was urgent yesterday?"

"We've identified Manuel Arroyo's body, sir." Hernández definitely sounded like a cat with cream. "Positively."

"What?" Tejada gave brief and fervent thanks that Professor Meyer had firmly declined to be arrested as an accessory to Arroyo's disappearance. Then he felt a rush of anger that the body had not been identified quickly enough to spare him the trip north, and his encounter with Elena. "How?"

"Well, you remember Saturday night, sir, I couldn't go to the Otero's party because of my tooth?"

"Yes. I'm glad you're feeling better, Sergeant, but—"

"Well, I finally got it pulled on Monday. And Dr. García was chatting a bit—he says he always does, to try to relax his patients, you know—and he started talking about how he never forgot the inside of a mouth. It seems that dentists take a lot of pride in their work. He says they're like jewelers, and that any dentist can recognize a tooth he's crowned. Something about shape, and color and all that. Quite an art form, according to Dr. García. So that gave me the idea. Because Arroyo's face was pretty smashed up, but his teeth were still there."

"You found his dentist?" Tejada interjected, interested despite himself. In a just world, he thought, men like Hernández would rise quickly.

"Yes, sir." Hernández sensed his commander's interest, and expounded happily, eager to share his discovery. "I got Señora de Arroyo to give me his dentist's name, and it turns out he had a whole fancy set of false teeth. Dr. Vargas took one look at the inside of the corpse's mouth and right away started matching it with his records. So it's absolutely positive. From now on I'm always going to find a dead man's dentist, sir!"

"Good work, Hernández." Tejada smiled, silently blessing the sergeant not only for conscientious police work but for cheering him up. "It looks like this was a wasted trip, then. But I did find one thing that might be interesting, so it's not a total loss."

"Very good, sir." Hernández sounded pleased. "And I've been going over the records, and there are a few interesting patterns there too, sir. Can you make it back to Salamanca this evening? We can compare notes."

"I'll be on the next train," Tejada promised. He was eager to leave the border country for both practical and emotional reasons.

The long train ride was not pleasant for the lieutenant. He had entered the station in San Sebastián with his eyes fixed firmly on the ground, and had minutely inspected the tiles by the ticket booth, the treads on the stairways, and the stripe along the platform, afraid that if he looked up at any moment he might encounter Elena and the fugitive professor. When he finally boarded the train, he realized with horror that he might have to spend several more hours staring downward if Elena was in the same car. Fortunately, she was not. He wondered if she was on the same train, or if she and Meyer had taken a later one. She would, he knew, have had to check out of the Hotel Maria Cristina, offering some excuse to the suspicious manager for her prior absence. Not that he would care, once he was paid, if Alfanador's guess was correct.

Tejada's own journey south had been delayed by Captain Alfanador's casual comment that hoteliers liked to be paid. He had left the post in San Sebastián, after thanking the captain with as much grace as he could muster. Before purchasing his ticket, he had stopped at the telegraph office, and wired what seemed like a safely obscene amount of money to the Hotel Miramar, care of Alain Yves, along with a mostly truthful note: "THANKS FOR HOSPITALITY. STOP. FATHER-IN-LAW'S CONDITION REQUIRES IMMEDIATE RETURN HOME." The expense eliminated the modest surplus provided by his monthly salary, but Tejada felt that allaying possible suspicion was worth the price.

The train chugged up into the golden Castilian plains,

leaving the cool green of the coast behind. Tejada hoped that the warm, dry air of the desert would clear his brain. The dark, rain-blown madness of the night seemed ridiculous here, where the sun's harsh spotlight illuminated a blond landscape under a cloudless blue sky. Tejada started to sweat slightly. He pulled out his notebook and began to review his notes on the Arroyo case, determined to avoid thinking about Elena. We can't establish an exact time of death, Tejada thought. So it doesn't make sense to ask who could have killed him. Better to figure out who wanted to. He began to scribble in his notebook. Two hours later, he had filled several pages:

Sra. Otero de Arroyo—she's anxious to inherit his money. Did she know he was sending it to Switzerland? Would she have the codes for his accounts? Why would she want his money now? Were they estranged?

Judge Otero Martínez—was embarrassed by Arroyo. Probably knew his brother-in-law was transferring money abroad. Protecting his sister???? Wanted to manage investments??? Weak case.

Tomás Rivera—body was found in his warehouse. Resented Arroyo's position and prestige? Weak. But why was body found there? If a false lead, why did murderer think Arroyo might be linked to Rivera?

Arturo Velázquez—Protecting Rivera???? From what????

~~Guillermo Fernández~~ Guillermo Fernández—No known motivation.

Unknown—Someone who Arroyo knew was a Red, and could have denounced. (Rivera?? Velázquez? *Another petitioner??*)

Someone who knew about Arroyo's connections in Switzerland. (Blanes, at BBV? But would he kill a client to prevent him from withdrawing funds???) Inheritance???? Blackmail? But wouldn't it go the other way?

Tejada frowned at the notes. They made little sense. It was warm in the railroad car, and he knew that he would be wise to catch up on a little of the sleep he had lost the previous night. He closed his eyes, steadied his breathing, and opened his mouth slightly, allowing his jaw to relax. The rhythmic clatter of the train and the murmurs of his fellow passengers began to sound further away, and his mind relaxed. *It must be very satisfying for you to have a Republican's daughter for your whore!* His jaw snapped shut on the memory of Elena's words.

He spent much of the next hour with his eyes resolutely screwed shut, thinking of the various cutting replies that he had been too surprised to make. She was, he reminded himself, not worth the effort of thinking about. She was a Red, and a subversive, and he had always known it, and he should consider himself lucky that she had not decided to blackmail him for the help he had given her and Meyer, and if she *did* hit on the idea of blackmailing him he would cheerfully . . . he would definitely . . . probably . . . he would pay. For Meyer's sake. And for Professor Fernández's sake, since he seemed like a decent old bird. Not that Elena would stoop to blackmail. At least, he didn't think she would. But a woman who could feign passion as she had feigned last night . . . If she had been pretending. How could he not have guessed something of her feelings earlier . . . but if she really was so devious there was no reason to feel guilty . . . Tejada's thoughts scurried around the question like a hamster on a wheel all the way back to Salamanca.

Sergeant Hernández met him at the station. "Good trip, sir?" he asked, as the two men headed back to the Plaza de Colón.

"Yes," Tejada lied. "Tell me about what you found in the records."

"Well, once I knew that it was Arroyo that we were dealing with, sir, I thought it made sense to look at his records as far back as we have them," Hernández explained. "And there's precious little really, but way back in '36, in the inactive folder, I ran across an interesting connection."

"Yes?" Tejada prompted, on the edge of irritability. It was only kind to allow Hernández to tell the story in his own way, but the lieutenant was not in the mood for discursive narrations.

"Arroyo was seeing Tomás Rivera," Hernández said simply. "And according to your interview with Rivera, they hardly knew each other. And he was found in Rivera's warehouse. So Rivera's lying about something."

"What do you mean he was *seeing* Rivera?" the lieutenant asked.

"It's in the surveillance file, if you know where to look," Hernández explained. "He had some kind of appointments with Rivera. Every week at three o'clock for nearly three months."

*Idiot*, Tejada thought, depressed. That's another thing I've overlooked. I'm supposed to be in charge of the files. I should have picked it up. I should have gone back to the older files. "Good job," he said, although the words tasted like sawdust in his mouth. "Have you talked to Rivera?"

"No, sir." The sergeant was apologetic. "I only picked it up on Tuesday, sir, and then yesterday what with meeting with Dr. Vargas and all, I didn't follow up. I should have, I know."

"No, it's fine," Tejada said absently as they reached the post. "You've done a lot more than I have."

Hernández hesitated. The lieutenant looked tired. He might reasonably want to take a few hours off, go to dinner, and then catch up on paperwork without further discussion of the Arroyo case. But Hernández was proud of his initiative, and unwilling to let it go. Tejada headed automatically for his office, and the sergeant, taking this as a sign that his superior intended to keep working, followed him, and risked a question. "You said you'd found something interesting, sir?"

"Not as interesting as your findings, Sergeant," Tejada's voice was dry. "I think Arroyo had a Swiss bank account."

Hernández looked startled. "Why? What did you find in San Sebastián, sir?"

Tejada rapidly summarized his search of Arroyo's house, and his discovery of the little address book. "I can't prove it though," he finished as they reached the door of his office. "And I can't think of any connection to Rivera."

The sergeant frowned, and shut the door as Tejada dropped into the chair behind his desk. "So, say that Arroyo was converting currency. Do you think anyone knew about it?"

Tejada hesitated. Then he gestured to the sergeant to be seated. "Would you confide a secret like that to anyone, Hernández?" he asked quietly.

Hernández hesitated. "Probably not. Well, not to anyone I wasn't close to."

"You're happily married, aren't you?" the lieutenant observed, lowering his voice even more. "Suppose you had a brother-in-law whose financial judgement you trusted?"

"I might tell him, I suppose," the sergeant said carefully. "But I'd have to be sure that he wouldn't object to anything illegal."

Tejada jabbed a pencil into the blotter on the desk. "But how much of a risk would it be?" he asked, his voice carefully neutral. "After all, supposing your brother-in-law did object? Would he be willing to involve his sister in scandal by denouncing you?"

The sergeant winced. "Murder is illegal too, sir," he pointed out.

"I know it."

The two officers' eyes met. "How much of this is guesswork, sir?" Hernández asked.

"A lot," Tejada admitted. "I just wondered if it was guesswork that made sense."

"The captain will have a fit," the sergeant observed.

Tejada nodded. "I know. I'd prefer Rivera myself. I wish the other didn't make more sense."

Hernández nodded, looking glum. Then he said, "What do you want to do about Rivera, sir?"

Tejada glanced at his watch. It was just past nine. "Pick him up this evening," he ordered. "I don't know if he killed Arroyo, but he lied to an officer pursuing a murder investigation. That's enough for an arrest."

"Yes, sir." Hernández sounded approving. "Do you want to send someone now, sir? Or wait until later?"

"Midnight, I think," the lieutenant said, after considering a moment. "I want to catch him at home. Bring a car. Oh, and Hernández?"

"Sir?"

"Don't wake me up," Tejada said firmly. "I'll talk to him in the morning."

The sergeant looked amused. "I'll make sure Corporal Jiménez doesn't confuse his orders, sir," he said.

"Thanks," Tejada said, with real gratitude. "I want this taken care of. But I . . . haven't gotten much sleep lately."

"Yes, Lieutenant. At your orders."

"Dismissed." Hernández stood, and turned to leave. Tejada jabbed at the blotter a few more times and then said suddenly, "Would you tell your wife?"

"Tell her what?" the sergeant turned, looking puzzled.

"If you were . . . I don't know . . . doing anything illegal."

Hernández considered. "I don't know. It's hard to imagine really." He smiled briefly. "After all, sir, I'm a guardia. Bit embarrassing to break the law, in our job."

"But if you did?"

Hernández was surprised by the lieutenant's tone. Then he remembered that his superior was unmarried. "She'd probably find out anyway," he explained. "Very hard to live with a woman and keep secrets from her."

The sergeant left to organize Tomás Rivera's arrest, wondering if Lieutenant Tejada was considering Señora Otero as a possible suspect in her husband's murder. Lieutenant Tejada hastily reviewed the towering piles of paper on his desk, ate dinner, and went to bed, where he lay awake until well past midnight, pondering the advisability of confiding information about illegality to a woman. He had reached no satisfactory answer the next morning, when he started work, but when Corporal Jiménez entered, swelling with self-satisfaction at a task successfully accomplished, the lieutenant was grateful for the distraction.

"Rivera's down in the cells, sir," Jiménez reported. "We brought him in last night, a little after midnight."

"Well done, Corporal," Tejada said, since Jiménez obviously expected him to say something.

"His family did an awful lot of caterwauling," the young man reported, looking vaguely dissatisfied. "Not like Señora Otero at all. One of the kids woke up and started crying and then his wife went into hysterics, and we had to pull them apart, and he was damn near hysterical too until we got him into the car and cuffed. And even then Gómez had to smack him to make him stop whimpering."

"It sounds as if you handled the situation admirably, Corporal," Tejada said patiently.

"Thank you, sir." Jiménez smiled for a moment, and then the worried look returned. "It wasn't like what I thought it would be though."

"Suppose you bring him down to one of the interrogation rooms now," the lieutenant suggested gently, ignoring his junior's faint frown. "I'll meet you there."

"Yes, sir." Jiménez saluted, and left. Tejada collected the notes he had made on the Arroyo case and headed down to the interrogation rooms. Jiménez was waiting for him, along with his prisoner.

The doctor did not look well. He was in shirtsleeves, and

Tejada guessed that the guardias had not waited for him to dress fully when they arrested him the night before. A purple bruise across one cheekbone showed where Guardia Gómez had administered his cure for hysteria. Rivera was radiating fear. Tejada took the seat behind the little table in the room without speaking. Then he deliberately spread out his notes and consulted them. Then he raised his eyes to inspect the prisoner. "I don't like people who lie to me," he said finally.

"Lieutenant?" Dr. Rivera's voice was a croak.

The lieutenant consulted the notes on his desk again. "You told me you were never close to Manuel Arroyo Díaz," he said. "I have your exact words here: 'He belonged to a different generation, a different profession, a different class.' You said you'd never been friends."

"And that's true." Rivera was white-faced.

"Odd." Tejada ran a finger down the yellowing sheet of paper Sergeant Hernández had pulled from Arroyo's old file. "According to our records, Arroyo visited you after the petition was signed. On August 4, 1936, at three p.m. And again on August eleventh, and again on August eighteenth. August twenty-fifth, September first, September eighth. . . . We seem to have a pattern here, Doctor."

Rivera shuddered. "I hadn't seen Arroyo in years, Lieutenant. I swear to you. . . ."

"Why did you lie about your connection with him?"

"I didn't. I—"

"Jiménez," Tejada interrupted, with a slight gesture.

The corporal, who had been standing behind Rivera, snaked an arm around the prisoner's neck, and jerked backwards, gently applying pressure to the doctor's windpipe.

"Don't lie to me," Tejada said mildly as Rivera struggled and gasped for breath. He made another gesture, and Jiménez relaxed his grip slightly, still keeping one arm around the doctor's neck. Rivera was sweating. It was difficult to tell in the artificial light, but Tejada thought that the doctor's skin had a yellowish tinge. He drew a few rasping breaths but said nothing. One of Elena's friends, Tejada thought. Someone she trusts . . . someone she cares for. "Do you know the effect of electricity on the human nervous system, Doctor?" he said, and took pleasure in watching Rivera's face go slack-jawed with horror. "The Guardia Civil have been experimenting with the process. Perhaps you'd be interested in a demonstration?"

"No." The word was a whisper.

"What was your connection with Arroyo?"

"He consulted me professionally. For a few months only," Rivera said, eyes on the ground.

Of course! The lieutenant thought, with a rush of relief. A bookkeeper! And someone Arroyo could trust absolutely! Thank God it's not Otero. He wouldn't have anything to do with this, of course! I must have been insane. "And exactly what did he require your financial expertise for?" he asked happily, sure that he was moving into the final phase of questioning.

"My what?" Rivera sounded genuinely bewildered.

"You said he consulted you as a bookkeeper, man," Tejada snapped. "What did he want to know?"

Rivera stiffened and shot Tejada a look of pure hatred. "I said he consulted me *professionally*. I'm a doctor, not a bookkeeper, Lieutenant." His voice was shaking with something other than fear now.

Tejada was about to make a stinging retort about such an obvious attempt to mislead him, but then he looked at the dates in his notes. Rivera had started working for his brother-in-law in the autumn of 1936, shortly *after* the visits from Arroyo had ceased. And Arroyo, the lieutenant realized, would have been far more of an expert at international finance than a fledgling bookkeeper who had come to it as a second career. But why would Rivera see the need to hide the fact that he had treated

Arroyo as a patient? "What did he require of your medical expertise, then?" he asked, still menacing, but also puzzled.

"He was an analysand."

"A what?" Tejada frowned over the unfamiliar word.

"One who undergoes analysis, Lieutenant." Rivera spoke dryly.

"Analysis of what?" Tejada demanded, thoroughly confused. "You mean blood samples and things like that? Did he have some health problem that he didn't want generally known?"

"Psychoanalysis, Lieutenant," the doctor explained wearily. "It's sometimes called the 'talking cure.' It was pioneered in Vienna, about forty years ago. The theory is basically that a patient can be cured of his neuroses by exposing their unconscious basis."

Tejada frowned, puzzled. "You're saying that Arroyo was crazy?"

"Not necessarily." Old pedagogical instincts were strong in Rivera, despite the situation at hand. It had been a long time since anyone had been interested in the daily subjects of his former life. "Neurosis is frequently partially defined by the patient. That is, if the patient feels that he has a problem, then the problem must be said to exist."

"Arroyo thought he was crazy?" The lieutenant translated uncertainly, after a moment. Behind Rivera, Jiménez rolled his eyes, and tapped one temple expressively.

"Trauma or extreme grief can sometimes trigger neurotic symptoms," Rivera said dryly. "At the time, Arroyo was rather traumatized. He had difficulty sleeping, or so he said. And he claimed to be suicidal."

Tejada was intrigued by the doctor's careful circumlocutions. "You didn't believe him?" he asked.

Rivera hesitated. Behind him, Jiménez raised one hand and then dropped it again, after a hasty gesture from Tejada. "I was not the ideal analyst for Professsor Arroyo," the doctor said finally. "I didn't trust my own judgment in his case."

"Why not?"

"The analyst is supposed to be detached. Preferably an utter stranger. I was not a total stranger, nor was I at all detached from what was happening to Arroyo. I may have been too close to be objective."

Rivera's answer seemed reasonably clear and plausible, but Tejada had the nagging feeling that the doctor was concealing something. He returned to the one definite charge he had against Rivera. "You didn't mention this when questioned earlier."

"I felt that Arroyo's privacy should be protected." There was definitely a false note there.

"You were arrested," Tejada pointed out. "You spent a night in prison; he had been murdered and couldn't be harmed by disclosure, and yet you kept it secret. Don't insult my intelligence, Doctor."

"The relationship between analyst and analysand—"

"Bullshit," Tejada interjected. "You practically admitted earlier that you didn't think anything was the matter with Arroyo." He suddenly heard what he was saying and added, with inspiration, "That was why you didn't say anything, wasn't it? Arroyo wasn't really sick, and you knew it and he knew it. The visits were a cover for something else, weren't they?"

Rivera frowned at the floor. Jiménez lightly touched his shoulder, and the doctor raised his head. "I didn't say anything because I have some pride," he spat, his eyes suddenly tear-filled. "I had nothing in '36, Lieutenant! Nothing! And Arroyo knew it! He invented the illness to give me a patient! Why do you think he was cured as soon as Ramón hired me? I took his charity because I have a family, but I didn't broadcast it to the world! Are you happy?"

Tejada blinked. "That's why you're sure he wasn't really insane?" he hazarded.

"I offered to treat him without pay." Rivera's voice was shaking. "And he refused. Every session, God help me, I told him he was cured. And he always just shook his head and laughed, and said he was nuts. It got to be a joke, the way he refused every week. 'Nonsense, Rivera. I'm crazy.' Every week." The doctor stopped, choking.

"And I'm supposed to believe this?" Tejada asked, not at all sure whether he did believe it.

"I don't expect you to believe it," Rivera said despairingly. "But it's the truth."

"You could have saved yourself a lot of grief if you'd come forward with this earlier."

"I'm sorry, Lieutenant."

Tejada nodded, accepting the apology. "Let's assume you're telling the truth. Who knew that you were in contact with Arroyo?"

Rivera looked puzzled. "Well, he came to my house. So, my wife knew. I didn't mention it to anyone else. I suppose he might have told his family."

Hell, Tejada thought. And that brings us straight back to the Oteros. He decided a direct question might be helpful. "Who would dump his body in a warehouse with ties to your brother-in-law's firm, where you would be likely to find it?"

Rivera shook his head. "I don't know."

"Is there anyone who might think that your contact with Arroyo was more recent than '36?" Tejada demanded. "Anyone who's been out of touch with you for a few years, but who knew about your connection then?"

Rivera hesitated. Then he said quietly, "I don't know. But Arroyo called me again, recently."

Tejada's eyes narrowed. "Oh?"

"I never met with him," the doctor said hastily. "I never saw him, after that last time in '36. But he telephoned me about a month ago, and asked if he could come in again. Someone might have known about the phone call."

"Why would he call you?" Tejada asked. "Do you think he thought you were in financial difficulties again?"

"I don't know." Rivera was puzzled, and glad of the opportunity to consider the question. "It was odd. He said he wanted advice from someone he trusted. And he made the joke about being crazy again, only he said someone else was as well. I wondered if maybe he wanted to talk to me about a friend who was having some sort of breakdown. I set up a meeting, but then he called back a few days later and canceled. I wondered at the time—"

"Wondered what?" Tejada prompted.

"If perhaps he was the one who needed my help after all."

"You mean if he really was nuts?" Tejada asked.

Rivera looked briefly impatient. "I wouldn't use that word, but well, yes. You see, when he was in analysis, he seemed quite sane to me. But that joke about being crazy, and the way he made it was always a little odd. And when he made it again . . ."

"What was the joke?" Tejada asked, interested.

"Well, that was the thing." Rivera was perplexed. "It wasn't really a joke, but he always seemed amused by it. He just always referred to his illness in German. I wondered a bit if it was a way of distancing himself. A defense mechanism, if you want the technical term."

"Isn't most psychoanalytic terminology in German?" Tejada suggested. "Maybe he was just being professional."

Rivera shook his head. "This wasn't jargon. It's a very colloquial phrase, actually. Almost an insult: *Ich habe einen Vogel.*"

"*What?*" Tejada snapped, in a voice that made Jiménez as well as Rivera jump slightly.

"It doesn't really translate," Rivera said apologetically. "I mean, it means more or less, 'I'm nuts' but it doesn't make any sense if you translate it literally."

"The literal translation being?" Tejada prompted.

"Well, it's something like 'I have a . . . a bird,'" the doctor explained, embarrassed.

"The last time he called you," Tejada said, in a slightly

strangled tone of voice, "he said that someone else *hat einen Vogel?* Is that correct?"

"Yes." Rivera looked puzzled. "Exactly. And that he didn't know quite what to do about it."

"He didn't mention who this might be?"

"No."

Tejada thought for a moment. Then he said quietly, "Corporal?"

Jiménez straightened to attention. "Sir?"

"Put Dr. Rivera in one of the cells, and then send word to his wife that he's being held in protective custody. Then tell Sergeant Hernández to meet me in my office." He rose. "If you're lying, Rivera," he said quietly, "I will personally make you sorry that you were ever born. But for the moment I'll take a chance that you're not."

# Chapter 20

The sound of a truck pulling up suddenly in front of her house had the same effect on María de Fernández as the sound of fingernails on a chalkboard. Guillermo was reading to her on Wednesday evening, in an ineffectual attempt to take her mind off of her pain, when the unmistakable screech of brakes recalled her worst nightmares. "What's that?" She interrupted him in the middle of a sentence, unable to pretend successfully that she had been paying attention. "It sounds like a car."

"I'm sure it's nothing." Guillermo raised his eyes from the book and scanned the room: the faded quilt; the half-open closet; the clock; the framed wedding photo on the wall. He memorized each detail hungrily, trying to fix it in his memory for future use, in the interval between the time the motor died and the inevitable knocking on the door.

The doorbell sounded downstairs. María reached for her husband's hand. He squeezed it briefly, and then the sound of the door swinging open filtered up to them. A moment later someone was running up the steps. "Papa? Mama?"

Husband and wife relaxed, and Guillermo laughed, two weights removed from his mind. "In here, Elenita!" he called, heading to the doorway.

"Elena!" María's voice clearly showed how much she wished to get up to meet her daughter.

Elena, who had deposited her bags in the front hallway in a mad rush for the familiar, enthusiastically hugged her father, and then bent over María's bed to embrace her mother.

"Thank God you're safe!" María did not let go of her daughter's hand.

Guillermo kept one hand on his daughter's shoulder and asked a little anxiously, "Are you alone?"

"No." Elena shook her head. "Or, well, yes, at the moment. But Theoklymenos is at the station."

"He made it across the border!" María smiled, pleased for her husband, for the refugee, and for the kind fate that had safely returned her child.

Elena looked suddenly grim. "Yes, we crossed last night." To forestall further questions she said hastily, "It was his idea. He thought, since you're under surveillance, that it wouldn't be a good idea to be seen arriving at your house."

"Given that I'm under surveillance, how is he supposed to avoid that?" Guillermo asked, appreciative of his colleague's logic, but annoyed that he could see no way to solve the problem.

"He said that if *you* were the one under surveillance, all you would have to do was go out. That way, whoever's following you won't be watching the house." Elena was careful to keep her voice expressionless. Professor Meyer's exact words had been, "*Your guardias seem very efficient. Let us hope your lieutenant gives them orders to follow only your father.*" "I gave him directions, and he can make it from the station alone," she added.

Guillermo nodded and stood. "We're out of aspirin," he said simply. "I'll go and see if there's any at the pharmacy." He turned to his wife. "You'll be all right?"

"Yes." María smiled at him, at peace with the world in spite of her pain.

Professor Fernández hurried out, anxious to draw attention away from his home, and wildly relieved that his daughter had returned, her mission apparently accomplished. After the door had closed behind him, María said to her daughter, "Have you eaten? There's bread still, from the morning."

"Sounds great." Elena hurried to the kitchen, eager to avoid further questions from her mother.

She was still downstairs when someone rang the front doorbell. Meyer was standing on the threshold, looking nervous. He relaxed considerably when Elena opened the door and smiled at her. "Your directions were admirable. And I did not see any policemen."

"Papa went out about twenty minutes ago," Elena explained.

"And your mother still cannot leave her room, no?" the professor asked gently. "You will please give her my thanks. And my apologies, for intruding on her house."

Elena nodded and hastily went back to her mother to report the professor's safe arrival. María thanked her daughter, and then added, "I thought he could have Hipólito's old room while he's here. It's not aired out, but I wouldn't open the windows anyway. We don't want to announce that he's here. Can you make up the bed?"

"Of course." Elena nodded and returned to their guest.

The professor humbly accepted the news that he was to sleep in a shuttered and airless room where the temperature probably was well over eighty degrees. "I'm sure I'll be very comfortable," he lied politely.

Elena's mouth twisted bitterly. "Better than last night, anyway."

Professor Meyer was unable to ignore her tone. He patted her shoulder. "Don't worry, Helena," he said comfortingly. "He's a good man. And a clever man."

To Elena's relief, the sound of the front door put an end to the discussion. Guillermo Fernández found them in the kitchen. "*Wilkömmen, Herr Professor.*" He held out his hand to his colleague.

Meyer rose to take it. "*Merci.*" To Elena's surprise, the words were in French. "There is no need to speak German."

Guillermo was mildly surprised also, but he contented himself with saying, "As you wish. You've eaten already?"

"Yes," the refugee replied, although he had in fact eaten very little. The lieutenant's comment about ration cards had reminded him of what he already knew; the Fernández family risked hunger as well as prison to shelter him. With that thought still uppermost in his mind he added, "I must thank you Professor Fernández. I did not think past getting out of France. But Helena tells me that you have made plans already?"

Guillermo nodded and sat down. "Yes, my son sent a wire yesterday."

"Saying what?" Elena interjected with interest.

Her father frowned slightly. "He sent us eight hundred pesetas, and said 'See letter for explanation.'"

"What letter?" Elena demanded.

"It hasn't arrived yet." Guillermo looked a little grim. "I assume it's something to do with Professor Meyer's passage. But I don't know when it was sent. And given the post office . . ."

"What a stupid thing to do," Elena snapped.

"Telegrams are neither cheap nor discreet," her father reminded her. He turned back to their guest. "For now, I'm afraid the best thing to do is to lie low. If you don't leave the house . . ."

"Understood." Meyer pushed himself to his feet. "For now, I think that I will go to bed. The last few days have been tiring." He smiled. "And no doubt you wish to speak with Helena."

Elena shot to her feet as well. "The bed needs to be made. I'll go and you can follow me. We never use that part of the house, so it would be suspicious to have a light there, and I know my way in the dark."

Elena made her way to her brother's old room by running one finger along the wall and found her brother's bed by hitting her shins against it. She shook out fresh sheets, reflecting as she did so that she was placing them over a mattress undusted for years. She left Professor Meyer in the stifling darkness, and made her way back to her own room by feel. She opened her own windows, and undressed without bothering to put on a light. She was already in bed when a glow under the door announced that someone had turned on the hallway light, and there was a gentle tap on the door. "Yes?" She did her best to yawn as she spoke.

"Elena?" The door opened, and her father appeared, silhouetted against the hallway light. "Are you going to bed now also?"

"Yes. I'm tired and it's been an exhausting few days." Elena hoped that she sounded too tired to continue the conversation.

"All right," Guillermo was hesitant. "I suppose we can talk tomorrow. I'm glad you're back safe, Elenita."

Elena fought back tears. "Thanks, Papa. Me, too."

"Good night, *niña*. I love you."

"I love you too." Guillermo shut the door, and Elena buried her face in her pillow. *Niña!* she thought despairingly. Oh, my God! I can't tell them. Papa will be disappointed in me. And Mama will feel sorry for me, which is worse. And I have to tell them something about how we managed to cross the border, and they don't know anything about Carlos, so they won't understand how I could have thought . . . but he won't say anything. Well, he can't, because of how he's involved, but he wouldn't anyway. At least, I don't think he would. Although she was tired, she tossed and turned for a long time, telling herself firmly that she did *not* miss the comforting presence of a lying, sneaking, hypocritical guardia civil.

Her insomnia was unexpectedly helpful. She woke late and when she finally made her way to the living room she found her father and Meyer with their heads together over a letter. "Oh, good, you're up." Guillermo greeted her. "Come and see what you think of this."

Elena took the piece of paper he held out to her. It was an aerogram, plastered with Mexican stamps, with the words *por avión* printed in one corner. She frowned at her brother's miniscule handwriting. The letter was rambling and affectionate, full of commonplaces about Hipólito's job and apartment, and many

things that he had already related. Elena read through an enthu-
siastic praise of the Mexican climate and temperament with
increasing impatience, and then her eyes narrowed. "*I've told you
before, and I'll tell you again,*" her brother had written. "*I wish you'd
join me here. There's no rationing, no war, and professors are respected
here. The Mexican authorities welcome refugees, and honestly it's not so
hard to book a passage. Take the SS* Rosas, *for example. She's an
Argentine vessel, and she must make twenty transatlantic trips a year.
This month alone she left Buenos Aires on the 2nd, stopped at Río
de Janeiro on the 4th, Veracruz on the 7th, and Havana on the 9th.
Then she headed for the Azores. She'll dock at La Coruña on the 17th,
head down to Lisbon, and then reverse her stops. (La Coruña again on
the 22nd, then the Azores, Cuba, Mexico, etc.) I happen to know her
schedule because a friend of mine (João, I don't know if I've mentioned
him) was talking about heading back to Lisbon. There must be a hundred ships like the* Rosas, *and any one of them could bring you, if you
could get permission to come. I think Mama and Elena would like it here,
too, and the money shouldn't be a problem now.*" The letter trailed off
into commonplaces again and Elena looked up. "The SS *Rosas,*"
she said.

Her father nodded. "At La Coruña, on Wednesday," he agreed.

"And the wire was money for the passage?" Elena hazarded.

Meyer looked troubled. "But there is still the question of
papers. I cannot pass customs."

"Hipólito seems to think that entering Mexico won't be a
problem." Guillermo's voice was reassuring. His expression was
neither as anxious as Meyer's nor as haggard as his daughter's.
It was the expression of a man facing an interesting challenge.
"At least, I assume that's what 'the authorities welcome refugees' means. So it's just a question of leaving Spain."

"*Just* a question of leaving Spain?" Elena repeated with some
sarcasm.

"With due respect, Dr. Fernández, your son may not be aware
that Jewish refugees are frequently regarded in a special category," Meyer said hesitantly at the same moment.

Guillermo shrugged aside the objections. "Hipólito knows who he's dealing with. And as to leaving Spain, do you think they'll care if you entered legally, as long as you're leaving? You entered in a large group, there was a lot of confusion, your passport never got stamped."

Joseph Meyer regarded his colleague with incredulity. "My passport never got stamped?" he repeated. "You think I should give them my passport? You must be joking."

"I don't see why not," Guillermo argued. "False papers are dangerous. And expensive. And I don't know where to get them."

"They'll want to know that the Mexicans will take him though," Elena commented. "They might turn a blind eye to his lack of an exit visa, but he'll need guaranteed entry."

"These came with the letter." Guillermo held up a series of folded papers, looking a little grim.

Elena took one and unfolded it. It was heavy card stock, unlike the thin paper of Hipólito's letter, and the stationery had an embossed seal. In a few formal phrases, the letter conveyed the Mexican government's willingness to accept Elena as a permanent refugee. She frowned. "I don't understand."

"Hipólito's provided *us* with papers for leaving Spain," her father said, a little grimly. "Or, to put it another way, he's given us three shots at altering an official document."

Elena inspected the visa Hipólito had sent more closely. It was printed, but her own name had been typed onto a blank line: "*Give permanent shelter and protection to Elena Fernández Ríos.*" She raised her eyebrows. "You think we can convincingly alter this?"

"Your father tells me he has a typewriter," Professor Meyer spoke. "Unfortunately, the capital letters do not fall in the right places."

"It's cream-colored paper," Elena pointed out, testing the visa between her fingers. "It will be hard to blank things out."

"We were about to go into the study to try." Her father spoke briskly. "Would you like to come and help?"

Elena shrugged. "All right. If Mama doesn't need me to do anything."

Since Professor Fernández had only one typewriter, it was impossible for more than one person to work at the forgery at a time. Joseph Meyer thoughtfully suggested that his colleague type a series of test copies, using the names Guillermo, María, and Elena Fernández, and then attempt to alter the test copies before moving on to the actual documents. Guillermo agreed, with a laughing comment about German logic which made the refugee wince slightly. He tapped away for a few minutes, and then presented the results to his daughter and colleague. "All right, how much of this should be altered by the machine, and how much do you think calligraphy will fix?"

Elena considered the regular black letters. "It's probably better to work on mine or Mama's. We both have a long vertical in the first letter that could be changed to a J pretty easily. And your name is too long anyway. It looks like the "a" in Mama's name could become an "o" without too much trouble . . . but then you have to turn "r" into "s" and I'm not sure how that would work. And then there are so many extra letters."

"The trouble is really the capitals, then," Guillermo agreed. "And what to do with the extra letters on the surname of course, although I suppose that could just be crossed out."

After some more debate, Elena settled down with a list of neatly typed *Elena Fernández*'s and a pen, and did her best to alter her name. Meyer took a list of *María Pilar Ríos de Fernández*'s and did the same. Guillermo tapped away at the typewriter, providing more sample copies. All of the inexpert forgers quickly hit setbacks, but Professor Meyer was inspired after about half an hour's work. "Try spelling my name with an 'f' instead of a 'ph' at the end, so the capitals coincide," he suggested.

"Is that the name on your passport?" Guillermo demanded.

Meyer shrugged. "Surely the Mexican embassy can make a mistake? And you use 'f' for the Greek letter $\phi$ in Spanish, do you not?"

"Yes." Guillermo nodded. "All right, try it that way."

Unfortunately, the best efforts of all three were unable to alter an "F" or "P" to an "M" without causing visible changes. "You'll have to say it's a typo," Elena commented finally, in despair. "Because they aren't used to foreign names."

"Yes," Meyer frowned. "But . . . I do not know . . . Helenka, do you type?"

"Me? You mean, really type? Like a stenographer? No," Elena shook her head, regretful.

"I do not either." Meyer sighed. "But I believe there are more common errors, for someone who types. If we could make the changes look like those common errors perhaps. . . ."

This set in motion a spirited debate about what might be considered a "common" error, which ended with Elena, her father, and the professor intently inspecting the typewriter, and all three of them miming the motions of an expert typist, to see which keys might well be interchanged frequently. They were in the midst of this debate when the clock struck two, and Guillermo started up. "My God, it's Friday. I'd almost forgotten. It would be just brilliant to be late today of all days, wouldn't it. Elenita, would you like a walk?"

For a moment Elena did not know what her father was talking about. Then she realized, with horror, that he was inviting her to go with him to report for parole. She shook her head, mute, and then forced herself to add, "I'll stay here, and try to work on this more. And . . . and Mama shouldn't be left."

"All right." Guillermo kissed his daughter and hurried toward the hallway, pausing only to grab his hat and say to his guest, "I have to report to the Guardia Civil every Friday. A formality, generally, but they've been very picky about it lately. I should be back soon." Guillermo was out of the door before Meyer had found the words to express his surprise that Elena did not wish to accompany her father, or to ask Guillermo to thank the lieutenant.

Elena took her father's seat at the typewriter and returned to her experiments. Professor Meyer considered her silently for a few moments, but finally decided to say nothing. How she conducted her affairs was no business of his.

Elena was grateful for Professor Meyer's tact. She had forgotten that her father would have to encounter Tejada. He doesn't have to say anything about Meyer, she thought, with sudden fear. He doesn't have to reveal that he knows me at all. He can arrest Papa for murder, or subversion, or whatever he pleases . . . but he won't. Or he wouldn't have if I hadn't said that to him. Her determination to shut out what might be happening to her father at the Guardia Civil post made her focus more intently on her work, and actually spurred her to produce a very creditable sample forgery by the time Guillermo returned an hour later.

The professor was in good spirits. "Very quick again," he reported cheerfully. "Mostly a formality. With any luck they'll drop it altogether soon." He inspected his daughter's work. "That's good, Elenita. Do you think you could do it with the real thing?"

Elena frowned. "I don't know. I'd like to practice a little more. And then there's the question of matching the ink, and how to blank things out on this color paper. Maybe we should practice with your visa first, so we get a feel for working with it."

Both Guillermo and Professor Meyer made a few more attempts at altering names, and then decided that Elena's attempt was not going to be bettered. After a practice run with Guillermo's visa (in which it was discovered that the "F" on the Mexican typewriter that had typed the visas was slanted slightly differently from the "F" on Guillermo's machine), the professor carefully slid Elena's visa into the typewriter and began to make the necessary corrections. Another tense half hour with a pen, and the final product was done.

"There!" Guillermo looked at his work, and found it good.

"Do you think they'll examine it closely?" Josef Meyer, possessor of an entry visa for Mexico, looked more dubious.

"The seal and everything is genuine," Elena reminded him comfortingly. "And so's your passport."

Meyer snorted briefly. "No one would want to forge one of those passports now. They're not worth the paper they're written on."

"The next question is how to get you to La Coruña." Guillermo was brisk.

"Is it far?" the refugee asked, apprehensive.

His host shrugged. "Another train ride. The question is how to get you tickets. *I* can't buy them, because I'm not allowed to leave Salamanca. And Elena's just returned."

"Perhaps you can draw off the surveillance again, as you did when I arrived," Meyer suggested.

After further discussion, the Fernández agreed to Professor Meyer's plan. Guillermo suggested that for him to leave the house again the same day would be suspicious. Elena quietly agreed to go to buy the ticket on Saturday, thankful that the day's preparations had kept her father too busy to ask her about how she had crossed the border. She volunteered to go and report the progress that had been made to her mother, hopeful that she would be spared the necessity of mentioning Lieutenant Tejada for another evening.

Her hope was misplaced. María took an eager interest in the preparations for Meyer's departure but she had (from her daughter's point of view) a depressingly good memory. When Elena had finished the story of the altered visa and explained her intention to go to the station the next day, María said, "That's a good idea. But the professor must be very resourceful. How did he make it to San Sebastián? Do you know, Elenita?"

Faced with a direct question, Elena was silent for a moment. She was tempted to lie, and say that she had no idea how Professor Meyer had crossed the border; he had not confided the details to her. But she was not in the habit of lying to her parents. She took a deep breath. "I met him in France," she said.

"You crossed the border? But how? Why did you take such a risk?" Her mother was concerned.

Elena was somewhat steadied by the telling of her trip to France, and her first encounter with Meyer. "So we agreed to rest in a hotel lounge until nightfall," she finished, feeling her mouth go dry.

"And you crossed on foot? My God, Elena, you poor thing! The professor must be quite a mountaineer."

Once again, Elena was tempted to let silence stand as the reply. But her childhood habit of total honesty was strong. "No," she said reluctantly. "As it happened we were found. By . . . by Lieutenant Tejada."

"Lieutenant who?" María asked, frowning both at the title and her daughter's tone of voice.

"The officer Papa reports to," Elena amplified, eyes fixed on the quilt. "Who gave us permission to travel. He said he was in Biarritz on other business."

María gasped. "The Guardia found you? But you got away? How? Why didn't you tell us earlier?"

Elena twisted her hands in her lap. "He drove us across the border," she explained unwillingly, wishing that she had simply let her mother think that she and Meyer had crossed the border on foot. "He . . ." she paused as it occurred to her that even if she had not wished to conceal details of her meeting from her parents, she could not think of a plausible motive for Tejada's help. A memory of his stubborn chauvinism came to her aid. "He said he wouldn't hand a Spaniard over to foreign authorities. And he didn't care what we'd done, so long as we weren't Communists." She swallowed remembering Meyer's last words to the lieutenant. "He's a good man . . . for one of them."

"Why didn't you tell us earlier?" María repeated, stunned.

"I didn't want to worry you. You know how Papa is about the Guardia."

María was quite sure that her daughter had not offered a full explanation, but years of war and surveillance had taught the professor's wife that the absurdly irrational and wildly implausible were sometimes a daily fact of life. María did not think her daughter was lying. Talking about her encounter with the Guardia Civil clearly made her miserable, but there were many possible reasons for that. María decided that forcing her daughter's confidence would be unwise. I'll talk to Guillermo this evening, she thought. And see what Elena's told him about all this. And give her a chance to recover from the whole business. "Thank God I didn't know about this at the time," she said aloud, forcing a smile.

"That was what I thought." Elena's smile became more natural as her mother dropped the subject.

To her relief, her parents seemed willing to let sleeping dogs lie. The next few days were tense enough anyway. There were no direct trains to La Coruña, and Elena had been forced to purchase a ticket with a connection in Madrid. Professor Meyer, who spent much of the time pacing the hallway and itching to go outside, accepted the news that he was to leave on Tuesday morning and arrive at La Coruña the following dawn with fatalistic calm. Elena devoted herself to giving the professor intensive Spanish lessons, and doing her best to recall the layout of the Madrid station, so that he would not need to ask for directions when he changed trains. Guillermo, who had pointed out that traveling such a long distance without luggage would probably attract comment, packed a small suitcase for his guest over Professor Meyer's embarrassed objections. The suitcase was far from full. It contained only an extra suit, a small toilet bag, and a few volumes of Homer. "So you'll have something to read on the boat," Guillermo insisted. "I have extra copies anyway."

Elena and Guillermo said their final good-byes to Professor Meyer early Tuesday morning. They had agreed to leave together, well before him, so that any surveillance would be drawn away from the house. "Good luck," Guillermo said quietly, shaking hands with his colleague. He smiled a little. "I hope we meet again."

"Next year in Mexico, perhaps," the Jew agreed. He turned to Elena. "Thank you for all of your help, Helenka."

"It was nothing."

Father and daughter left the house and wandered down to the market, patiently standing in line for bread, glad that they had an excuse to spend so much time away from their home. They returned a little after ten. The house was empty, except for María. "He left around nine-thirty," the professor's wife reported.

Guillermo looked at his watch. "His train's in less than an hour."

"If all goes well, we won't hear anything for at least a month," Elena reminded her father. "Until Hipólito writes."

"If all goes well," María agreed.

# Chapter 21

"We probably won't hear anything for at least a month," Hernández said gloomily.

The lieutenant grimaced. "You're an optimist, Sergeant. We probably won't hear anything at all. The Swiss haven't gotten rich by releasing information."

The two men were sitting in Tejada's office, ostensibly filling out requisitions for ration cards, but actually worrying away at the Arroyo case. Captain Rodríguez, who had thoroughly approved Tejada's decision to arrest Tomás Rivera, had been indignant when he discovered that the lieutenant had not charged him with murder. "You've had the man for three days, Tejada!" he had snapped the previous evening. "That's long enough to get a confession."

"I'm not sure if he murdered Professor Arroyo, sir," Tejada explained.

"Then why are you holding him?" the captain demanded.

"Protective custody, sir," Tejada replied. "He may well have information about Arroyo's murderer and we may need him as a witness. I don't want him to turn up dead also."

Not surprisingly, the captain had seized on Tejada's last statement as proof that the lieutenant did in fact know who had killed Arroyo, and demanded that the felon be arrested immediately. Tejada had attempted to explain that while Rivera's evidence provided a clear motive, the doctor had not mentioned a specific person, but the captain had been unwilling to listen to him. "I want an arrest by the end of the week, Lieutenant," he'd snapped at the end of an increasingly tense interview. "Or I'll move ahead with charges against Rivera." Tejada had saluted stiffly and marched out, wishing that the post had a firing range so that he could relieve his feelings.

Now, in spite of Hernández's sympathy, the lieutenant was depressed. He had written to the address listed for Adolf Vogel in Arroyo's address book, politely requesting information about more recent clients from Salamanca, probably referred by the professor. But he knew that the threat of the Guardia Civil would be blunted in Zurich. Even Spanish banks were reluctant to release information to the Guardia. The Swiss, with nothing to lose, were not even likely to bother with a flat refusal.

"Do you think it would have been better to find out what bank this Vogel worked for, and then written to them?" Hernández asked.

Tejada shrugged. "I was in a hurry. And I thought that a man might be easier to deal with than an institution."

The sergeant nodded. "Looks like Rivera's in for it then," he commented.

The lieutenant sighed. "We've done all we can." He spoke as much to himself as to Hernández.

"I know it," Hernández agreed. He made a dismissive gesture. "At least it's one less file to keep track of."

Tejada made an affirmative noise, and returned to the memo he had been drafting. For a little while the only sounds in the office were the sharp clatter of typewriter keys and the scratchings of Hernández's pen. Tejada finished typing and pulled the sheet from the machine. "Anything happening with the other petitioners?" he asked abruptly.

"Nope." To his relief, Sergeant Hernández seemed uninterested. "We might think about dropping surveillance on them as well soon. There are only the two of them left, after all, and they're not likely to get into much mischief."

"Something to think about," Tejada agreed, and dropped the subject, relieved that the idea had come from Hernández and not from him.

The lieutenant spent the next few days taking care of paperwork. He had more than enough to do and managed to think very little about Manuel Arroyo and his murderer. His faint twinges of conscience grew slightly stronger as the end of the week approached. Captain Rodríguez would probably bring formal charges against Tomás Rivera on Monday. I've done all I can, he reminded himself. Rivera's a Red, even if he didn't kill Arroyo. Most men wouldn't have gone to so much trouble. And it's not as if I have nothing else to do. The necessity of keeping the interview appointments of all the other parolees on Thursday and Friday was a relief. They made it impossible for Tejada to worry about anything else.

Sergeant Hernández had neatly rescheduled the appointments so that there was no longer a hole where Manuel Arroyo's had been. Tejada had succeeded in pushing almost every thought of the petitioners out of his mind by Friday afternoon when Guillermo Fernández showed up for his appointment.

Tejada nodded at the professor and asked a few desultory questions. Fernández was alone. The preceding week the lieutenant had feared that Elena might once more accompany her father to the post, and had reproached himself for his idiocy in fearing such a thing as soon as Guillermo had entered his office unaccompanied. Of course Elena would do anything to avoid him now. Tejada, who had carefully read the reports of the Fernández surveillance for the previous week, and noted with infinite relief that none of them contained any reference to a mysterious guest, hurried through his interview with the professor, anxious to get Fernández out of his sight.

The lieutenant was too preoccupied to notice that his

parolee was nervous. It was not until Tejada issued a curt dismissal that he realized that Guillermo Fernández seemed to have something on his mind. Instead of scuttling for the door, the professor coughed, turned his hat in his hands, and hesitated slightly. "Lieutenant?"

Tejada, who had returned his attention to the folder on his desk, forced himself to meet Professor Fernández's eyes. "Yes? Was there something else?"

"I wanted to thank you." Fernández sounded embarrassed. "I understand my daughter's trip north wouldn't have been possible without your help."

Tejada tensed, as a series of wild speculations raced across his brain at lightning speed. Elena must have told them something about crossing the border, he reminded himself, deliberately trying to unclench the muscles in his neck. That's all he means. He was proud of how steady his voice was as he said, "A permission to travel was the least I could do. I hope Señorita Fernández enjoyed her vacation."

The professor nodded, and Tejada reflected that he had never seen the older man smile before. "My wife and I are of course glad that she *returned* safely," Fernández said.

Tejada nodded. "There's really no need to thank me." His voice was held steady by the bitter knowledge that the professor almost certainly would have had a great deal more to say had he known the full circumstances of Elena's encounter with him in France.

"I wanted you to know that your kindness was noted." Professor Fernández spoke with a kind of gentle dignity. "I hope Elena thanked you as well," he added.

"She was very gracious." Tejada's voice was slightly strangled, but the professor seemed relieved by his reply.

"I'm glad," he said simply. "She normally remembers her manners, but she can be temperamental sometimes. Like her mother."

"I didn't notice that," Tejada managed. *I don't deserve this*, he thought.

The professor looked slightly amused. "If you'll forgive my say-ing so, Lieutenant, when you marry, you will find that *all* women can be temperamental. I wouldn't have said my wife was, when I first met her. And then, before our son was born sometimes I won-dered what had happened to the woman I'd married. When she was carrying Elena, too, although at least by that time I was pre-pared." Professor Fernández was startled out of his reminiscences by the look on Tejada's face. "Are you all right, Lieutenant?"

"Fine, thanks," Tejada lied automatically. "Professor . . . I need to meet with your daughter."

The parolee drew back slightly, looking anxious. "She's not under suspicion of anything, is she?"

"No!" Tejada took a deep breath, and made sure that his voice was steady enough not to betray him before continuing. "No. I . . . I have . . . a question—some questions, for her. But there's no need for her to come to the post. If I could meet with her briefly at your home . . . this evening perhaps? I would be . . . very grateful."

"We will be at home." The professor spoke with gentle irony. "And I take it that you know the address."

"Yes," Tejada nodded, unhappily. "Until this evening, then."

Tejada saw the rest of the parolees in a daze, and responded absentmindedly to Hernández's questions about patrol routes for the following week. He began clearing his desk a few minutes before eight o'clock. He was locking the office door before the church bells in the square had finished tolling the hour. Corporal Méndez hailed him as he left his room a few minutes later. "Sir! I'm glad I've found you. Estrada and Gómez are scheduled for patrol in the north sector, but Estrada's due for leave and he says that if they do the north route he won't get back until—"

"Talk to Hernández," Tejada interrupted. "I'm off duty."

"I couldn't find him, sir. And the schedule—"

"Can wait until tomorrow," the lieutenant finished without breaking stride. "I'm busy."

It was still hot, and rays of the afternoon sun hung in the dusty streets, nearly as palpable as the folds of a shawl. Tejada paced through the warmth aware only of a cold knot in his stomach. Elena could not be pregnant. Or, more accurately, she could be but it had never occurred to him that she might be because . . . because it had never occurred to him. But if she was, regardless of how she felt about him, he had to see her. Her contemptuous words echoed in his ears. "*I imagine rubbing my parents' nose in it will be your favorite part.*" Tejada winced. He emphatically did *not* want to explain his relationship with Elena to the anxious, grateful, gentlemanly Professor Fernández. But the professor was owed some explanation. The walk to the Fernández's house was both too long and too short.

Somewhat to the lieutenant's surprise, Guillermo Fernández himself opened the door to his home. "My wife is bedridden, due to an injury," he explained, in answer to the lieutenant's raised eyebrows. "And we have no servants." Then, seeing that Tejada seemed disinclined to respond, Guillermo added, "I believe Elena is upstairs. The second door on the right."

"Thank you." For the first time, Tejada blessed the professor's liberal opinions. He had not been able to think of a way of tactfully asking to speak to Elena without the presence of a chaperone and he was grateful that he would not be required to do so. Still, when he knocked on the door the professor had indicated and pushed it open, he was surprised to realize that he was standing on the threshold of Elena's bedroom.

She was curled up on a window seat at the far edge of the room, her hands clasping her knees, her forehead resting against the panes of glass. She would have looked like a child if it were not for the waves of hair piled loosely on her head. She did not turn her head as the door opened. "Go away." Her voice was weary.

Tejada cleared his throat, embarrassed. "Your father said I'd find you here. I'm sorry to intrude."

Elena whirled around at the sound of his voice and was on her feet more quickly than he would have believed possible. "What are *you* doing here?"

Tejada had taken a few steps towards the window seat as he spoke. Now he hastily retreated to the doorway. "I had to see you."

"This is my *room*." Elena spoke indignantly and then turned crimson as she realized that she could hardly expect the lieutenant to be as awed by this fact as most men.

"I . . . I'm sorry to intrude," Tejada repeated, flushing also. The setting had already made him uncomfortable without Elena's reminder. The room had clearly belonged to her as a child. The row of girl's novels on the top bookshelf, the slightly dusty dollhouse in one corner, and the garishly painted jewelry box below the mirror on the dresser were things no man should ever see. He was out of place here, a toy soldier carelessly dropped among a little girl's treasured possessions. His gaze slid over to the narrow bed in one corner, and hastily looked away; a brown-eyed doll resting against the headboard seemed to be staring at him reproachfully.

"What do you want?" Elena's first wave of surprise and anger was over. Her voice was quiet, but it trembled a little. She was standing still and straight, with her hands at her sides.

"I wanted to be sure that you were all right." Tejada spoke hoarsely.

"I'm fine." She hardly opened her lips.

"Oh. Good." The lieutenant hardly knew what he was saying. "Also . . . I wanted . . . to ask . . ." He took a deep breath, prepared to ask her about the suspicion that Guillermo Fernández had innocently raised, and found himself saying incoherently, "What you said that night in Biarritz . . . Was it because of Meyer? Because you thought that I would . . . if you didn't . . ."

Elena felt her lips trembling. "Yes," she whispered, determined not to let him see her cry. To her surprise, she felt no satisfaction at the lie, although she had obviously succeeded in hurting him. Hurting his *amour propre*, at any rate, she thought, desperately searching for spitefulness.

"I'm sorry." Tejada's voice was shaking. "I didn't know. I . . . forgive me."

Elena shrugged, wishing that she could simply believe him and walk into his arms and cry. "It doesn't really matter."

"It matters if you're with child," Tejada retorted, too shocked to properly formulate his opinion that a woman's virginity was of moral as well as practical importance.

Elena went white. "I'm not pregnant!" She retreated a step, wondering if his uncanny ability to put her worst fears into words was a trick learned as an interrogator, or if he was particularly attuned to her preoccupations. To add weight to her denial she added forcefully, "And even if I were, why should you care?"

Tejada was suddenly sick of negotiating the minefield of Elena's perplexing values. "Because I'd like my child to bear my name!" he snapped. "*And* my child's mother. That's what any normal, decent man would want, and what *you* would want, if you weren't so hell-bent on proving that you're as warped as any Red whore!"

"And why didn't your daughter's mother get this handsome offer?" Elena blazed. "Was she too poor to have any decency? Or did she turn you down?"

"My what?" Tejada said, taken aback.

"Your 'little protege's' mother. The one you foisted onto your brother." Despite her best efforts, Elena heard her voice crack treacherously. The lieutenant stared at her, open mouthed, and she swept on, before her wave of righteous anger could abate and leave her stranded. "His letter fell out of your coat. He seems very tolerant about raising your bastard."

Automatically, the lieutenant's hand went to his coat pocket and drew out the crumpled letter. He looked from it to Elena's face several times, his lips working silently. Then he said quietly, "My brother likes to imagine scandal. The child's a war orphan."

"All war orphans are cared for by the state!" Elena cried.

"Not Aleja Palomino!" the lieutenant said shortly, his eyes on the letter.

It took a moment for Elena to place the name. Then she said slowly, "Aleja Palomino? My student, Aleja?"

"Probably none of your students receive government pensions," Tejada muttered, still avoiding her eyes.

"No," Elena agreed softly, yearning to believe that he was telling the truth. "But why?"

Tejada's fingers tightened into a fist. "I'd rather not say."

"Why?" Elena's eyes narrowed. "Was her mother—?"

"No," the lieutenant interrupted hastily. "Elena, look, I've never . . . I've done things that would probably make you hate me, but I swear to you none of them involved women. I mean not *because* they were women. I'd rather not explain about Aleja because . . . it's not a story I'm proud of . . . and not all of it is completely mine to tell. . . ." He glanced up, saw her face, and added hastily. "But I *will* tell you, if you ask. Because I won't lie to you. Isn't that worth anything?"

Elena took a deep breath. Then she retreated to the window seat and sat down. "Tell me," she said quietly, gesturing for him to be seated in a rocking chair facing the window, and then folding her hands in her lap.

Tejada perched himself on the edge of the rocking chair, and gazed downward. Without raising his eyes he began to explain why he had made provision for Aleja and her mother, and why he had made himself responsible for the daughter and widow of one of the men who had fought against him. Halfway through his recital, he slid out of the chair to grasp her folded hands. She did not move. She remained still when he had finished speaking. Finally, desperate, he looked up. "You do believe me?"

"Yes." She sounded slightly dazed. "And I'm glad Aleja's not your daughter."

He swallowed. "Elena, I'm so sorry."

She stood, dislodging his hands, and he scrambled to his feet, feeling foolish. When she spoke he realized that she was crying. "I'm not a priest to grant absolution. But thank you for telling me the truth."

"I love you." He knew the words were inadequate.

Elena turned away from him and bent her head. "I love you too," she admitted softly, reflecting wearily that in another time and place he might have been a good man, and wondering if she was really grateful for his honesty.

Tejada lightly put his hands on her shoulders. "Then marry me," he said quietly.

Elena shuddered. She wanted to turn around and be kissed and comforted and reassured that fear and hunger would never touch her again. But faces she had known during the war appeared like ghosts, and held her still: the children killed by bombs; the young men, barely more than children, who had frozen and died at the Front; or been starved and shot as prisoners. She folded her arms across her stomach. "I can't."

His hands slid down her shoulders, and over hers. "Why not?" His voice was gentle. "Is it because I support General Franco's government?"

She nodded, not trusting herself to speak. Tejada sighed. "Elena, love, the war's over. It's not that I . . ." He paused, trying to formulate his thoughts carefully. "It's not that I don't care that you were a . . . a Socialist, but there can't be two Spains forever, Elena. We're compatriots, after all. We can't go on holding ourselves separate."

"It's not that," Elena protested faintly, aware that she should be trying to break free.

"Suppose you were with child," the lieutenant said softly. "That child would have a new history, no? A history without war. He could be a new beginning. But you wouldn't want him to cut off half his heritage, would you?"

Elena finally turned around. "No. But you would."

"No," Tejada protested.

"Yes, you would." Elena sighed. "And your child would have to. To survive." She choked slightly. "*You* may believe that, about how there can't be two Spains, but other people don't. And you couldn't marry me, Carlos. For your own good."

"What do you mean?" He frowned.

She smiled sadly, touched by his naïveté. "It would be the end of your career. You'd lose your friends, your colleagues—"

"Nonsense," he interrupted, although her words shook him a little.

"You'd be a security risk." Elena saw that she had given him pause and unthinkingly touched his cheek to comfort him. "Everyone would know that you'd married a Red."

"My private life is no business of the Guardia's," Tejada protested vehemently, tightening his arms around her.

"And my father's is?"

"That's different."

"Yes," Elena agreed. "Because my father's life really *isn't* political. But yours is. And you'd never be able to trust me, you know. You might avoid talking about your work with me, but sooner or later you'd take something home to work on, or leave something in your coat pocket like that letter of your brother's."

"Don't be silly." Tejada absentmindedly kissed her palm, and Elena smiled at him.

"I've seen your desk, darling. You leave papers out all the time."

Tejada stiffened suddenly. "That's true," he said in a subdued tone of voice.

Elena, who had unconsciously been leaning against him, suddenly felt as if a large bucket of ice water had been thrown at her. But she straightened her shoulders and pressed her advantage. "You might remember to be careful for a while, but not for the rest of your life," she persisted. "And what do you think I would do if it was something about my father? Or Dr. Velázquez?"

"Yes." Tejada dropped his arms. His voice was distant. "That's it, then."

Elena swallowed. She tried a watery smile, which was a miserable failure. "At the very best, it would end any chance of promotion," she finished, wishing that she felt more triumphant.

Tejada blinked, and then, to her astonishment, smiled brilliantly, seized her shoulders and kissed her. "Promotion be damned," he said when he let her go. "This is the second time you've helped me solve a murder and I'd be an idiot not to discuss my work with you whenever the opportunity presented itself. Here, take a look at this." He dug out his notebook, flipped it open to his notes on the Arroyo case, and handed it to her.

Elena stared at him, too bewildered to speak. "Because I trust you," the lieutenant said, smiling at her. "Read that. And that part there." He pointed.

Elena blinked, sat down, and automatically began to read. "So?" she asked, puzzled. The lieutenant squeezed himself onto the window seat beside her, and indicated several more passages. Then he gave her a few more pieces of information. Elena frowned, and then advanced a hypothesis.

Tejada nodded. "It makes sense, doesn't it?" he asked.

"The only thing that doesn't fit are the dates," she pointed out.

"I know." Tejada sighed. "That was what made me think that Arroyo had disappeared in the first place. Because he was so scrupulous about all his other parole dates."

"We all are," Elena pointed out dryly. "No one wants the Guardia knocking on the door at three in the morning."

Tejada laughed briefly and then suddenly seized her hand. "Elena! Did your father miss any of his parole dates?"

"Of course not!" She stared at him, surprised.

"That's it then," Tejada said quietly. "Your father's last appointment with Captain Rodríguez wasn't checked off. I assumed that it was just the captain's carelessness. But Rodríguez must have checked off the wrong folder—Arroyo's. He probably never got the petitioners straight. Damn idiot."

Elena laughed. "Tactful way to talk about a superior officer!"

The lieutenant grinned at her. "I have implicit trust in my fiancée."

"I didn't say—" Elena began a half-hearted protest, and Tejada kissed her.

"You were saying?" he asked a little while later, when she was resting her head comfortably against his shoulder.

Elena flushed. "I was saying you'll never find proof. And he's not the sort of person you can just arrest."

"No." The lieutenant spoke with obvious regret. "And Rodríguez wants to start prosecuting Rivera on Monday."

"This would be Rodríguez, the damn idiot?" Elena inquired mischievously.

Tejada raised his eyebrows. "This would be the future Señora de Tejada who's asking?"

Elena sighed. "All right. You win." She grimaced slightly. "Again. I don't know how I'll tell my parents though."

"That's my job," Tejada reminded her gently. "Now, either kiss me, or tell me how I can find enough evidence to save Rivera's neck."

"You could try a telegram to Switzerland," Elena said, choosing the second option, to his disappointment. "Now that you know the right questions to ask."

"I doubt they'd answer. And it wouldn't be fast enough anyway."

"A confession?"

"How? If I can't lay a finger on him?"

They discussed the problem for a while longer, reached no thoroughly satisfactory answer, and ended up kissing anyway.

Finally, Tejada's dormant conscience yawned and stretched. He reluctantly disentangled himself and stood up. "I suppose I had better speak to your father," he said. And then, in consideration of Elena's liberal upbringing, added, "Do you want to come?"

"Of course!" Elena's indignant surprise at his question made the lieutenant very grateful that he had thought to ask.

They went downstairs with their fingers intertwined but Tejada's sense of propriety made him drop her hand before knocking on the door of the professor's study. He had the vague feeling that Elena should not be present for his interview with Professor Fernández, but when he pushed open the door in response to the professor's muted, "Come in," he forgot his scruples and was simply glad for the moral support.

Guillermo was sitting in an armchair with a pad on his lap, apparently absorbed in a lengthy piece of writing. He stood a little awkwardly, allowing the pad to fall to the floor. "Lieutenant?" And then, with some surprise, "Elena? I hope nothing's wrong?"

"Errr . . . no." Tejada shook hands with the professor, and then stood, facing him, uncertain how to continue. After a moment, Guillermo resumed his seat. Tejada gulped. "I wanted to inform you . . . to ask you . . . that is, I realize this must be a somewhat unexpected question . . ." Only his pride prevented him from turning to Elena for help. She took his hand and squeezed it encouragingly. "A startling question," Tejada repeated, more strongly. "After all, you don't know me, or my family, but . . ."

"I am sure that they are honorable people." Guillermo's voice, slightly amused, filled the awkward silence. "And," for an instant his smile was bitter, "at the moment you are far better able to support Elena than I am." Tejada gasped. Guillermo stood and held out his hand. "I don't know that I have reason to like you, Lieutenant, but I have excellent reason to trust you. And Elena seems to have made her choice already. In Biarritz."

"You *knew*?" Tejada and Elena spoke at the same time, in identical tones of outraged embarrassment.

"And you said—?" the lieutenant choked.

"And you didn't say—" Elena stammered.

"Professor Meyer and I have been friends for a long time," Guillermo said mildly. "We had a chat the evening before he left." The professor smiled at his daughter. "He was worried about you, Elenita."

Elena made an embarrassed noise, somewhere between a groan and a giggle. Tejada absently folded one arm around her shoulders. "Well," he said, almost dizzy with relief, "that makes my next question much easier, then."

# Chapter 22

The Roman bridge over the river Tormes had been a favorite spot of the university's old rector. He had frequently crossed it, sometimes spent half hours staring down into the sluggish water, and had even made it a part of his novels. Guillermo had avoided the bridge since his old colleague's disgrace and death. It belonged to a world that no longer existed. So it was with a little shock of recognition that he turned a corner and saw the Roman arches once more, as if he were coming face-to-face with his own past.

It was the middle of the siesta and the bridge was deserted. Guillermo moved toward it hesitantly and placed a tentative hand on the sunbaked stones before starting across. They were almost unpleasantly warm against his bare skin. He leaned on the ancient wall and squinted down into the courtyard of the Church of Santiago, situated in the little park by the river. The brightness of the sun on the flagstones almost blinded him and he turned his head toward the yellowed grasses that clung to the dusty bank and the slow, greenish water beyond them. The river was low at this season. The paths through the park were dusty, and the scrubby bushes and crabgrass that grew in the shade of the ancient arches were coated with a fine golden grit. It was breathlessly hot. No whisper of wind touched the sweat pooling on Guillermo's forehead, or disturbed the footprints along the

path by the river that wound into the welcome shade and continued on by the water's edge. No women scrubbed clothes on
the opposite shore. No children splashed in the shallows. The
relentless sun had driven everyone indoors.

A rhythmic tap on the cobblestones of the street behind him
interrupted Guillermo's thoughts. It was regular but not quite
symmetrical. *Tap-tap. Tap. Tap-tap. Tap.* He turned, looked up
and shaded his eyes with one hand, and the taps resolved themselves into measured footsteps and the click of a silver-handled
walking stick. "Professor Fernández?"

Guillermo nodded. "Good afternoon. It was kind of you to
meet me here."

"Not at all." The voice was hearty, self-assured, not low or
furtive in the least.

I hope he's the right one, Guillermo thought, with a trace
of nervousness. He doesn't seem worried. Aloud he said simply, "I thought you might prefer it. I am known to the Guardia
Civil. People are sometimes reluctant to associate with me too
publicly."

"What a shame." The words were a social reflex. To the professor's relief his companion brought the conversation to the
point. "Why, exactly, did you wish to consult with me?"

Guillermo considered what to say for a moment. "I was a
friend of Manuel Arroyo's," he said finally. "He and I . . . had
certain interests in common. I understand that you had his
complete confidence. And now, in his absence, I wished to ask
your advice."

"It's kind of you to say that Professor Arroyo trusted me.
And certainly I hope it's true. I'm at your disposal, Professor
Fernández."

Guillermo bowed slightly. "Thank you. I merely wanted to
know if you were the other signer on Arroyo's second account."

"What?" The question was startlingly, unnecessarily loud.
Guillermo glanced around involuntarily, although the area was

obviously empty. His companion caught Guillermo's sign of nervousness, but did not lower his voice. "I have no idea what you're talking about."

"Arroyo's other Swiss account," Guillermo explained, keeping his voice low. "I held the number for one of them, but I know there was another, and I thought that now that he was dead, it was important to have the number for it as well."

Guillermo's companion frowned. "What makes you think I would lend myself to such an illegal enterprise?" His voice was still loud, but it was no longer hearty.

Guillermo looked apologetic. "Because Arroyo mentioned to me that you had similar investments. A few days before his unfortunate demise."

*Tap-tap-tap.* The cane bounced thoughtfully on the stones. "I am afraid that I can't help you, Professor Fernández. But I think it might be a good idea if you provided me with the number of Arroyo's account."

"Why?" Guillermo demanded, startled.

The other man smiled. "You do realize, Professor, that you have just provided yourself with an excellent motive for Arroyo's murder? After all, now that he's dead, you are presumably the only person who can access his wealth. And, as you say, you are already known to the Guardia Civil."

The professor looked apologetic. "Well, yes. But on the other hand, if I were arrested, I would certainly tell the Guardia all that I knew about Arroyo's investments and yours."

"Are you attempting to blackmail me, Professor?" The words were amused.

"Blackmail is an ugly word," Guillermo said gently. "Why don't we call it an exchange of mutually profitable information? I can tell you the account number that I know and you can tell me the number that you know. Or the numbers."

To Guillermo's surprise, his companion actually laughed. "And what would my clients say about my sharing such private information? I'm sorry Professor, but one account number isn't enough *mutual* benefit—no matter how much Arroyo had squirreled away."

Guillermo shrugged and turned away to hide his confusion. "I'm sorry you feel that way. You don't leave me much choice."

"Or you, me." Something in the tone of voice made Guillermo turn back, just in time to be blinded by a flash of sun on silver as the walking stick was raised, handle first, and brought down with savage swiftness.

The professor dodged instinctively; his ear stung from a glancing blow. He staggered against the wall of the bridge and clumsily tried to roll sideways as the glittering silver-headed cane was raised again. Blood spattered on the warm stones. Guillermo dodged again, panting for breath, aware that his opponent was twenty years younger and considerably more experienced at this type of combat. He yelled for help, a futile gesture in the deserted street, and then kicked out desperately. His foot connected with something solid, probably a shin, and he surprised a grunt out of his attacker. But the counterattack had been a bad idea. Guillermo felt himself lose his footing. He stumbled to his knees, clutching the rough stones of the bridge's railing to remain semiupright. He cried out again as another blow landed, clinging stubbornly to consciousness, though nearly blinded by his own blood.

Then, quite suddenly, the shadows under the bridge erupted into motion and noise, there was the report of a pistol as some-one fired into the air, and footsteps clattered on the cobble-stones. Guillermo's last thought before he passed out was that he had never been happy to hear the words "Guardia Civil! Hands up!" before.

When he awoke, the first thing he was aware of was the unpleasantness of the beads of sweat dribbling down his upper lip. He licked them away and realized that they were blood. Someone was pressing his forehead, and a voice was saying, "No, head wounds always bleed like that. Why don't we just take him back to the post?"

"Because the university clinic is closer." Guillermo cautiously opened his eyes, squinted against the sun, and made out the vaguely familiar shape of Sergeant Hernández. "And because the lieutenant will kill me if we bring him in looking like that."

"Yes, sir." The first voice was submissive. Guillermo had closed his eyes again, but he guessed that the sergeant had turned away when he heard the voice above his head add in a rebellious mutter, "I still don't see why. It makes a better case for attempted murder this way."

Something in the mutter made the professor suspect that the boy holding his head was the same age as an undergraduate. He smiled, and realized that he had a splitting headache. "Have you ever had a broken head?" he demanded with a slight groan.

"Are you awake then, sir?" This voice might have belonged to another student; young, deferential, slightly embarrassed.

"More or less," Guillermo agreed. He tried to sit up, and discovered that he could not. "But I can't move."

"He caught you a couple of good cracks." The guardia kneeling by the professor spoke comfortingly. "But you were only unconscious for a couple of minutes or so. You'll be fine."

"Good." Guillermo had the feeling that he ought to ask about the success of the operation. But his head hurt and he found himself uninterested in anything beyond his immediate physical discomfort. He kept his eyes shut and allowed the conversation of the guardias to flow around him, responding only when they asked him direct questions to make sure that he was still conscious. The pair of guardias who sounded like students stayed with him until a stretcher arrived, and then took him to the hospital, where—deference forgotten—they managed to obtain surprisingly fast service.

It was only several hours later, when his head had been neatly stitched and bandaged, and a brisk nurse had forced him to

drink a seemingly huge quantity of water, that Guillermo managed to interest himself in external practicalities. When he
emerged from the consulting room the two guardias who had
escorted him were waiting. They started to their feet and moved
toward him, and Guillermo reflected that they were probably
only half aware of the menacing picture they presented. "We're
here to take you home, sir," one of them explained as they took
the places of the nurses at Guillermo's elbows. "Lieutenant's
orders. There's a car waiting."

"Thank you." It occurred to Guillermo that if María saw one
of the Guardia vehicles drive up and deposit him on the
doorstep in his current state she would probably have hysterics.
"Do you think it would be possible for me to call my wife and
explain what's happened?"

"The lieutenant's already spoken to your daughter, sir."

"Of course." Guillermo allowed himself to be led out of the
hospital and driven home without further protest.

Elena met him on the doorstep, her eyes full of tears. "I'm so
sorry, Papa," she whispered as she hugged him. "We should
never have asked you to do this."

Guillermo returned her hug, and thought, a little sadly, that
she already said "we" when she spoke of the Guardia. "At least it
worked," he said, resigned to the inevitable.

"Oh, yes, it worked like a charm," Tejada assured the Fernández
family that evening at dinner. "We have enough evidence to con-
vict Crespo of attempted murder right now, and we'll have
enough to try him for murder and money laundering within a
week, I think."

"Has the captain given you a week?" Elena asked.

Tejada smiled at her. "Yes. He won't let us touch Crespo
because he's afraid of his powerful connections, but based
on the evidence we have, he's letting us hold on to him. And

I think he'll let us be a bit more persuasive once I talk to Judge Otero."

"You think Judge Otero will support you?" Elena was dubious.

"I think so." The lieutenant sounded pleased with himself. "After all, I can give him two very good reasons. First of all, that walking stick Crespo used is a twin to Otero's. I'm going to suggest that Crespo deliberately chose it and planned to abandon it by the body as evidence to implicate the judge."

"But that's nonsense!" Guillermo protested. "He couldn't have come definitely intending to kill me. And lots of men must have canes like that."

"True," Tejada admitted. "But I think if I plant a little seed of doubt about Crespo's loyalty, His Honor will be more willing to listen to my second argument: that it would be very unpleasant to be charged with illegal money laundering."

"Arrest Judge Otero!" Guillermo laughed. "You must be joking. He'll know you're bluffing."

Tejada shook his head. "Not if he thinks Crespo will finger him. And Crespo *will* finger him if the captain allows us to question him properly."

"Which he'll only do if Otero withdraws his support," Elena pointed out.

"Which Otero will do, if he thinks that Crespo will betray him first," Tejada finished.

"Classic prisoner's dilemma," Guillermo commented.

"It's not just used in philosophy classes, Professor," Tejada smiled. "And thanks to you we know that Crespo had more than one client with a Swiss account. With any luck, by the time we go through his office we'll have half a dozen pressure points."

"What do you mean?" Elena, who had only heard a summary of Guillermo's encounter from the lieutenant, looked puzzled.

"Crespo didn't just have a Swiss bank account for himself," Tejada explained. "He specialized in setting them up for other people. If we can find a list of names in his files, we'll have that many more men to lean on. One of them is sure to crack."

"You think that was what he meant when he said his clients wouldn't like him sharing that information?" Guillermo asked.

Tejada nodded. "It was smart of you to ask for the number *or numbers*. I thought Arroyo might have been blackmailing Crespo based on one account. It didn't occur to me that Crespo might have been handling a large number. It makes sense though." He sighed. "Crespo told me that his clients would have been uncomfortable with a man of Arroyo's political sympathies working for him. I should have guessed that maybe it wasn't Arroyo's politics that was the problem."

Guillermo frowned slightly. "But most of them are probably men in good standing. They'll be hard to arrest. Especially only on my word."

"We won't get all of them," Tejada said frankly. "But we'll get Crespo." He fell silent, and realized that Elena was regarding him steadily. He flushed. "A penny for your thoughts?"

"Why does getting Crespo matter to you?"

Tejada considered. "I didn't particularly like Arroyo Díaz," he said at last. "He struck me as a windbag when I knew him and he was certainly involved in illegal currency transfers. But he stuck up for his friends. For Unamuno, of course." The lieutenant smiled briefly. "And then for Tomás Rivera."

"For Doctor Rivera?" Guillermo interjected. "What do you mean?"

"He knew Rivera was broke in '36," Tejada explained. "So he went through some kind of analysis with him to funnel a little money his way. He was very clever really. He told Rivera he had to do it because he "*hat einen Vogel.*" And that was the exact truth, in a way. He did have a banker, named Vogel, who provided him with enough spare cash for a little charity. And I think . . ." Tejada paused.

"Yes?" It was Elena who prompted him.

"I think he was very . . . loyal." Tejada tested the word like the rung of a shaky ladder. It creaked under his weight but held firm. "He called Rivera again, a little while before he died. I think he'd found out about Crespo's accounts then, and was trying to decide what to do about them. He might have tried to blackmail Crespo, but I think he might have just decided to keep quiet too. He was loyal to Crespo for giving him a job . . . even though the job wasn't much better than an insult."

"But if he just kept quiet, why did Crespo kill him?" Guillermo protested, unwilling to let the lieutenant romanticize his late colleague.

"Rivera says Arroyo called him on a Monday evening," Tejada said quietly. "I think he called from Crespo's offices. And I suspect he was overheard." The lieutenant's mouth twisted bitterly. "At any rate, the last time his wife saw him alive was on his way to Crespo's offices. They would have been empty. And he was an old man, and unarmed. It was easy enough for Crespo to club him and then dump the body in a place where it would implicate Rivera, or at the very least cast doubt on anything Rivera said, just in case he'd gotten too much information from that phone call. And it was even easier for him to suggest that Arroyo had been planning to disappear and send me running off in the wrong direction. Especially since we didn't even notice that he was dead for two weeks, thanks to an administrative screwup!"

Elena put one hand on his arm. "It wasn't your fault."

Tejada shrugged, impatient. "I know. As I said, I had no opinion of the man. But he didn't sell out his friends. And he deserved better than to be murdered by a former protégé who didn't even think to keep a clear desk because it didn't occur to him that someone who had once been a professor might still be able to read." The lieutenant lowered his voice, a little embarrassed at his own vehemence. "It's bad enough that Crespo killed him. He didn't have to humiliate him as well," he finished illogically.

"Anyone who gets mixed up with the Reds runs that risk, you know," Elena reminded him quietly.

"Arroyo wasn't really a Red," Tejada protested. "He signed a petition. That was all." Skeptical silence greeted his remark. He shook his head, flushed. "It's not the same thing. Anyway, Arroyo wasn't a hypocrite like Crespo. And he wasn't a coward!"

"That Fernández has guts, I'll say that for him," Sergeant Hernández remarked a few days later.

"I don't think he would have signed that petition in the first place if he didn't," Tejada commented thoughtfully.

Hernández shot a surprised look at the lieutenant. Tejada had been odd and abstracted for the last several days, he thought. Ever since they had planned Crespo's arrest. He said, "Well, his testimony ought to be worth something, anyway, even if he is a Red."

Tejada winced slightly. "Have you dropped the surveillance on him?" he asked.

"Yes, ever since Crespo's arrest." The sergeant looked thoughtful. "Was that how you got him to agree to act as a decoy, sir?"

"Not exactly." Tejada shook his head.

"What then?"

The lieutenant aligned the folders on his desk with mathematical precision. "Favor to a family member," he said, eyes on the folders.

Hernández looked surprised. "Is he a relation, sir? You never mentioned it before."

"I'm going to marry his daughter," Tejada said, still avoiding his subordinate's eyes.

"What? You're joking!" The lieutenant's head shot up, and Hernández realized that he had crossed a line. "I mean . . . I mean . . . congratulations, sir. But . . . But have you thought about . . . well, about the implications?"

"That any chance of promotion will be extremely slim; that I'll be pitied or despised by friends and colleagues; that I'll be considered untrustworthy at best and a traitor at worst?" Tejada ticked off the list on his fingers.

"Well . . . no, I meant . . . well, yes." The sergeant was embarrassed.

"No, I hadn't thought about them," Tejada said dryly. "But my fiancée has spelled them out for me."

"Oh." Hernández coughed. His superior's last statement had glowed with the sort of possessive pride that told him, far more than any words could have, that his incredible statement was true. The sergeant hesitated. Tejada was sitting quietly, apparently unconcerned by his fellow officer's reaction. But his knuckles, gripping one of the folders, were white. Hernández took a deep breath, conscious that his own career might well be affected by his next words, but too curious to remain silent. "Why don't you bring her to dinner sometime," he said, with forced casualness. "I'm sure my wife would love to meet her."

The lieutenant relaxed his grip on the folder. "Thanks, Hernández," he said quietly, expelling a silent breath. "We'd love to come. That is if you're sure it wouldn't be an imposition?"

Hernández shrugged. "You've never met *my* in-laws," he said.

Tejada laughed. The telephone on his desk rang, and he picked it up, still smiling. "Guardia Civil, Tejada . . . Yes . . . Yes, Your Honor, thank you for the clarification. . . . Thank you, I'm honored. . . . Yes, Your Honor. . . . Good-bye." He hung up the phone, and his smile gained a touch of malicious satisfaction. "Speaking of in-laws," he said. "That was Judge Otero. His Honor is worried that we are under a misapprehension as to his relationship with Eduardo Crespo. He called to reassure me personally that any steps the Guardia needs to take to discover the identity of his brother-in-law's killer have his full approval."

Hernández smiled back. "Let's go have a little chat with Crespo," he suggested.

"My thoughts exactly, Sergeant." Tejada stood. "Before Judge Otero finds out about Elena," he added.

"My thoughts exactly, sir," the sergeant admitted, as he followed Tejada.